THE
SECRET CASEBOOK
OF
SIMON FEXIMAL

KJ CHARLES

First published by Samhain Publishing. This revised edition published 2017 by KJC Books

Cover design by Kanaxa, spine and back by Lexiconic Design
Interior design by eB Format
Edited by Anne Scott

Print ISBN: 978-1-9997846-0-7

For Lydmila Tsapaeva, a wonderful artist
and
for the real Beatrice Phan, a kind and generous soul

Contents

The Caldwell Ghost — 1
Butterflies — 15
Remember, Remember — 41
Silver — 77
Cakes and Ale — 99
Devils on Horseback — 125
An Eye for an Eye — 157
The Writing on the Wall — 187
Turn of the Century — 217
The End — 233

The Caldwell Ghost

A note to the Editor

Dear Henry,

> *I have been Simon Feximal's companion, assistant and chronicler for twenty years now, and during that time my* Casebooks of Feximal the Ghost-Hunter *have spread the reputation of this most accomplished of occultists far and wide.*
>
> *You have asked me often for the tale of our first meeting, and how my association with Feximal came about. I have always declined, because it is a story too private to be truthfully recounted, and a memory too precious to be falsified. But none knows better than I that stories must be told.*
>
> *So here is it, Henry, a full and accurate account of how I met Simon Feximal, which I shall leave with my solicitor to pass to you after my death.*
>
> *I dare say it may not be quite what you expect.*

Robert Caldwell
September 1914

I am, my friends agree, a fairly easy-going sort of chap, not quick to anger or to fear. Thus, when I came to live in Caldwell Place, I paid no mind to the screams in the night, which could well have been foxes or cats (never mind that they sprang from the empty air of my bedroom). I scarcely objected to the muffled moans, which could have come from a neighbour's pleasures (if the house had not stood alone, with no neighbour for a mile to either side).

But I did feel it was a bit much when the walls began to bleed.

Simon Feximal, ghost-hunter, stood in the imposing entrance hall of Caldwell Place, the ancestral home that I had inherited from my uncle along with a fortune far insufficient to restore the dilapidated property. Mr. Feximal was observing his surroundings. I was observing him.

He was worth the observation. A little above medium height but with very broad shoulders and an erect stance, he held himself like a pugilist. His face was more like that of a priest, albeit not one of any religion practised today. The sort of priest who wielded a sickle, or a ceremonial dagger, I thought: stern, unsmiling, dedicated. He had a beak of a nose, heavy brows over deep-set dark eyes, and a thick head of steel-grey hair, although his face suggested he was not many years older than my own twenty-five.

Mr. Feximal turned, looking around him, brows drawn together.

"Have you inhabited Caldwell Place long, Mr. Caldwell?" His voice was a deliciously deep baritone. I repressed the urge to shiver at the sound.

"Not six weeks," I told him. "I inherited it from my uncle three months ago. The house has stood empty for many years because of its evil reputation. I felt that was an absurd superstition, and I need to sell the place, so I thought I could come and put paid to the nonsense with a bit of nineteenth-century common sense." Both of us looked at the dull brown-red streaks on the wall, where the blood had bubbled, flowed and dried. "I have now decided I was wrong."

Feximal nodded. He had doubtless heard many similar openings to many similar stories. "May I see the portrait?"

I took him into the Blue Drawing-Room, lighting all the candelabras and lamps there. The night had drawn in, and I felt the atmosphere was sufficiently sinister without dark shadows. He stood in the middle of the chamber, slowly turning to take it all in, and once again I seized the chance to observe him, admiring his strong thighs and muscled back. Apparently ghost-hunting kept one in excellent shape.

The room was also worth observing, although less attractive. It was furnished in the style of seventy years ago, and although the dustcovers had been removed and the upholstery cleaned, the stiff-backed chairs were still faded and ancient. The parquet floor was bare of rugs. A large, speckled mirror dominated one wall with its heavy gilt frame—I saw Feximal pay particular note to that—and a handful of family portraits hung on the wall opposite. It was one of those that we had come to see, the one whose image had appeared all over the house, etched in shadows, woven in spiderwebs, and finally outlined on the walls in blood. I had taken this to be a hint.

"Randolph, Lord Caldwell," I said, walking towards it. Feximal came to stand at my side. He smelled faintly of an odd spice that I could not place. "My ancestor of some two centuries."

"The story, as you know it, please?" Feximal contemplated the picture with a frown in his fine dark eyes. The man in the painting looked back with a faint smile. He was a handsome chap, with green eyes rather like my own, but a much more assured, aristocratic demeanour, and he wore the curled white periwig adopted by gentlemen in those bygone days.

"I can't vouch for the truth of this," I began. "It's family history, and not the kind that's preserved in the books. What I've heard is that Randolph here was a degenerate of the most unrepentant kind."

"Meaning?"

"He had a fondness for men." I glanced over. Feximal didn't look shocked, or disgusted, or even very surprised. "He apparently spread his attentions widely, from the stableboys to the butler, from his tenants to his neighbours. He seems to have been indiscriminate."

Feximal looked again at the portrait. His gaze was assessing.

It is a strange phenomenon that men of my tastes often have a knack for sensing when another man shares those tastes. Without signals, hints or touches, one can often simply *tell*. I possess that knack. It had prevented me being assaulted or arrested on many occasions, and now I felt the slightest bat-squeak of awareness and it struck me that the stern, mysterious, powerful Mr. Feximal and I might possibly have something in common.

Not that I would have pressed the issue, alone in a haunted house with a ghost-hunter. But still.

Feximal's attention remained on the portrait. "What sort of man was he? Is he said to have forced his attentions on the unwilling?"

"Not that I know," I was pleased to report. "He was not a brute, to my knowledge. Simply a man of decided inclination, applied widely and enthusiastically."

Feximal's mouth twitched. I wondered what he would look like when he laughed. If he laughed.

"He met a violent end," I went on. "It seems that he was in bed with someone—a man—when he was shot to death. The murderer was never caught or tried, because of the possible scandal, I suppose. Whether it was a spurned lover, a current lover that he had yet to spurn, his own wife, a neighbour's wife..."

Feximal held a hand up. "I grasp the point. Did he have decent burial?"

"I suspect it would have been hurried. He was taken in the act, and the law was even less kind then than it is now."

"You sound sympathetic."

"Of course I am. The poor fellow was murdered."

"I find most of my clients lose their powers of empathy when the screaming starts."

I shrugged. I had a fellow feeling for the deceased Lord Caldwell, but it seemed something of a risk to say so. "I don't suppose he wants to be here any more than I want him here."

His dark eyes turned to me with clear approval. "You are quite right. If I can find a way to free him, it is as much in his interest as yours." Feximal peered at the portrait again. "If you will go over it once more. The symptoms of the haunting include—?"

"The bleeding walls, of course. That's happened several times now. Screams at night. And other noises."

"What sort of noises?"

"Moans. Lots of moans."

"Of pain?"

"Er, no, not precisely." I felt myself blush.

"Then of what nature?" Feximal asked.

"Of pleasure."

"A man's pleasure?"

"Precisely," I said, and wondered if he might speculate how closely I was acquainted with the sound of men's pleasure.

He didn't seem to, instead looking away to assess the room. "I see."

"Mr. Feximal, do you think you can deal with this?" I asked. "I have no knowledge of what you do or how you do it. Can you make it—him—go away?"

He turned back to me then, his eyes rather stern under the heavy brows. I felt a decided quiver at being the object of his full, commanding attention. "It is not a matter of making anything go away, Mr. Caldwell. A wrong was done here, a pain caused, a circle opened that has yet to be closed. Only when the story is finished, by whatever means, will the haunting be over."

"I am a journalist," I blurted out, because his deep, authoritative voice and chiding demeanour were giving me quite inappropriate sensations. "I know about stories. They must have endings. A story without an ending is an unbearable itch to the reader."

"And worse to its protagonist." He looked at me, and there was a connection there now which warmed me even more. Did I see appreciation in those dark eyes, too, an awareness of me as a man? I could not tell. "So I shall find the ending, and end the haunting. I fear I must ask you to leave me to do that alone, and to depart this house."

That was a bitter disappointment. As a journalist, my curiosity was boundless, and I had been anticipating the spectacle of a ghost-hunter in action. As a man, I should have liked to hear more of that deep voice that seemed to press like dark velvet on my nerve endings.

"I should rather not leave you alone here," I said. "It is an uncomfortable place even without the haunting, and the manifestations of the thing's presence have become stronger and angrier by the day. I should not like to be alone here myself, and I worry for your well-being. May I not assist you? After all, the ghost is my family responsibility."

"I am used to working alone."

"Might you not benefit from companionship, even so?"

He did smile at me then, almost reluctantly, as though he was not used to the act. The expression was surprisingly warm on such a stern face. "Thank you, Mr. Caldwell. That is a rare consideration. But this is my profession, and I have secrets to keep."

There was no hint of concession there, and I gave in to his will. In truth, I had not enjoyed the experience of being woken by screams to see blood bubbling out of my walls, and the old house was uncomfortably chilly tonight. I should doubtless be more comfortable elsewhere.

"Very well, if you insist. I shall bank up the fire for you and go." I glanced at the fire as I spoke, and blinked. It was already burning brightly, far too brightly for the icy tang in the air. "That's odd, it's quite high. I wonder why it's so cold in here."

Feximal turned sharply. As he did so, the fire went out. One moment, it was a cheerful blaze to the eye, the next black, cold, dead coals, without a hiss of steam.

I stared, disbelieving. Feximal spoke urgently. "Go, Caldwell. Go now. Run."

I will admit, I bolted, scurrying to the door, tugging on the handle. Then again. And again.

"It's locked," I said. There was nobody else in the isolated building. The door had never stuck before. It would not open.

Feximal strode over. He gave the doorknob a tug.

"It seems to be locked," he agreed. "Although I should point out that there is no keyhole."

Nor was there. Yet the door was, without question, closed, and staying that way. The fire was out, and as I stared frantically around the room, the candle flames began to wink out, one after another, each tiny bulwark against the darkness extinguishing as I watched.

I may have whimpered.

Feximal was delving into his black Gladstone bag. He produced a squat, wide-necked glass bottle which appeared to be full of sand and bits of dried plants.

"Come here. Stop. Stay there." I stopped a few feet from the mirror as directed, and watched in alarmed confusion as he placed a candelabra by my feet then hastily walked around me, spilling the bottle's contents to form a circle. Pins and rosemary needles stuck out of the white sand.

"You should be safe now. Do not, under any circumstances, leave or break the circle. Stay still and do not fear, no matter what you see." He gave me another, very swift smile. "Trust me. I shall keep you safe."

I nodded my obedience. "But what about you?"

"I'm used to this," Feximal said, and stripped off his coat.

Even in these most unpromising circumstances, I had to look. There were only a handful of candles left alight still, except for those in the sand circle, and the rest were snuffed out as I watched Simon

Feximal disrobe. He removed his plain dark waistcoat, threw down his cravat, and unbuttoned his white shirt.

I swallowed. "What are you doing?"

He didn't reply. He didn't have to. As he dropped the shirt, what I saw was answer enough.

He was covered in writing. It was scrawled in black and red ink, from wrist to shoulder of both muscular arms, across his broad, powerful shoulders and chest. None of it was in a language I recognised, or could read, but it was unmistakably writing…and it was still being written.

I gaped. The lines, some spidery, some looping, still others jagged, etched themselves over his skin, a constant silent chatter of messages.

"What—" My voice failed.

"The stories write themselves," he said, very matter-of-fact. "I serve as their page."

"Er…"

"Ssh," he added, quite kindly. "Try not to worry."

Easy for him to say.

He stood, stripped to the waist, steepling his hands in an odd, almost prayerful posture in front of his face. He was still and silent for a minute in the dark room, and I could hardly help wondering how far down the writing went, what might be marked on his powerful thighs and buttocks and even further into forbidden territory.

He murmured a sentence in a language I did not know, and walked over to the mirror. He looked into it, and I looked too, and I uttered an oath as I saw.

In the mirror, the writing over Simon Feximal's body was English. Huge angry capitals that looked nothing like the writing I could see on his body. MURDERED, said the reflected capitals, hastily scrawling themselves and sinking into his skin again. INJUSTICE. JAMES. JAMES. PLOT. HATE. UNDONE. UNFINISHED. JAMES. BASTARD.

"He had a bastard?" I asked breathlessly.

"I suspect—that's an—expletive." Feximal jerked the words out, and I realised his face was lined with strain. "He's—angry."

The screaming came then, so loud and sudden that I leapt like a rabbit. Louder and louder it shrieked, the sound circling us like a gale. Feximal bowed against the force of it, a force I could not feel in my circle, muttering to himself. The moans were back, too, under the screams, and a terrible gibbering laughter, and I had never heard a noise I liked less than those sounds of pleasure, pain and madness combined in that awful way.

Feximal stood straight, with an obvious effort. The writing on his skin was frantic, tangling lines of incomprehensible scrawl. The writing I saw in the mirror was all too readable, and I gaped as I saw the words forming on his body in an old-fashioned script: *fuck me suck my cock spread your hole and take it*

I'm quite fond of that sort of literature in its place, but its place was not a man's skin. I looked away from the obscenity and saw instead the portrait on the opposite wall.

My ancestor, Randolph, Lord Caldwell, was smiling at me. Not the faint smile I was familiar with, but a broad, lascivious grin. As I stared at the painting in the mirror, he licked his lips.

"Feximal!" I yelped, pointing, and the portrait lifted his hand and pointed at me in response. I staggered back, consumed with fear, and as I did, my heel breached the sand circle.

Immediately I was plunged into a vortex. Strange winds howled around me. The screaming was ten times louder, rasping on my nerves and skin like some saw-toothed plant. I was buffeted by impalpable forces, heard howling in my ears and inside my head. I cried out in sheer terror, and Feximal's strong arms closed around me, pulling me to the shelter of his body, and I heard his voice in my ear, shouting over the unearthly noises. "Quiet, Robert. It's all right. I'll look after you."

And it all stopped.

We stood together in the dark room, he behind me, his arms pinning me close, his chest pressed to my back. The unnatural cold had gone. The silence rang in my ears.

"Did you do that?" I whispered.

"No," said Feximal grimly.

Then I heard the laugh again. A chuckle, now, a throb of amusement. With it, gently this time, the moaning began, little sighs and groans of carnal enjoyment. Feximal had one bare, muscular arm around my neck, the other around my waist, holding me brutally tight, and despite my sheer, sickening terror, I realised, to my own astonishment, that I was growing hard in my drawers.

That was madness, I thought, but it was as if my body and mind were separate things. I was frightened, confused and desperate to run for my life, or soul, but my prick was being called, and it seemed to intend to come.

I felt, rather than heard, breathless grunts and groans. My mind threw up the faces and bodies of lovers I had never seen. My skin flared with the touch of fingers that weren't there. I cried out, through fear or arousal, I could not tell which, and Simon Feximal shouted something aloud.

Now, with my hard-won experience, I know that he had begun the Third Line of the Saaamaaa Ritual, on which he and his fellow ghost-hunter Carnacki had done such perilous research. Then, I only knew that the guttural sounds of those strange words in his deep voice boomed like a pagan gong, and the barrage of sensation was snuffed out as instantly as the candles had been.

I gasped for breath and slumped back against his bare chest, held by that hard, unwavering grip. My legs were shaking, but my prick was still rigid as a tent pole.

I became aware of a hard length pressing against my arse, and I realised Feximal was in the same state.

"I think I know what it wants," I whispered.

"So do I." His voice was strained. "The power of this thing… I cannot master it and protect you at once. I can hold it off a little longer. You must run to the window. Break it. Climb out. Otherwise…"

"Otherwise what?"

His breath rasped hotly against my ear. "Damn it, man, you can feel what it wants. I can feel it. It is old, and powerful, and it has a way in. It is very easy for a spirit to direct the actions of the living as it desires, if…" He tailed off.

"If the living share the same desires?" I asked.

He stood, absolutely still and silent, holding me pinioned against him. Then he murmured, very softly, very deep, "It's coming upon us. You really should run away."

I was bewildered, terrified. I was aching for his touch, for more than touch. I could hear the moaning starting again, beginning to build. And, I was not leaving a fellow human alone in this house of madness.

"Is it evil? What it wants?" I panted.

"No. It's…angry, betrayed. Lonely. Frustrated. It wants satisfaction."

"So do I." I leaned back against him so that my head was on his powerful shoulder, my prick, restrained by close-fitting trousers, trying to push upwards and out.

"Robert… You can still run," he rasped.

"No."

"This will not be controllable." His voice held clear warning, and clearer desire.

"Please, Simon. Please."

Feximal—Simon—took a shuddering breath. Then his hand on my waist moved down, stroking over my arousal, pulling me hard against his hips, his own stiff prick. His other arm was wrapped over my shoulders, forearm against my throat, and he increased that pressure too.

I was held there, trapped, in a haunted house, with a strong arm gripping my neck and a strong hand opening the buttons at my waist.

My cock sprang free. I groaned aloud. Simon gave a little exhalation of satisfaction and took it in his hand, rubbing his thumb over the tip, spreading the dampness that already beaded there. I rubbed back against his hips in wanton invitation, and he pushed at my drawers and trousers, shoving them down, tucking my shirttails out of the way.

"Kneel," he ordered me, and I fell to my knees, or tried to. His arm was hard against my windpipe, and I grabbed at it, for balance or freedom, as for a second I was held off the floor by that pressure.

He was strong as an ox, and he was going to fuck me.

I whimpered, and he let me down to the floor so that I knelt obediently before him. I did not look round, or into the mirror, for fear that I might see what was written on that thickly muscled body now.

Simon reached a long arm for his bag, without releasing my neck. He fumbled within, pulled out a small bottle, flicked open the stopper one-handed. I smelled an unfamiliar perfume, one that made me think of the Arabian Nights.

He was slicking his cock, readying himself.

I tried to bend forward, to get on hands and knees. He didn't let me. His finger slid down the crease of my arse, his knee nudged my legs apart into a wider stance, he moved his free hand forward once more to control my hips, and his cock shoved forward into my entrance.

I gasped aloud. I was no virgin, had had a fair few men ride my arse, but never with so little preparation. I bit my lip as he pushed again, not too far or too fast for what it was, yet it stung painfully. I shut my eyes.

Simon pushed again, and this time my arse took the invasion with more readiness. I grunted, breathing in and out, feeling the burn recede with each breath. He rocked into me, further each time, until I made a small sound of pleasure that somehow rang out clear against the ghostly moans.

Simon shifted his arm from my hips to my chest, encircling my own arms, hand closing over one wrist to hold my arms tight by my sides. He pushed again then, and this time he slid all the way in, thick cock stretching me wide, until I felt his hips pressed right against my entrance. I was trapped by his arms round my neck and chest, by every inch of his erect member inside me, pinioned and stuffed like a Christmas goose.

I groaned aloud. As if in answer, Simon pulled out, slowly and carefully, till only the head of his thick member was inside me, leaving me feeling empty.

Then he began to fuck me in earnest.

I am no Goliath, but neither am I weak. I had never felt the urge to submit to another man's will, let alone to force. I had always approached physical satisfaction as I did everything in those days of youth: as a pleasant game.

This was no game. Simon held me captive. My legs were splayed, my arms trapped, and I could do nothing but groan and grunt and take the fucking he administered. I was hopelessly mastered, utterly subject to his will, and I had never been so hard in my life. I thrashed against him with a dark, unspeakable joy at the commanding usage, and as I cried my pleasure aloud, I felt something else.

A tongue in my mouth. A pinch to my erect nipple. A hand gripping my cock.

Not Simon's. Not anyone else's; we were miles from the next human being. Nobody's, in fact, because as I opened my eyes and stared, I saw nothing but the dark and empty room.

I shut my eyes again and felt something rub against my erection. It was, without question, a stiff prick. A hand closed around me, pushing them both together.

"The ghost," I gasped. "It's touching me."

Simon didn't respond. He simply lifted me slightly to change the angle, and as he drove into me now, he hit that spot that sends ecstasy leaping through a man's flesh. I cried out for more, and he gave me more, more than I thought I could take, again and again, forcing his solid cock deep as the ghostly member thrust and twitched and jerked against mine.

Simon came, buried in my arse, with a savage grunt as his seed spilled. I came a second later, crying out with my release. And I will swear that I felt something else, cool and silvery, splash against my belly, and as it did so, the spectral moans died away.

I lay back against Simon as he loosened his grip—only slightly; if he had released me I would have fallen. I was shaking. He inclined his head so it rested on me, chest heaving with desperate breaths.

When I opened my eyes, the fire burned brightly in the grate, the candles shed their merry glow and, in the mirror, the painting of Randolph, Lord Caldwell was no more than a simple picture.

I will not detail the rest of that night. Simon tended to me with an absurd attentiveness that charmed me beyond words, until I was ready to walk the house with him to check for any evidence of further haunting, an exploration that ended inevitably in one of the more habitable bedrooms. I am pleased to report that the subsequent moans and screams that disturbed the silence of Caldwell Place were mine.

The ghost never returned, its story concluded that frantic evening. Simon called it a case of two centuries' *coitus interruptus*. One can only sympathise.

Butterflies

A Note to the Editor

Dear Henry,

I had not intended to write more of what I find myself calling The Secret Casebook of Simon Feximal. *(Such is the jobbing author's habit, to create a book out of nothing!) I told you how we met, tied up the tale, and it was done. Yet there are so many more stories, so much of my history with Simon that I should not like to disappear.*

I met him in 1894. For two decades we have been lovers, the best of friends, the bitterest of enemies. We were partners in work and in crime, of more than one sort. We have shared secrets so dark that the stories I have published in The Casebook of Simon Feximal, *which you begged me to amend for the sake of readers' weak hearts, came to seem to me almost light entertainment. For two decades, we have been everything to one another, yet to the world I am no more than the famed ghost-hunter's friend and chronicler, witness to his deeds. In writing Simon's stories, I have written myself out of my own life. I wonder, Henry, if you can imagine what that is like.*

I have decided. I shall write the Secret Casebook, *record the truth of our lives—not Simon Feximal's life alone, but Robert and Simon, together. It is for you to decide what to do with the tale when it is told.*

Your friend,
Robert Caldwell
October 1914

It was a fortnight after my first and, so far, only meeting with Simon Feximal. He had rid my inherited house of a lustful ghost, opened my eyes to a concealed world of strange forces and arcane knowledge, and buggered me twice. The next day he had departed, with a nod of thanks and a final-sounding farewell. There was no hint of regret in his stern dark eyes. I had wondered whether to propose another meeting, but looking at that remote face, I lost my nerve.

It was hardly unusual behaviour. Those of us who prefer the company of men know that many of those men want to leave one's company as quickly as possible after the fact. The only dignified response is a smile and a shrug, even if one should wish for more. And Simon Feximal, with his strange air of a pagan priest, and the occult writing scrawling itself over his skin, was not a man to bother with importunities.

I was disappointed, but not surprised. My own features—medium stature, green eyes and unimpressively brown hair—were pleasant but undistinguished. My profession as a journalist would doubtless be repulsive to a man with secrets to keep.

I could understand his indifference to my person and forgive his dislike of my profession. What I found a great deal harder to swallow was the bill for his services.

He did not send it. A fee for the visit had been agreed, but he was to give me a final amount depending on the work required. In the natural excitement of the moment, and the next day's awkwardness, I had certainly not thought to request it. And it was not sent.

I wrote to him, a businesslike note, asking for the amount due. He ignored the letter. I wrote again, and received a letter by return.

I will admit, I had butterflies in my stomach as I opened it. I wondered if there might be a personal response. Perhaps even a suggestion that we might meet again.

There was no such suggestion. Merely a few lines in a clear, vigorous hand, stating that there would be no charge.

I read the note with incredulity, then dawning fury, as it came upon me with stunning force that Feximal apparently considered my services as bed-partner would suffice in lieu of payment. Whether he believed that I had been paying him by offering my body, or far worse, that he was paying me for my services by waiving his fee for his, I did not know. I did not care. I damned his eyes, the patronising swine, and sent a twenty-guinea payment that I could ill afford along with a note nicely judged to convey my sense of offence, and I resolved to be relieved that I would never see him again.

In fact, it took ten days.

"Get down to Winchester," Mr. Lownie told me. He was the editor of the *Chronicle* then, a tense, compact man with a habit of chewing his pipe stem to splinters. "Extraordinary reports. Two deaths, against all nature. There's a train at quarter past."

He pushed a paper into my hand and thrust me out of the office. I was used to this unceremonious method of briefing, and I did not so much as glance at my orders, concentrating only on the seemingly impossible feat of catching the allotted train. I ran to the Underground, fretted until I reached the station, secured my ticket, and leapt aboard the second-class carriage almost as the train drew away with the angry cries of a guard ringing in my ears.

The carriage was empty, and I sat back in my seat, took a much-needed breath, and looked for the first time at my brief, which included two reports from the local Winchester newspaper and a transcribed statement from the local doctor. I read them with curiosity mingled with growing horror.

It appeared that some five days ago, a young lady and her governess, taking a walk in the woods, had stumbled upon a strange discovery. From a distance it looked to be a great pile of brightly coloured paper, a vast heap of trimmings and cuttings piled into a mound some six feet long and perhaps two feet high. As they approached the peculiar sight, they realised with astonishment that it was constituted, not of paper, but of butterflies. Butterflies in their thousands, of the most extraordinary variety of hues, of species not native to England or ever seen here. The insects were all dead or dying, with barely a flutter to their wings, and the two ladies approached to look closer. Then a drift of the lovely dead things slipped to the ground, and what had seemed merely extraordinary became terrible.

It was not simply a heap of butterflies, as if there was anything simple about such a thing in a chilly English October. The bright wings hid a corpse.

He was Thomas Janney, Old Tom, a vagrant of the Winchester woods. Known to the police as an itinerant and a drinker, prone to foul language in his cups, but with little real harm said of him at any time these past two decades. And he was dead, face suffused with blood, skin shrivelled and dry, and inside his mouth, down his throat, in his lungs, were butterflies.

An appalling discovery, but the passing of a tramp makes little impact on the world, however mysterious the circumstances. It was the second death that had set the news wires alight.

This time it was a local schoolmaster, Hubert Lord. No weakling he, as unlike the broken-down wanderer as could be imagined. A young, healthy man in his twenties, he had set off into the woods for a cross-country run, as was his peculiar habit, and he had not returned. Alarmed for his safety, his young wife contacted the police, and it was not long after that his body was found, his face distorted with fear and horror, his throat crammed with butterflies.

Where were the creatures coming from? How could two such swarms arise? Why should they kill?

The local journalist, though his account was verbose and greatly too conscious of its own styling for the taste of a brisk London professional like myself, had included a few valuable pointers in his story. Chief amongst these was the interview with Dr. Merridew, an amateur lepidopterist apparently held in high regard by those who shared his interest. He had been asked to give his views by the police, as Winchester's only "butterfly man", and had volunteered the information that some of the species had never been seen outside South America, that none of them were equipped for the rigours of an English climate, and that it was as impossible for butterflies to be directed to kill as it was for such a peculiar mix of species to be bred in captivity, or for them to swarm together.

And yet they were bred, and they did swarm, and two men had died.

I took a room in the Wykeham Arms, a pleasant inn set in winding red-brick streets. Compared to London, everywhere was convenient in this little cathedral city, but I was pleased to note that it was just a short walk from Dr. Merridew's address on Culver Street. My first step was to send him a note requesting an appointment at his earliest convenience. My second was to go down to the crowded dining-room, ready to plead with the staff to find me a seat for luncheon.

I walked in and saw Simon Feximal.

He sat alone at a table for two, directly in front of me, intent on a newspaper as he ate, and I stopped dead, gaping with the shock of recognition, and with that unwelcome, unstoppable quiver of sensation in my gut as I took him in. I had told myself that my memory and the dramatic circumstances of our first meeting had exaggerated his attractions, but he was every bit as commanding a presence as I remembered. That hair like spun steel, that beaky nose, those powerful shoulders that I had clutched as he drove into my body…

The landlady made a politely impatient noise, urging me forward, and as she did so, Feximal looked up.

"Robert?" he said blankly. "What are you doing here?"

"Oh, you gentlemen know each other!" cried the landlady, and swept me forward to the spare seat at his table with relief. "Then I dare say you won't mind sharing. We've steak and ale pie, sir, sit you down and you shall have a plate."

I would have turned away. My injured pride and his less-than-warm welcome both stung, and in truth, more than my pride had been hurt. To have shown the tenderness that Feximal had demonstrated that night, the second time, the murmurs of endearment, the gentle touches, and then to walk away from me—that had felt like a lie. Like a promise made and not kept. Like a cruelty.

Two things stopped me from rejecting the offered seat and taking my meal elsewhere. The first was that he was surely here for the same reason I was, the inexplicable butterflies, and I was determined to have that story. If Simon Feximal, ghost-hunter, discovered anything to do with this mystery, I intended to make it worth three columns of the *Chronicle*'s paper, with a byline.

The second was that, though his greeting had hardly been a welcome, he had called me Robert.

I sat. Feximal looked at me, deep-set eyes unreadable, waiting. I arranged my napkin. He put the side of his fork through a hard piece of pie crust, shattering the pastry into shards and crumbs.

Someone would have to speak first, unless we were to sit here in silence for the next hour. It was inevitable that the someone should be me.

"You're here about the butterflies?"

"And so are you, I take it." I had forgotten how deep his voice was. It seemed to vibrate in my chest as he spoke.

"For the *Chronicle*," I said. "Have you been called by a private individual, or the police, may I ask? Or are you here on your own account?"

He gave me a grim look in place of a reply. Whether his discomfort sprang from his habit of secrecy or our previous connection, I could not tell. The landlady arrived at that moment with a laden plate for me, and Feximal took the opportunity for a forkful of pie, avoiding an answer.

As if that would work on a man whose trade was questions. "Have you learned much of interest?" I enquired.

Feximal swallowed, with some annoyance. "Mr. Caldwell, are you intending to pump me much longer?"

The double meaning—very clearly not intended—rang in the air. I saw a slight flush stain his cheeks as he realised it, and my own riposte was so obvious, it barely needed to be said. I said it anyway. "Turn and turn about, Mr. Feximal."

Feximal put down his fork. "You're angry."

"No," I responded automatically, then, "Yes. Yes, I am."

"I had no intention of insulting you."

"When you waived your fee in consideration of services rendered?"

Feximal reached for a piece of bread, tearing it with his strong fingers, not looking at me. "That was not my meaning. I did not think of—that evening professionally. I prefer to remember it as personal."

"Oh." I felt my face turning hot. I had put the worst possible interpretation on his behaviour. It had not even occurred to me to consider the best. "Oh. I thought…"

"I gathered what you thought." His stern mouth relaxed, just slightly. "I can see why you are a journalist. You have a gift for self-expression."

Now I knew I was scarlet, thinking of that cursed note I had sent him. "I must apologise—"

"You must not. If you misunderstood me, that was my fault." He looked for a moment as if he would say more, then turned his eyes to his plate, dropping the crumbled bread sops into the plentiful gravy. He resumed eating, and I followed suit, not quite sure what to say now, feeling a flare of quivering excitement. Surely, if he wanted no more of me, he would have allowed me to dwell in my misapprehension. Was there, perhaps, a second chance?

I had no grand dreams, I need hardly say. I had spent a few hours in his company, during which I could count on one hand the number of his smiles. I had no illusions that there would be more than a repeat of our first encounter—ideally, without supernatural interference this time—since I could not imagine what this strong, remote man would want from me other than physical relief.

But if he wanted that, he should have it, and welcome. I had brought myself off half a dozen times in the last few days with the memory of that first, merciless fuck, Simon Feximal imprisoning me with his powerful grip, taking his pleasure as I cried out under him. The thought made me half-hard now, and I shifted uncomfortably in my chair.

Fortunately, my musings were interrupted by the arrival of the postboy at our table with a note for me. I opened it, and was startled to see a brief handwritten line signed by Dr. Merridew, to whom I had written not an hour ago.

"A problem?" Feximal asked. He was watching my cursedly expressive face.

"A rejection." I dropped the note on the table. "Dr. Merridew, the local lepidopterist, declines to see me. He has an ill opinion of journalists, it seems. That's a nuisance."

"Do you need to see him?"

"Unquestionably. If I'm to write a story on this business, he is a useful source of information, which I will have to travel far to find elsewhere. I can hardly pretend to expertise on butterflies myself."

"Nor I." Feximal was regarding me with a slight frown. "Why do you want to write the story?"

That would seem an entirely unnecessary question from anyone else. Writing stories was my job. But Feximal wrote stories too, or had them written on his skin in alien alphabets and unknown hands. *The stories write themselves*, he had said. *I serve as their page.*

"Two men are dead," I told him. "I want to know why."

"To know it, or to write it?"

"Both. My calling is to bring information to light." I spoke with all the pride of my journalistic ideals. "To tell the world the truth."

It was twenty years ago. I was very young.

Feximal did not laugh at me, though he might have done. He considered me for a moment, examining my features almost dispassionately. "Yes. But what of those truths that should not be told?"

"Surely knowledge is always preferable to ignorance."

"No," he said, looking straight at me. "It is not."

I felt the hairs on my neck rise at the bleakness in his eyes. It occurred, belatedly, to me to wonder what he had seen. What he wished he could forget.

"No," he repeated, more gently. "But… If I offer you an olive branch, as an apology for my clumsiness, will you take it in the spirit I intend?"

"There's no need to apologise. The misunderstanding was mine." He looked as though I had pushed him away, his face closing, and I added hastily, "But if you have a proposition for me, I shall gladly accept."

His eyes gleamed at that—I may say that any double meaning was entirely intentional on my part—and what he said then was one of the two things I had most hoped to hear.

"I have an appointment with Dr. Merridew in half an hour. If you should wish to accompany me, as a colleague, and not under the rejected name of Caldwell, I should be glad of your sharp eyes."

I accepted with thanks, enthusiasm, and hardly any disappointment. He was staying in the same inn, after all. Anything else could wait.

Dr. Merridew's small house stood at the corner of the narrow street, on the edge of a large area of open ground. Simon and I—I had given up trying to keep my distance by thinking of him by his surname—were shown in by a young tweeny maid, who ushered us down a corridor to face a large heavy door, knocked, and fled.

There was no answer from inside the room. I glanced at Simon and knocked again.

This time, I heard a fumbling, and the scrape of a key in the lock, and the door was pulled open.

The man who faced us was in his fifties, at a guess, with a scholar's stoop and wire-rimmed spectacles. He looked somewhat gaunt, but not feeble. Indeed, he seemed to be bursting with energy, judging by his little hopping skip back from the door.

"Mr. Feximal?" he demanded in a reedy voice, looking from one to the other of us. "I did not expect two visitors."

Simon held out his hand. "Good day, Dr. Merridew. This is my colleague, Mr. Robert."

I held out my hand in turn and received the most perfunctory grip from the lepidopterist, a flat palm against mine and the merest brush of a couple of fingertips. Evidently the doctor's energy did not extend to greetings.

He ushered us in, shutting the door and turning the key in the lock. "Mr. Feximal, you requested my time in the name of the Chief Constable. Without that I should not have seen you. I am a busy man with no time for mumbo-jumbo or idle curiosity."

"Then let us get to the point." Simon seemed perfectly comfortable with the open rudeness. "Why would butterflies attack a man?"

"They would not." The doctor took a tall stool that stood by a workbench, and did not invite us to sit. Simon stood, impassive. I glanced around.

We were in the doctor's study. It was a crowded room, very warm thanks to an iron stove. A small, barred window let in a little daylight. Glass cases hung on the walls, not displayed but jammed up against one another, and in each was pinned a butterfly.

There must have been hundreds. Huge iridescent blue things, smaller ones in every shade and pattern, some the simple creatures I recognised from my boyhood, others with great sweeping oddly shaped wings from which tendrils fell. Splayed and pinned, the dead things lined every available wall, each displayed with its accompanying cocoon and labelled in thin handwriting.

A long bench ran around three sides of the room, piled high with the scientist's paraphernalia: killing bottles, jars, bottles of preserving solutions, pins, haphazard stacks of books and papers. Dirty plates lay out with the congealed remnants of old meals. A large marble mortar, its bowl and pestle stained with yellowish dust, stood at my elbow, next to a pile of local newspapers at least a foot high. The floor was swept very clean, though, except that crumpled at the base of the bench, half under a leg of the doctor's stool, was a dead butterfly. It looked to me like the common pest known as a Cabbage White.

"Do you say that the dead men lost their lives to some other agency?" Simon was asking.

The doctor tutted. "No. I say that butterflies are not killers. There is no species that can bite or sting. They did not attack those two unfortunates. They simply sought refreshment."

"Refreshment?" I repeated, feeling a vague horror at the commonplace word. "What sort?"

"Fluids." Dr. Merridew's eyes glinted. His hands were splayed flat on his bony thighs as he sat, the position seeming oddly eager, as though he were restraining himself. "Butterflies sip solutions of sugars and salts. Sugar water, the nectar of flowers, sweat..." He looked directly at me. "A man's tears."

"You believe that the butterfly swarms descended on those men to drink from them?" Simon asked.

"It is winter. Where else could they feed? And one man oozing a drunkard's sweat from his grimy pores, another in a lather from his bodily exertions—well, that would be a movable feast."

"So the butterflies descended for no other reason than to satisfy their thirst—"

"And then it is simple enough," Dr. Merridew concluded. "The sight would be startling. The men cry out. The hungry butterflies detect more moisture in their mouths and throats, and they seek it."

I had to turn away. I could imagine with sickening vividness that multicoloured, paper-winged silent swarm descending on me, the feel of crawling legs in my mouth, the probing of a million probosces at my ears and eyes and nostrils, until every breath I took simply sucked the creatures further in…

"Robert?" Simon asked sharply.

I shook my head, waving away his concern, pulling myself together. "Please go on."

"That is all," said Dr. Merridew. "The deaths were entirely natural, in the circumstances."

"And the circumstances?" asked Simon. "Where did the butterflies come from?"

The doctor's thin hands flexed on his thighs. "I cannot say. Perhaps a freak wind. One reads of storms carrying swarms of insects over great distances in the Americas. I have no other explanation. I should know if anyone in England was breeding butterflies in such vast numbers, as it would require a huge and well-heated facility to accommodate so many species. I certainly do not possess such a facility," he added with a humourless smile, clearly anticipating the question. "I do not breed butterflies. I buy my specimens dead."

"I understood from the newspapers that they were varieties from all over the world," I put in. "Where would the wind have blown them from?"

"I could not say." The doctor's pinched face was taking on a familiar expression, that of a man tired of questions. He would ask us to leave in a moment, unless greased.

"You have a remarkable collection," I said. "I have been advised that it is one of the most impressive in the country."

"In private hands." Dr. Merridew made a poor attempt at a modest look. "My life's work is to acquire an example of each known species. It is my ambition to present my collection to the Museum in Kensington when it is complete. The Merridew Bequest, you know."

"A most generous ideal," I said warmly. "How close are you to completion?"

"I have much of what I need. This has been my life, Mr. Robert." The doctor began to lift a hand in a gesture, and slapped it back down on his trouser leg. "I have dedicated many years to accumulating these. Some of the rarest, most valuable butterflies in the world are here. I *own* them. Soon I will have them all."

"I'm sure you will. Which is the rarest butterfly?" I asked the question purely to keep the man on his hobbyhorse, but his face closed over as if it had been a deliberate dig.

"The Cobalt Saturn." He seemed suddenly to be on the verge of fury. "It is found only in a single valley in an island of the Philippines. I have tried to obtain a specimen. I sent messengers. Begged traders. Offered far in excess of a fair price. I have tried, and tried…" His teeth were set. "I will have one. I will."

"I'm sure your efforts will bear fruit," I assured him. "What is so remarkable about this creature? Is it a particularly beautiful type?"

"Beautiful?" Dr. Merridew turned on me as though I were an idiot, his voice scathing. "Remarkable? It's *rare*. What else is there?"

Simon and I left the house together. I could scarcely contain my relief at escaping the stifling heat.

"What an odd man," I said.

Simon nodded. "It seems a strange ambition, to pursue a collection without any pleasure in either the hunt or the beauty of the creatures he acquires."

"That is strange," I agreed. "And so is the fact that his specimens are sent to him dead, yet he has killing jars on his workbench, ready for use."

Simon looked round at me, his rare smile dawning. "Sharp eyes indeed, Robert. I am fortunate to have you with me." I looked ahead, trying not to betray my absurd pleasure at that crumb of praise. "But, as Dr. Merridew said, to breed that quantity of butterflies would require a great expanse of land and equipment, which would not have gone unnoticed by the police in their investigation. Hmm."

"Where to now?" I asked.

Simon's wry glance suggested that he had noticed my transparent attempt to include myself in his work. "I must see the corpses. It is unlikely to be pleasant."

I believed that, and took the warning. "I might go and speak to the police, then. Perhaps we could compare notes this evening?"

"I shall look forward to it."

The police sergeant was more welcoming than the butterfly collector. Many provincial policemen swell with pride at being interviewed by a real London journalist, and the greatest difficulty is to stop them talking. This one was much of that type, except that he evidently felt that the whole butterfly business was an embarrassing nuisance.

"It's peculiar, yes," he said. "Very peculiar. But peculiar ain't my business. The Chief Constable's brought a fellow down here to look into it, a Mr. Feximal, I expect you know the name. Peculiar is *his* business. My business is law-breaking, and I've quite enough of that to be getting on with."

I made noises of sympathy, and he launched into a recital of his woes. I had covered many a crime in London, and it seemed to me he had very little to complain about: a few burglaries, the usual cases of drunkenness and wife-beating, a nasty piece of vandalism in the cathedral involving the desecration of an ancient tomb. He cast no light on the butterfly killings, or much else, but his story of the tomb caught my attention and I considered it as I nodded along to his monologue.

I doubted Simon would be finished with whatever he was doing in the morgue yet. The cathedral was no great distance. It would be worth a glance, and if the vandalism was as dramatic as the sergeant claimed, it might make either excellent local colour or even a short article of its own. I was paid by the word; these things count.

I headed off to Winchester Cathedral and soon found myself in its chilly stone interior. It is a building of extraordinary beauty, the soaring pillars and arched roof like a petrified forest above me, and I paced through it in some awe, feet ringing on the flagstoned floor.

I asked a verger for what I sought. His face showed reluctance, but I dropped the sergeant's name into his ear and a shilling into his hand, and he took me to a tomb, concealed from the public by a temporary curtain.

"Here it is, sir," he said. "The tomb of Peter des Roches. Appalling."

The medieval effigy of a reclining man carved in stone had doubtless been beautiful once, but time, or perhaps the touches of the faithful, had worn away the statue's features until he had the appearance of a leper, pitted and noseless. Underneath the effigy, the side of the tomb was cracked and splintered, with a jagged-edged hole exposing its black interior. I ducked down to look at it, and recoiled.

It was *cold*. I could feel the icy air stealing out from the dark interior. And it was dark inside, too, not just an absence of light but darkness as a force, a hungry, waiting thing that would devour all attempts to see in. I looked at the broken edges of stone, and perhaps it was merely the shadows, but it appeared to me more than that. As though the darkness was staining the stone. Slowly spreading outward, into the light.

The hole in the tomb was sufficiently large to admit a man's hand. I should not have put my hand in there at any price.

I stood, wanting to be away. "What on earth happened?"

"Someone broke into it," the verger said with a despairing shrug. "With a crowbar. Who knows why. Maybe they thought to find treasure, but…"

"In a tomb this old?"

"It has not been opened before to my knowledge, sir. But why would a bishop's tomb contain treasure?"

"Who was this gentleman?" I asked.

"Peter des Roches, sir. Bishop of Winchester in the reigns of King John and Henry III. He was a good man, by all accounts." The verger named a few of the bishop's achievements, founding this and supporting that, then, seeing he was losing my attention, went on, "And there's a fine piece of local folklore too, sir, a charming tale, if you'd care to hear it?" He didn't wait for my assent. "The story goes that one day, Peter was out hunting in the forest instead of caring for the souls of his parish, when he met—who do you think?"

He seemed to expect an answer. "King John?"

"King Arthur. Of the knights of the Round Table, sir."

"Really." I wondered how long this fairy tale was going to take.

"It's said that King Arthur invited him to dinner in a great hall under a hill. The two ate a fine meal together, with many a glass and many a tale to make the evening a success. And then, as they parted Peter bemoaned that nobody would ever believe who he had met that day, and he asked the king for a token to prove that it had truly happened. So King Arthur told him to close his fist and open it again, and when he did so, a butterfly flew from his palm."

"A—"

"A butterfly, sir. Ever after, whenever Bishop Peter opened his fist, the miracle was repeated. People came from far and wide to be blessed by him. He became known as the butterfly bishop, so the tale goes." The verger paused, evidently struck by his own story. "And that's a funny thing, sir, now I think. I don't know if you've seen the news—"

I didn't wait for him to tell me. I was already hurrying out of the great, shadowy hall, walking as fast as respect for the holy surroundings allowed, and the second I passed out of its doors, I broke into a run.

Simon and I stood together, staring at the broken tomb. I had met him on the way out of the morgue, which was fortunate, else I should have doubtless forced my way in to get him, given the urgency I had felt. Now, standing in front of a centuries-old relic, I wondered if I had just made something of a fool of myself.

Simon was crouched down, one hand on the tomb to balance himself, the other hovering over that dark opening.

"What could it mean?" I asked.

"I don't know."

"That hole is big enough to reach in. What might someone have taken from in there?"

"I don't know." Simon's face was intent. He murmured something under his breath, and then, quite suddenly, he pushed the tips of his fingers into that awful, waiting hole. The colour drained from his face so fast I thought he would faint. He snatched his hand back, and I felt pure relief to see it emerge intact.

"What is it? What's in there?"

"Cold." He swayed slightly, and his knuckles whitened where he gripped the sepulchre's stone.

"Are you all right?"

Simon's mouth moved slightly. It was very dark now, the dim lamps casting long shadows. His deep-set eyes were black pits, and his skin looked not just pale but oddly colourless.

"Simon?" I put my hand on his arm and felt the violent shudder that ran through him. "Simon!"

His hand shot out, grabbed my coat, pulled me down. I landed hard on my knee on the cold flagstones. He grasped the back of my head, forcing my face close to his, and I had a momentary flash of alarm that he might mean to kiss me, and in a cathedral, of all places—but he did not. He pushed his face against the side of my head, forcing words into my ear, so close I felt his lips move on my skin, still barely audible. His breath was very, very cold.

"Help—me. Get me—out."

It was only a few hundred yards, thank God, and though I had not Simon's strength, I was sturdy enough. I dragged him along, his arm over my shoulders, his feet stumbling. I suppose people thought he was drunk.

By the time we reached our lodgings, Simon's weight was making me stagger. I pushed him up the stairs, past the landlady's disapproving gaze, and into my room, where he half fell onto the bed and then, in a sudden spasm of activity, began tearing at his shirt.

"Simon?" I said helplessly.

"Get this off!"

He was dragging at his coat, like to tear it. I joined him—this was not how I had imagined undressing him—and unfastened his shirt, and recoiled at what I saw. The writing on his skin was frantic, far worse than before, huge jagged letters, the ink stabbing itself up and down over his chest. His face was grey.

"Mirror," he rasped.

I grabbed the looking-glass from the wall and brought it over, twisting round so that I could see his reflection too.

The last time, the mirror writing had been clear, if obscene, English. This time, it was utterly incoherent. The letters had the rectangular form of those one sees in illuminated medieval manuscripts, utterly indecipherable.

"I can't read it," I said.

"Nor can I." Sweat beaded on his forehead. "Trying to talk. Too old. I can't. I can't understand. Stop it!"

I was close to panic now. "Simon? What can I do?"

Simon was pushing and scraping at his chest with his nails, leaving scratched trails that beaded red, as though he were trying to rip off his own skin. It had no effect on the scrawl which became, if anything wilder.

"Stop it!" I dropped the glass and grabbed his hands. He pulled back, hard, far stronger than me, but I didn't let go, and he jerked me forward into his lap, and whether it was him or me I could not to this day say, but we were kissing then, his lips and teeth hard and desperate on mine. He shoved me backwards, and I fell onto the bed with his muscular bulk pinning me down, and his hands pinioning mine.

It was scarcely kissing now. He forced his tongue, thrusting, into my mouth, and I moaned my surrender around it. His hand moved, so that one held both my wrists while the other went to his waist, and shoved clothing aside. He shifted above me, still holding me down, and knelt over my face, and like that, without a word, he pushed his stiff cock into my bruised, wet mouth.

I almost choked. I almost came.

I did not know, I still do not understand, why it should be such a pleasure to have Simon manhandle me so. I do not lack self-respect. No other man has ever used me ill, and I should resent it extremely if any tried. But then, no other man has ever held on to me as though he were lost in darkness, as though my body were his last connection to the light.

I knew more later. God help me, I was to discover so much, and to learn the truth of Simon's words, that some knowledge would be better lost forever. But even then I think I understood that he was dying inside, and he found life in me.

So he fucked my mouth, desperate and bruising, and I squirmed and moaned underneath him, unable to take even the slightest control and painfully aroused by his need, and when he came, hard and deep, in my throat and his grip on my wrists relaxed, I fought my hands free and unbuttoned myself frantically. He was still in my mouth as I frigged myself no more than twice and spent with a cry of painful ecstasy muffled only by his prick.

Simon pulled away from me, breathing hard, and rolled off me.

I was hanging half over the edge of the bed. I slid down to the floor with a thump.

"Robert." Simon sounded exhausted. "I…" He did not try to finish the sentence.

"Are you all right? What happened in the cathedral?"

"The story." He gestured at his chest. The writings had calmed now, still moving, but more like the gentle pace of a fountain pen than the insane skittering script of before. "The story was too old. It's distorted. Decayed. I couldn't read it, and it needs to be read. It was so angry, and it would not stop. It filled my mind, until…well, until you filled it instead. Robert, please, I had no intention of distressing you—"

"The only thing that will distress me at this moment is if you apologise. I should take that very ill indeed."

"I forced you." His voice was raw.

"On the contrary. I should have insisted." That got his startled attention. I put a hand up, resting it on his thigh. "And I am delighted to have been of assistance."

There was a pause, and Simon began to laugh. He laughed like a man who was not used to the act, and who was not quite sure why he was doing it. I hauled myself back onto the bed and leaned over to kiss him with my bruised lips, and he pulled me close and held me there. I ran a finger over the skin of his chest and felt nothing but coarse hair and warmth.

"You are quite remarkable," he said. "So matter-of-fact. Does nothing dismay you?"

"I was not matter-of-fact just now," I pointed out. "I enjoyed myself exceedingly. And while I may be dismayed on occasion, I have never seen the point of having vapours. Are you recovered?"

"Thanks to you." His arm tightened.

"What's in the tomb?"

"So many questions, Robert." It was not a rebuke, but he clearly did not intend to give a full answer. "A grave has been violated. That must be set right."

I asked the question that had been burning in my mind since the verger spoke. "Do you think that the folk tale is true? Butterflies from empty hands? King Arthur? Because, the thing is, Dr. Merridew kept his hands flat. When he shook my hand, he did not close his own at all. And when he spoke he had his palms on his legs, open, pressed down, as if he was trying to keep them still. Could it be that he did not want to risk closing them in front of you? Is he creating the things?"

Simon sat up and began to pull his clothing back to decency. I went to get my spare shirt front, since the one I wore had taken the brunt of my excitement. "I think it likely," he said. "Merridew was…wrong. I found the atmosphere peculiar. Did you sense something in there?"

"Me?"

"You felt something, I think."

"The butterfly deaths gave me the horrors, that was all. I imagined them somewhat vividly."

"You, who are so matter-of-fact." Simon did not smile, but his voice was warm.

"But how can Merridew be doing it?"

"I don't know. But it seems clear that he took something from the tomb, and it has been missed, and it must be returned." Simon stood. "It is my experience that gifts are very dangerous things to steal."

We stood together at the doctor's door, knocking relentlessly for some five minutes, before the man opened it himself. He looked flushed, and there was a butterfly on his shoulder. A Red Admiral, a creature that should have died well before this time of year, wings moving slowly back and forth, open and shut.

Merridew attempted to slam the door. Simon pushed back hard—very hard, considering the apparent frailty of the elderly man on its other side. In the end, it took our combined weights, shoulders to the door, to force it. Merridew stepped away with a gasp. We were inside.

There were butterflies in the hall, spread-winged on the walls, crawling on the ceiling, moving slowly underfoot. Some were those I recognised, Cabbage Whites and Painted Ladies. Others were the bizarre shapes and colours of the pinned specimens. All were alive.

"What is the meaning of this intrusion?" demanded the doctor.

"Shut your hand and open it again," Simon told him.

"I shall do no such thing."

"Do it, and we will leave."

The doctor glared at him, looked at me. He held out a scrawny fist, turned it palm up, opened it.

A huge black-and-white butterfly slowly opened its wings and flew off in a papery flurry.

Simon nodded, then took an unceremonious stride forward, past the doctor, and threw open the study door.

There were thousands of the things in there, crawling and flying and hanging in great heaps and mounds, many smashed to pulp underfoot. I clamped my lips shut and grabbed for my handkerchief.

"What did you take from the tomb?" Simon asked.

"Oh, you are clever." There was a fanatic light in the doctor's pale eyes. "It will do you no good, you know. What have you to accuse me of? I have done nothing wrong."

"You desecrated a tomb. Two men are dead."

The doctor gave a shrill laugh. A huge butterfly landed on his head, sitting at a jaunty angle, like a fashionable hat. "Superstitious nonsense. You can prove nothing. And the butterflies killed those men. Not me. I had no motive. No intention."

"You made the butterflies. You let them go. The deaths are on your shoulders, Doctor."

"Well, I could scarcely keep the damned things in here, could I?" Merridew gestured around. "Look at them. They get everywhere! You'll find them in your boots, you know." He turned up his palms, appealing for understanding, and gave an involuntary little clench of one fist. A white butterfly appeared on his palm; he glanced at it, and clapped his hands together.

"A Cabbage White," he explained, brushing the broken thing to the floor. "Worthless. Look, Mr. Feximal, the men were accidents. The butterflies were hungry, they swarmed. A tramp died, and some other fellow. That was unfortunate but it's hardly my fault."

"Why don't you stop making them?" I demanded as his hand closed and opened yet again.

The doctor frowned at my failure to understand. "I have to keep on. I must have a Cobalt Saturn."

I looked at his face, so intent, so dedicated, and at his hand, clenching and unclenching, dropping butterflies. I took a step away, towards the workbench, and my elbow hit something. The marble mortar, I realised. It was perhaps the only item in the room on which butterflies did not crawl.

Simon was wearing a singularly intimidating scowl. "Dr. Merridew, you are perhaps unaware of what you have done. You must return what you took from the tomb. You are turning a gift to ill uses, and you have awakened something that should be asleep. It must end."

The doctor laughed again. It was almost a shriek. "Return what I took? Oh, that will not be possible, I fear."

"It is not yours," Simon repeated, voice hard and commanding.

I looked down at the mortar, next to my elbow. I saw the fine yellow-brown dust.

"What did you take?" Simon was demanding. "Stone from the tomb, jewellery, a piece of the body? What have you done with it?"

There was a feverish glitter in the doctor's eyes. His hands opened and closed, butterflies rising from them every second. I stared at him, and the mortar, and the words of the old tale were ringing in my mind. *I'll grind his bones to make my bread...*

"Simon." I could not say more.

He turned to me. I pointed at the mortar, and the dust within. He looked down, and up, back at the doctor. Dr. Merridew laughed and laughed, pitch rising, and any lingering doubts about his sanity fled, because no sane man would have found amusement in the expression on Simon Feximal's face.

"You damned fool," Simon said, and the commonplace expletive rang out like a funeral bell.

"I see you understand." The doctor giggled. "The bishop's gift is within me now. I have consumed it, and it is mine. Mine."

Simon's jaw was set as he looked at that elderly madman, alight with energy, the fragile creatures rising up in a thin, twisting stream from his clenching hands. "Will you cease this?" he demanded.

"No. Why should I?"

"You must. Stop using it. Come to the tomb now, make what apology you can, and hope you may earn forgiveness. This is your only chance and there will not be another."

"Certainly not. What nonsense you speak."

"Very well." Simon turned abruptly. "Come, Robert."

"Come?" I echoed. "But—"

"There is nothing the police can do. Dr. Merridew has committed no crime in the eyes of the law, except for desecrating the tomb, which we cannot prove. There is, as he says, no way for him to return the bishop's bones now. We can do nothing, so let us leave."

"No." I could not understand this. "Two men are dead. Hubert Lord left a wife and a child. Others might die if he lets more butterflies go. How can you—"

"Come, Robert," Simon repeated. He grasped my wrist and pulled me to the heavy door. I pulled back angrily, uselessly. Simon stopped in front of the door, powerful grip still tight on my wrist, and paused, not turning back to face the doctor. "I hope you find your stolen gift worth its cost, sir."

Dr. Merridew did not reply. He was batting another Cabbage White off his hands.

I had stopped resisting. We stepped out of the foul, infested room, and Simon shut the heavy door, then pushed me gently in the direction of the front door. "Leave. Wait outside."

"No."

"Robert, I must ask you to go now."

"No. I saw you take it."

He looked at me, eyes steady on mine, and in that long moment of mutual regard, a partnership began.

"Go on," I said. "Do it."

Simon opened his hand to reveal the key that he had taken from the other side of the door. He put it in the keyhole and turned it, and with that act he locked Dr. Merridew in that hot little room filled with butterflies of his own creation.

It was Simon who locked the door, but it was I who took the key out of the keyhole, led the way out of the house, and dropped the key down the first drain I saw.

We returned to the inn without a word between us. I don't know if Simon thought of what we had done as an execution, or a murder, or as justice. He did not speak, and nor did I, but we went together to my room, and there we stripped each other wordlessly and he laid me down on the rumpled bed and took me then, gasping with each thrust as though that was the only way he could breathe.

Afterwards we lay together. I ran my fingers over his chest. I did not attempt to trace the patterns that wrote themselves at a leisurely pace on his skin. That seemed like a very bad idea, somehow.

I said, "I should like to meet again."

Simon gazed at the ceiling. "You have seen what I do. My life is not always safe, or clean. I should not like to see you stained by it."

That was, I observed, not the same thing as a "no".

I had little doubt that he was right. What I had seen of his strange work was frightening and disturbing, and my complicity in the night's work was something I had yet to allow myself to think of. Any sensible man would have walked away. But I was fascinated.

"I think I must insist," I said. "You may refuse, of course, but I warn you, you will be in grave danger of receiving another letter."

Simon shook his head, but I felt the muscles of his arm tighten around me, and the beginnings of a reluctant smile curved his lips once more.

The next night, with the verger's permission, Simon and I stood alone in the cathedral, before the tomb. I do not quite know what Simon did, and I could play no part in it, but I held the candles that lit him as he murmured incantations that closed the strange rent that the doctor's desecration had opened, until the crack in the tomb was no more than a piece of broken stonework, no darker or colder than the rest.

The alarm was raised by Dr. Merridew's housemaid when she could not enter his room in the morning. He was found under a shroud of butterflies more than two feet deep. What made this death different from the others was one peculiar feature. Over his face, in his lungs, every butterfly was of the same type.

Dr. Merridew had choked to death on Cabbage Whites.

Remember, Remember

I sat in Wyatt's dining-rooms by the Strand and waited for Simon Feximal, who was late.

It was the fourth of November, and this would be my first meeting with him since our return from Winchester. He was occupied with his strange duties of course; I had my career as a journalist to pursue.

It was blossoming. My account of the abominable Dr. Merridew and his death by butterflies had thrilled even the jaded palates of London readers. I had not given a complete account of events, wishing to steer clear of the laws governing defamation, gross indecency, obscene publications and possibly manslaughter. Still, my story increased the *Chronicle*'s sales by more than a third, and caused my editor to give me a grunt of approval and a gory murder to cover. I was becoming noticed as not just one of the penny-a-line crowd but a scribbler to be reckoned with. I was building the career of which I had so long dreamed, and I was proud.

I had therefore written to Simon suggesting dinner, phrased in terms that also suggested other evening entertainments—one develops a knack for writing in a way that no policeman could point to as criminal—and he had accepted. I named Wyatt's as the venue, since one can get a capital chop there, it was halfway between our respective addresses, and most significantly, it was very close to Holywell Street and its environs, where gentlemen can take a room for two hours with no awkward questions.

I had, therefore, come to this evening with some anticipation. But the clock ticked on and Simon did not arrive.

I waited. I ordered a dish for myself, and ate it, since I could not afford to leave a meal unconsumed. I took more wine than was good for me, and at last I abandoned my solitary dinner and left the chop house in a fury of disappointment, curiosity, anger. He could, surely, have sent a note, were he occupied with work. Had his interest lapsed in the intervening weeks? Or perhaps he had been unavoidably detained, even injured?

I stewed over these thoughts as I walked, aware of my own absurdity but unable to shrug off his defection. I walked home through Old Compton Street, where a telegraph boy can be had for a shilling, and the thought crossed my mind to look for consolation there, but I could not find the enthusiasm. The fact was, Simon Feximal had come to occupy my thoughts to a degree that was not entirely welcome.

Of course one dreams of forming a deep connexion, but for most of us, a dream is all it can be. Even were Simon to return my interest— and on the strength of this evening I had no reason to suppose he did— then what? He was a most extraordinary man living a most extraordinary life. I had my career to pursue. And the law condemned us both to a hole-and-corner existence when it came to personal affections. What on earth did I expect of him, or of myself? Why indulge in fancies that could only lead to disappointment?

No, I thought. I would do well not to think more of Simon Feximal. I would expect nothing, plan nothing, hope for nothing, and not allow foolish imagination to paint pictures of what could not be.

I was checking proofs of my latest article the next morning when I heard my name resound across the room.

"Caldwell! Where the devil's Caldwell?"

Mr. Lownie, editor of the *Chronicle*, pushed his way through the desks and piles of paper, cursing a compositor who blocked his way.

"Here, sir," I cried, lifting a hand.

"There you are," he said, with an accusatory note, as though I had been hiding under the desk. "You know the ghost-hunter. Feximal."

It is always a little unnerving to be told that one knows a man if one's knowledge is in the Biblical sense. I adopted an expression of, I hoped, intelligent curiosity. "I do, sir. May I ask the matter?"

"Can you use him?"

"I doubt it, sir, he is not a man to be used. But he owes me—" An explanation, at least. "A small favour. What's the matter?"

"Hartley House." Mr. Lownie rapped his pipe on the edge of my desk, spraying dottle. "The residence of his grace the duke of Sarum."

"And her grace his wife, and Lord Mitcham their son," I added. The infant thus named was the latest great-grandson to her imperial Majesty. Her Majesty had had the house built for the young duke, her favourite grandchild, and their graces had removed there some few months before the birth of their first baby. "What has Mr. Feximal to do with dukes?"

"That is what you shall tell me, Caldwell." Mr. Lownie pulled a twist of tobacco from his pocket and began to stuff his pipe with stained fingers. "Your ghost-hunting acquaintance was summoned there most urgently last night— What?"

"Nothing, sir."

"Along with Miss Kay and Dr. Berry. Carnacki's in Ireland chasing up some haunting, else he'd be there too, I hear."

I whistled. That list encompassed the best-known ghost-hunters in England, with the exception of the reclusive Dr. Silence. I had looked into the field in some detail when I had inherited a ghost along with my crumbling and so far unsellable house. What I had learned had left me with a powerful desire to avoid Dr. Berry, a powerful relief that my case did not require Miss Kay, and a choice between Messrs Feximal and Carnacki that I could only be grateful had been settled in Simon's favour by Carnacki's absence. "Three ghost-hunters to the ducal residence?"

"They have been in constant attendance since last night. The gates are locked and the servants silent. No journalist is admitted, and even callers of the highest society have been turned away this morning." Mr. Lownie patted me on the shoulder. "Get in there, Caldwell. I want to know what's going on."

I took the Underground to Green Park and the elegant new mansion of Hartley House. The corrosive touch of London fog had not yet begun to eat away at its white façade, and the house shone brightly, light spilling from the great windows on this dull day. Outside the wrought-iron gates lurked a disconsolate gaggle of my fellow scribblers.

Murchison of The Times raised a hand in weary greeting. "I don't know why you've bothered to haul yourself here, Bobster. Nothing doing."

"You must have some idea what's happened," I said. "You, stewing in ignorance?"

He snorted. "All I know is, there were screams and cries last night, an urgent fuss made, and all the spook-shyers called up in a lump. The place has been closed up like a nun's quim since."

Rodericks of the Gazette gave me a knowing look. "You are acquainted with the man Feximal, are you not?"

"I am."

"I saw your copy from Winchester. Good stuff." Rodericks narrowed his eyes. "You wouldn't be planning to steal a march on us with personal association, would you, dear boy?"

I denied it utterly and insincerely. Murchison and Rodericks closed in on me.

"Listen, my boy," Murchison told me quietly, while Rodericks glared our fellows away. "Hopkin got inside this morning, but the spook-shyers wouldn't talk to him. Your pal Feximal marched him out. Poor fellow looked scared half to death, couldn't say a word. The fact is, we're all stumped, because it's no good to get in if you can't stay in. Now, if we can finagle you inside, do you suppose you can persuade Feximal to talk to you?"

"I might," I said cautiously. I did not think it likely, but one should never say no before hearing the offer.

"You'd want to be reasonably sure. He's a bruiser of a fellow." I knew that well; his finger marks had lingered on my hips for days. "Because I've greased a servant here, and not used her yet, and I believe I can get a man inside."

"Put him in his shirtsleeves," Rodericks said, with a rude nod in my direction. "He'll look just like the baker's boy."

"But it's halves on the story, Bobster," Murchison insisted. "I'll want something exclusive."

"Thirds," Rodericks said over his shoulder. "The maid was my lead in the first place."

"Halves, and you two split what I give you," I said firmly. "If Feximal doesn't want me in there, he's liable to tear me limb from limb." What a thought. Simon truly angry with me was not a sight I wished to see, but Simon venting his outrage with a stern and punishing hand… I reined in my thoughts before they wandered too far from decency.

Murchison and Rodericks exchanged looks. "Halves," they agreed without further argument, and I knew then that the task ahead of me should not be taken lightly.

The disloyal kitchenmaid met us round the back of the house. She had a bowl of slops in her hands, and a baize apron bundled under her arm, ready to act as my disguise. Her face bore a surreptitious look and her pinched mouth spoke of dissatisfaction.

"Don't you point the finger at me when you get caught," she muttered.

"I shan't," I assured her. "I trust you won't be suspected?"

"Don't know as I care if I am. I'd give up my place for two shillings and welcome." She sniffed meaningfully, my cue to offer a sympathetic ear.

"What's so bad about it? Is it the family, or the Upper Ten?" The senior servants set the tone of the backstairs, and a cruel Cook was the bane of many a kitchenmaid's miserable life.

She shook her head. "It ain't that, I been in worse-run houses. But I never been in a haunted one before, nor I don't want to, and put up with it I shall not."

"Tell me," I said.

She gave me an expectant look. I found a couple of shillings in my pocket and passed them over with a secretive hand.

"Crying." She leaned forward, speaking softly. "Littl'uns, crying like their hearts was broke. Ever since the baby came, we've heard the crying." She looked round sharply at a raised voice from inside the house. "No time for this now. You get inside, and I know nothing."

She shoved an earthenware bowl of slops into my hands, and I followed her meekly in. Normally I should have taken the opportunity to pump the servants for information, but we had the kitchenmaid on our payroll already, and I was after bigger game. I slipped through the back ways of the house, abandoning the bowl and stripping off the apron as I moved from the servants' domain to the family rooms.

The house was brand new, of course, warmed with great hot-water pipes to the point where I was quite glad that I had left my topcoat outside with Murch. I paced the halls, trying to look as though I belonged here. The halls were silent and empty. I could hear the sounds of speech from ahead, and I quickened my pace as my sharp ears caught a particularly low and resonant tone.

Only one man of my acquaintance had a voice that deep.

I could have hurried forward then, but I was caught by uncertainty. No gentleman would invade the privacy of another's home thus; but I was a journalist, not a gentleman, and I had a story to pursue. Simon would understand that, would he not?

Or perhaps he would not. I had thrilled at the thought of his disapproval earlier, but it seemed rather more probable and more menacing now. If he was truly angered, or disgusted, so that he did not want to see me again…

Well, that would be as it might. Had I not resolved already to let the cards fall as Fate decreed? Journalism was my ambition, nothing more, and I had a career to build.

With that decided, I crept forward along the bright hallway to a great panelled door, and paused a moment to listen.

The voice inside was unmistakeably Simon's. It was hard to hear through the thick wood, but he sounded frustrated and even worried.

"I can't," he insisted. "There's nothing. It makes no sense."

A woman's voice came back, somewhat testily. I could not make out the words. Simon responded, a little quieter, so that the door muffled his words altogether. I heard "stubborn" and no more.

A hand touched my shoulder.

I had not had the slightest sense of another's approach. I turned with a startled cry and found myself facing Dr. Berry.

The famous ghost-exterminator was very close to me. He was not much over my own medium height, and aged at least fifty, his pale eyes magnified behind thick lenses, the sallow skin of his bald head sagging. His white moustache and neatly pointed beard were stained yellow with a lifetime's use of tobacco, and I smelled the stale fug of the weed on his skin and clothes.

"Who are you?" he said softly. His voice was sibilant, and the smell of smoke rolled off his breath.

"Just pausing in my duties, sir," I said as any servant might.

I doubted he would believe me, and it was clear he did not. His eyes widened a little, seeming as round as the lenses that framed them.

"Who are you?" he repeated, moving closer, so close that the lines of his skin seemed to impress themselves on my vision.

I leaned back. He leaned in, and I realised I had my back to the wall, and the man was up against me, and…

And I was frightened. Out of nowhere I was deeply, profoundly afraid, not of being evicted, or the physical chastisement that might come with it, but afraid as prehistoric man feared the noise in the dark cave. Afraid of something I could not apprehend, but which I knew and dreaded in my bones.

Dr. Berry's face was inches from mine. His eyes were huge. His teeth had vertical lines marked in brown, stained by years of smoke. The hairs just under his nose were of a browner shade too, fading out to yellow and then the natural white. All these details impressed themselves on me with a force so stunning that I could scarcely drag breath into my lungs. The gaping pores of his skin. The obscenely soft bulge of a mole, pushing its way out of the rough, pitted side of his nose. And the eyes, threaded with red veins, staring at me.

"Who are you?"

"Caldwell," I managed. My tongue felt thick.

"You're going to tell me everything." Dr. Berry raised a hand. He was not a stout man but his fingers were oddly plump, and pallid. They did not look like the swollen fingers of a drowned corpse. I told myself that they did not.

I did not want him to touch me with those soft fingers.

"Please," I whispered.

Dr. Berry's lips (a little cracked, a little dry, tobacco stains in the lines and ridges of dry skin) curved at my plea. There was nothing in the world now but his eyes behind those awful refractive thick lenses. His dead man's fingers closed on my jaw—

There was a solid thump, and he wasn't there any more.

"What the devil?" demanded a deep voice. I gasped, pulling in air to my parched lungs, and as the blackness around the edge of my vision receded, I saw Simon's powerful body protectively in front of me, and Dr. Berry straightening from where the blow had sent him stumbling down the hall.

Dr. Berry gave Simon a look of such blank malevolence that it shuddered down my own spine. Simon stared back, unmoving, his mouth curled with contempt. He seemed to feel none of the fear that had gripped me at the doctor's snakelike gaze.

"Another snooper." Dr. Berry pulled out a darkly stained handkerchief and dabbed at his lips. "I was merely teaching him a lesson."

Simon exhaled through his nose, then turned to me, and I cringed at the expression on his face. I had been a fool to do this, it dawned on me far too late. To bring my presence, with our illegal connexion, into his work.

"Mr. Caldwell," Simon said with grim intent.

"You know him?" enquired the doctor.

Simon ignored him. "I suppose I need not ask what you are doing here."

"Prying," Dr. Berry said. "Prying and spying. Eavesdropping and earwigging."

"Am I to do this entire task on my own?" said a sharp female voice from the door to the room.

I turned. She was a tall woman, in her thirties or perhaps older, with dark hair plainly dressed. Her face bore the marks of suffering, the irritable twitching of her hand suggested it had not always been borne with patience, and she was looking from Dr. Berry to Simon with an expression of some annoyance. She ignored me entirely.

"I found a scribbler," Dr. Berry explained. "But Feximal has interfered."

"I should hope so," replied the woman, who had to be the third of the ghost-hunters, Miss Kay. "Just throw him out, Simon." She flicked a finger at me.

"I am acquainted with Mr. Caldwell," Simon said. "The butterfly business last month."

"Then throw him out gently."

"That is not good enough," Dr. Berry said. "The scribblers keep coming in, like cockroaches, like rats. We must make an example."

Miss Kay looked at Dr. Berry and said, her tone quite dispassionate, "Everything about you revolts me."

I sagged against the wall, avoiding looking at Dr. Berry. I could feel his eyes on me like a wet touch, like a tongue on my skin, even as he answered Miss Kay in a tone of equal dislike to her own. If Simon would only escort me out, so that I did not have to go near Dr. Berry, I should not complain.

Simon said, "Well, Mr. Caldwell," moving towards me, and then all three ghost-hunters looked up as one.

"Get him *out*," Miss Kay snapped.

Dr. Berry reached a hand towards me. Simon smacked it away, with a force that sent the older man's limb flying upwards. Dr. Berry's pale eyes shone with anger, but that was when I heard it. A baby's cry.

It rose in sobbing crescendos, the mewing cry of a young infant, but it was loud. Very loud, and very close, and under it there was another cry starting. It sounded like the heartbroken sounds of a lost child, of perhaps two years, interspersed with gasps and sobs of fear. I stared, wide-eyed, as the sound came over and upon us, and with it a wave of sensation that made me cringe into myself.

Simon's jaw was set. Miss Kay bowed her head over clenched hands. Dr. Berry's eyes were narrowed as he murmured something under his breath.

The younger child cried out, and the sobs of both changed into a high-pitched moan that rose and wailed and sharpened with agony.

"For God's sake!" I cried, as the keening sound rose intolerably. "How can you stand there? Can you not help them?"

Dr. Berry gave a hiss of contempt. "Devils and demons. Mockery."

"A suggestion," Simon said to Miss Kay, over the spectral sobbing. "What?"

Simon jerked his head at me. "He has heard it now. He has sense. If we have one in, it will fend off the rest."

"Are you mad?" said Dr. Berry, with the most animation I had seen from him. "A filthy penny-a-line merchant, observing our work?"

"Mr. Caldwell has discretion," Simon said, without looking at me, or at Dr. Berry.

"And he has heard the cries," Miss Kay added. "What do you propose to do about him, Doctor? That I shall permit," she added icily, as he made to speak.

"I do not require your permission," Dr. Berry said, with a corpse's smile.

"Then we are agreed," Simon told Miss Kay. "Mr. Caldwell, a word."

I followed him into the next room, a lavishly appointed drawing-room that stood at the front of the house, very conscious of the other ghost-hunters outside. Simon glared down at me. "For God's sake, Robert, what were you about?"

"My profession," I told him. I would not apologise, not now I was away from Dr. Berry and his unmanning influence. I had rendered myself loathsome in Simon's eyes, no doubt, but he would allow me to stay. I would still get my story.

I might yet be forgiven.

"Be damned to your profession," Simon muttered. "There are interests at play—" He straightened away from me a second before Miss Kay stalked in, and went on, "If we allow you to stay, it will be as the sole representative of the Press. Your fellows must not intrude further. And we will see your copy before it is submitted."

"Of course," I said with promptitude.

"Very well." Simon sounded a little surprised at my ready agreement. Evidently he was not aware of the distinction between seeing my copy and having right of approval over it.

"What is happening?" I asked him, as he drew me over to the window, away from the centre of the room, where Dr. Berry and Miss Kay settled themselves, a good eight feet apart. It was a comfort even to have his solid body near me. Had I been permitted to touch him without disgracing us both, I might well have flung myself into his arms like a whimpering child and thus disgraced myself alone. Since I could not, I bade myself play the man, although I did turn around so that Dr. Berry was not in my peripheral vision. This did not prove comforting, as it simply meant he was behind me. "Are those children?"

"We do not know." Simon looked worn, and I realised that he must have been up all the night. "This is a new building. No child has died here, so we are told. But there has never been a haunting reported on this spot before."

"And…" I gestured at his burly chest, hidden by his frock coat, under which the runes on his skin would be moving.

"Nothing," he said shortly. "I have tried. But a child too young to tell its story…" He shrugged.

"Can they not do anything?" I asked quietly, with a jerk of my head towards the other ghost-hunters.

"We have tried. We will keep trying." He pushed a hand through his grizzled hair. "In truth, Robert, I am at a loss, Miss Kay too. And Berry has only one technique and that…" He made a face.

"What?" I asked.

Simon took a pace closer to the window, hand closing on my arm to bring my head nearer his. I felt his breath on my ear, and my skin shivered delightfully at the sensation. "Dr. Berry is an exterminator," he said softly. "He does not understand stories. He does not find the conclusions. He simply cuts the thread."

"I don't understand."

"I believe that each haunting is an unfinished tale, of some kind," Simon said. "If the story can be concluded, so is the ghost's presence. The untold story is agony, whether it is the fact of a murder or the location of a will, or simply…unfinished business, as with your ancestor's spirit." There was a slight reddening on his stern face at the mention of that business, as I'm sure there was on mine. "I believe, I *know* that the story must be concluded for the spirit to find rest. Dr. Berry disagrees."

"What does he believe?"

"That any ghost is a manifestation of evil. That they must be sent away howling, without sacrament or comfort. That we do not listen, we simply extinguish."

"But they're just children," I said. "You heard them."

"I know." He shut his eyes briefly. "The duke of Sarum wants them gone, by whatever means prove effective. Dr. Berry can do that. Miss Kay and I, it seems, cannot."

I was here for my story. It had cost me already, and it was foolish to focus on anything else. But I saw the pain in his eyes, and I still had the sound of lost children in my ears.

"Let me help," I said. "What can I do?"

The approval in Simon's face was reward enough. He gave me one of his rare, brief smiles. I felt, I was sure, that had we been alone, he would have kissed me, and the awareness tingled through me almost as much as the kiss would have.

"Thank you, Robert," he said softly. "You comfort me."

"Simon!" called Miss Kay.

Simon turned from me and strode over, I following. The lady ghost-hunter sat on a chair, hunched over in a way that suggested her governess had not made sufficient use of the backboard. Her fingers were ungloved and tightly interlaced, and she stared at her thumb. So did I.

The left thumbnail was very long, ludicrously so, over an inch and a half at my estimate. And the nail was…black? Bruised? No, neither. It was a dark, oily colour, with swirls of green and blue—and they moved, I realised, staring down at it. Her thumbnail was a pool in the world, opaque to my eyes, but deep, very deep indeed…

"I should not look too close," Simon murmured at my side.

"He might as well, for all the use it is." Miss Kay straightened her back with an irritated grunt. "There's foulness here, why can I not see it?"

"What can you see?"

She gave a frustrated wave of her hand. "Death, unnatural death. Fear and pain. But nothing clear, blast it."

"If we cannot see, we cannot act." Simon scowled.

"In which case Dr. Berry will. Must," Miss Kay added. "God forfend their graces should endure an unpleasant noise for an hour if it might alleviate the suffering of others."

"Theodosia," Simon said wearily. "It is not the family's fault they are haunted, or that they want the spirits gone."

"It will be their fault if that repellent brute extinguishes those souls before we can free them."

I was taking a liking to this forthright lady. "Are their graces safe here?" I asked. "Could they endure a few more days without danger?"

"Could, but won't," Miss Kay snapped.

"We don't know what danger there might be," Simon rejoined.

"The family could move out."

"It's their house."

"It's their ghost!"

I noted for future consideration that implacable Mr. Feximal and intimidating Miss Kay bickered like children, and enquired, "But you do not predict immediate danger for their graces?"

"Probably not," Miss Kay said brusquely. "This house is protected."

"By what?" It is a measure of how much I had already learned that I did not ask *By whom?*

"There are various means to hold back that which is outside," Simon told me. "Some as simple as a horseshoe, cold iron over the door—"

"Others more complicated," Miss Kay added. "This is the latter. The house is undeniably protected. And it is also haunted, and we cannot tell why."

"There is no why," said Dr. Berry right behind me, breath hot on my ear.

I started. No, let me be honest: I cried out with fear. Simon's eyes darkened with fury, but Miss Kay was already surging up from her chair with a snap of, "*You*," jabbing her forefinger into Dr. Berry's chest.

Simon pulled me to one side as Miss Kay hissed savagely at Dr. Berry. "Stay if you must, but I want you to leave before Dr. Berry acts," he told me, voice low.

"What will he do?"

Simon's jaw tightened. "Tear them from this world. Hurl them into the outer darkness, where there is…wailing, or nothing at all."

"Will you witness it?"

"I must. They should have someone who regrets their passing." His face was full of pain, and at that moment I decided I should not let the foul Dr. Berry do this, to children or to Simon, if there was any means by which I could prevent it.

"I asked you if I could help," I reminded him. "Could I…" I searched for any way in which I might be useful. "Have you researched the history of the house? I could visit the archives of the *Chronicle*. See if there is anything to be learned."

"It was only built a year or so ago. If there had been any mysterious deaths, they would be remembered." He evidently saw my disappointment, because he went on, "But it is a better idea than any I have. If you think it worth your time—"

"I could not bear to think of Dr. Berry doing—what he does—and to know I had left a single stone unturned to prevent it."

Simon regarded me steadily for a moment, then leaned forward, dropping his deep voice to a low rumble. "I have not sought your forgiveness for my absence yesternight."

"Oh, I understand—"

"I hope you will allow me to earn it."

I could feel my skin heating under his steady regard. "If you choose to give me an explanation, Mr. Feximal, I am very willing to be satisfied by you."

That brought the colour to his cheeks in a most pleasing manner. Braced by anticipation, I found the courage to leave the room without escort, although also without turning my back on Dr. Berry, whom I edged past as I might a dangerous dog.

Some hours later I was in the *Chronicle*'s archive room with box upon box of index cards in front of me, paper dust coating my fingers, and the beginnings of a headache.

Simon was right. The house was new; any tragedy there would be fresh in memory. It had been built on an unremarkable site of which nothing was to be found in the records. Nothing had happened on Hartley House ground before this.

Something *had* happened to its architect, one Mr. Glasport. That was the first thing I found when I started my search. Glasport had drawn up the plans, laid the foundation stone and applied the mortar to it with his own hand, raised a celebratory glass, gone home and hanged himself. His body was found in his rooms the next day.

In the normal course of things—I use the word "normal" in Simon's idiosyncratic sense—self-murder would surely be significant. I had scrawled a note to inform Simon of my discovery, with a promise of further researches, and sent it round to Hartley House by messenger boy. But my initial excitement had faded quickly. Our problem was not a despairing architect, but two young children.

Could they have died near the house? Beggar children, abandoned babes? My fertile imagination sketched a scenario: the duke of Sarum fathers children upon a mistress and rejects her, she leaves his starving babes by the palace walls…

It was possible, I supposed, but unsupported by evidence. By all accounts Sarum was a decent young man. And, in truth, if every abandoned child on the London streets left a wailing ghost, the living would not hear ourselves speak for their cries.

No: these children had died an unnatural death, and an unrecorded one, too. I had nothing to tell Simon. No way to prevent Dr. Berry doing his work.

I scrubbed at my face with the heels of my hand. I still had to write my piece. My editor was waiting; I had promised Murchison and Rodericks exclusives. I had not promised Simon copy approval, although he might think I had, but frankly, I had nothing worth approving. No scandal, no facts, no story.

Then again, perhaps a description of the scene might jog some memories. Could I frame the article as an appeal for information? That would add weight to a very slim tale and perhaps it might even work. It was quite possible a reader would come forward to solve the mystery. This was truly a way in which I could help Simon's work and my own at once, and I felt a pulse of excitement. I scribbled a note advising him of my intentions and gave it to one of the messenger boys, then got down to work.

By eight o'clock I had placed my story on Mr. Lownie's desk and arranged for one of the boys to send a fair copy to Simon. I had yet to meet my obligations to my fellow scribblers, but I was hungry, having missed the opportunity to take luncheon, and tired of eye. I would drop in at an eating house on the way home and write something more there.

Perhaps I could give Roddy and Murch a sketch of the spook-shyers at work, I thought, as I took down my coat and hat. They could offer their readers pen portraits of Miss Kay, Simon Feximal and Dr.

Berry. I should greatly enjoy describing Dr. Berry to the reading public, if the description was to appear under somebody else's byline.

The *Chronicle*'s offices stood on Fleet Street. I pulled open the door to a chilly, damp night with a peculiar tang to the foggy air, and almost at once heard a report, as of a pistol discharged close by. I jumped and turned, only to realise that it was a firecracker, thrown by a shadowy lout.

Of course. It was the fifth of November, Bonfire Night. That would enliven my walk, and I decided on the instant to walk home along the Strand, rather than taking my usual route through Drury Lane, in order to see the procession. I had always enjoyed the celebrations of Guy Fawkes Night in my village, with hot spiced cider, coloured lights and showers of bright sparks, and the burning of the guy atop the bonfire. We boys would cheer and throw brands plucked from the burning as the traitor's effigy blazed.

I was murmuring, "Remember, remember the fifth of November," under my breath when a man stepped into my path. He was respectably dressed, with a hat of the bowler type and a good-quality greatcoat.

"Mr. Caldwell?" he asked politely.

"I am he."

The man leaned in. His moustache bristled a little as he spoke. I have always preferred a clean-shaven face. "You sent a message to Mr. Feximal today. I am to ask you, sir, if you have any further discoveries or ideas."

"I do indeed. Are you sent by Mr. Feximal?" He seemed rather well dressed to be a messenger, more of an upper servant, but doubtless their graces of Sarum were supporting the ghost-hunters with all the means at their disposal.

"I am, sir. What message may I convey?"

I did not want to tell their graces that I had found nothing. If this man was to report back to them, he should convey a message that would incline them to listen to Simon's representations rather than Dr.

Berry's. "As I advised Mr. Feximal earlier, I believe we have now a path to the solution. I have already submitted my story to my editor."

"Story," the man repeated. "To the *Chronicle*'s editor."

"Yes, that's right." I wondered whether to let him bring Simon's copy of the story over to Hartley House, and decided against it. It would probably not be typed out yet and, in any case, I preferred to leave its delivery to him as late as possible. Once it was set, Mr. Lownie would resist any changes with all the strength at his disposal; he was notorious in Fleet Street for refusing to bow to pressure. "That has all been put in motion and sent on to him. I fear you've had a wasted journey, sir, but I hope the mystery may be solved and its effects undone."

The bowler-hatted man looked at me with odd intentness, his gaze skimming over me from head to foot. There was nothing indecent in it, more a dispassionate assessment, as if he were committing me to memory. "Very well, Mr. Caldwell," he said at last and turned on his heel.

I ate a meat pie at a Lyons coffee house on Fleet Street. The noise of the crowd was audible even inside, and when I emerged and headed left onto the Strand, it was to find a great mass of mostly unwashed humanity blocking the streets. The Bonfire Night procession had begun.

Hundreds of people were congregated along the Strand, where ordinary traffic had been stopped. A band played up ahead, and the procession shuffled along: men in the costumes of olden days, officers of the army and navy, clowns and masqueraders. Societies marched under bright banners and scattered along the slowly moving stream were torchbearers. Along the length of the street, houses and commercial premises blazed with coloured lights, flags, Chinese lanterns and other such gay adornment. There were cheerful cries, some chants, the pop and bang of firecrackers, the scent of gunpowder in the air. It was highly pleasing to the eye, and I did not have the remotest chance of making my way through such a mass of humanity towards Brewer Street.

I decided to wait and watch, then head up Aldgate to take my usual path home. Accordingly I found a place on a shop's doorstep that gave me a small advantage over the crowd (I am not a man of great stature). It was on the corner of an alley, in which a group of ragged children played a game, already bored by the spectacle before them, or unwilling to make an attempt on the crowd.

They were singing that ancient rhyme:

London Bridge is falling down, falling down, falling down
London Bridge is falling down, my fair lady.

I leaned my shoulders against the door, watching a group of masqueraders clad as Chinamen dance around the edges of the procession.

Build it up with wood and clay, wood and clay, wood and clay...

The simple melody combined with the smell of smoke, hot chestnuts and warm mulled wine took me back to my childhood. I found myself mouthing the words of the song along with the children.

Wood and clay will wash away, wash away, wash away...

We had played at this game in my village as these London urchins did. Two children made an arch of their arms through which the others passed, ducking under the bridge thus formed, and hoping not to be trapped when it fell.

Bricks and mortar will not stay...

Strange that a child's song should be about man's work coming to ruin, I thought, and considered Caldwell Place, my mouldering, once-haunted ancestral heap. The bricks and mortar there certainly would not stay, and I had no means of paying for its repair. I pushed away the worrying thought.

Iron and steel will bend and bow...

I tried to remember what came next. *Build it up with silver and gold*, I recalled, which would be duly *stol'n away*. The poor scansion of that stanza had always annoyed me.

That was not what the children sang. Instead, in the piping tones of childhood, came:

Build it up with blood and bone, blood and bone, blood and bone
Build it up with blood and bone, my fair lady.

They were playing intently, the two tallest girls joining their hands high, the rest snaking through and winding around in an endless loop. Their eyes reflected odd lights, the reds and greens and golds of the night, with a bright, animal sheen.

Blood and bone will keep the stone, keep the stone, keep the stone
Blood and bone will keep the stone, my fair lady.

We had never sung it like that at home. I wondered if children all over England had different versions of the tune, and if the city children's versions were always such gory horrors. Probably: most traditional songs were, and this sounded deeply traditional. It reminded me of something, in fact, something... King Arthur? I had been reading a volume of Arthurian tales just last week, after my encounter with the legend of the butterfly bishop.

Build it up with stone so strong...

"Ah, Merlin," I exclaimed aloud. *That* was what the song had brought to mind, of course: a Welsh tale. Merlin and King Vortigern and...the palace...

My breath stopped in my throat.

Stone will last for ages long, ages long, ages long
Stone will last for ages long, my fair lady.

I had to talk to Simon. I ducked off the step, into the teeming crowd, careless of who I shoved in my urgency to get to Fetter Lane. Please God he would be there. I did not want to seek him at Hartley House. I did not want to set foot in Hartley House ever again.

I had left the children behind me, playing a new game, but their song rang in my ear. *Build it up with blood and bone...* It could not be so, I told myself. But I knew, with an awful soul-deep certainty, that it was so, and I feared that knowledge.

The procession had come down Chancery Lane. I shoved my way back towards Fleet Street through the jostling crowd, cursing my modest stature. Simon could have shouldered through without effort. Crowds probably parted before him.

I wished he were here now. I wished for him as a child in the dark wishes for its nurse.

Fetter Lane ran north from here but I was on the wrong side of the street. I looked around, assessing how best to force a passage through the procession, and saw a man look back at me. I registered the bowler hat and moustache as familiar before I recognised him. The man who had asked what I had learned, who had not gone back to Hartley House with my message but was staring at me now.

His face was empty of feeling, betraying no human sentiment at all, but he began to shove through a group of masqueraders, coming towards me, and I turned and ran like a hare.

He stood between me and Fetter Lane, and I had no desire to play tag with him in a crowd. I fled instead into the dark alleys of the Inns of Court, that little maze of barristers' chambers and legal buildings. It was scarcely lit, and the shadowy lanes appeared almost black after the torchlit Strand. The cries and cheers from the procession were still audible, as were my pounding footsteps in the quiet lane, and—oh God—the other footsteps following.

I dived through Pump Court. There was a small enclosed garden ahead to my left, through which I might reach Old Mitre Court and double back onto the Strand. Or such was my intention, until I realised that of course it had been locked and the high railings would take too long to climb.

I had not enough breath to curse, or time to do it. I ran on through the imposing buildings, damning the legal profession and its winding ways, and the footsteps behind me came closer.

I had to make it back to the Strand. It had been a foolish error to leave the highway, with lights and people about. He could cut my throat in the dark and silence of the Inns without a soul by to hear my last cry. And he would, because if he was protecting the truth I suspected, there could be no alternative.

I took a violent left onto Kings Bench Walk and pounded on, gasping in the icy air. From there a little alley that ran up to Old Mitre Court would lead me to the Strand, and the protection of the crowd.

I glanced behind. That was a mistake. My pursuer was close, not twenty feet behind, running with a ferocious, silent determination, and as I looked, he raised his head and met my eyes.

I tripped, stumbled, slid. Regained my footing and sprinted on, fuelled by desperation, because I had seen murder in that look. I did not turn again.

Old Mitre Court brought me onto Fleet Street just opposite Fetter Lane. I hurtled over the road, praying that I could just make it to Simon's door, that he would be at home, and heard the cry behind: "Stop thief!"

The devil. Heads turned, hands grabbed—a running man is a guilty man. I slid out of their way, wrenched myself free of someone's grasp, losing precious seconds, and fled with the last breath in my body up Fetter Lane.

Simon lived at number 166. I had only written to him, had no idea which end or side of the street that might be, and no time to look around with my pursuer close behind and catching up.

"Simon!" I called desperately. I could barely draw breath into my labouring lungs to shout. "Simon Feximal! Simon!"

A strong hand grasped my arm from behind, its impetus pushing me forward. My pursuer grappled me, shoving me down a side alley as I attempted to gather my wits. His shoulders were heaving too, but he was big, and powerful, and as he shoved me against a wet, cold brick wall, he brought up a knife and set the point to my throat.

"Tell me what you know," he rasped. His face was patched red, and his eyes glittered with anger, as though I had inconvenienced him with my resistance to being murdered. His bowler hat had somehow stayed on his head throughout that mad chase. "What you know and who you told."

"I haven't told anyone," I gasped, and realised my mistake at once. If I had claimed Simon knew, or my editor, I could perhaps have used that to bargain for my life.

Or perhaps I could not, because the man in front of me did not look as though he bargained.

He increased the blade's pressure on my neck. I tried not to breathe deeply in case I cut my own throat for him with the movement of my flesh, but my lungs were starved of air and shallow breaths felt like slow suffocation. I needed to gasp, but if I did the knife would dig deeper into my throat. The panic must have been writ clear on my face, for I saw satisfaction bloom on his.

"What does Feximal know?" he demanded, twisting the blade's point against my skin.

I could not meet his eyes. I stared past him, over his shoulder. "Stop," I gasped. "Please. I'll tell you anything. Just let me breathe."

"You'll tell me everything," the man insisted, giving me an extra little prick with the knife point.

"Yes, yes. Please, I beg you," I wheezed, with shameless servility.

The man gave a grimace of satisfaction at my collapse, and moved the knife an inch or so. That allowed me to gasp for air. It also allowed Simon, standing behind him like a masculine image of Nemesis, to take a grip on his collar and pull.

The man went spinning away from me, stumbling several paces. He recovered his footing fast, but not fast enough because Simon was on him.

I have often had occasion in my published stories to remark that Simon has the physique of a heavyweight boxer. That is because he *is* a heavyweight boxer. I did not know then that he spent an hour a day in the gymnasium and had won a number of amateur contests, but I could have made an informed guess from the coldly scientific manner in which he eliminated my assailant, while I sagged against the wall, trying not to fall over. It took him, I think, four punches in not many more seconds, and the man in the bowler hat was still holding the knife when the last blow landed on the point of his chin and snapped his head back. He went down into the mire of the alley. Simon stooped to pluck the knife from his hand and came over to me.

"Robert." He put a careful finger to my throat. Even in the dim light, I could see the dark stain when he took it away. "Good God."

"I need to tell you," I croaked. My knees, to my shame, were shaking. "I know about the children."

166 Fetter Lane was just around the corner from Crane Court, the noxious alley where I had nearly been killed, and where Simon had left the unconscious man after going through his pockets. I huddled on a worn leather settee in the cluttered drawing-room, gripping a mug of sweet tea with both hands, with Simon sitting by me and Miss Kay in a chair by the fire. I had not asked how Miss Kay came to be there.

"Well?" she demanded of me.

It was difficult to know where to begin. I turned to Simon. "Did you get my messages today?"

"I had one. About Glasport, the architect."

"I sent two. The second may have been intercepted."

Miss Kay's brows shot up. Simon frowned and motioned me to continue.

"I wrote the first time to advise you about the architect. Glasport applied the mortar to the foundation stone of Hartley House, then went home and died with a noose around his neck. I wrote again to let you know that I intended to print a story on the haunting, appealing for information. My attacker came to the *Chronicle*, posing as a messenger, before my second message could have reached Hartley House. I thought that he came from his grace of Sarum and I hoped to persuade him that we were close to an answer, to buy time to stop Dr. Berry."

A look flashed between Simon and Miss Kay at that, but neither spoke.

"So I told him that the solution was in the message I had sent you, and that I had already written the story. I was referring to my second message. I believe he thought I meant my first. He tried to kill me because he thought I had found out about the architect's death, and written a story accordingly."

Miss Kay frowned. "Why would he try to kill you because you knew about the architect's suicide? Is that not a matter of record?"

"I know why he had to die," I said. "That is the story someone does not want written."

"And that is…?"

I steeled myself, afraid it might sound absurd, though there was no doubt in my mind. "Do you know the tale of King Vortigern and the boy Merlin?"

The marvellous thing about scholars of the arcane is that they very rarely ask tiresome questions such as, "What has that to do with anything?" Miss Kay did not even blink. "Of course. King Vortigern's new palace was built every day, and every night it fell down. His wizards told him that it could only be built by—"

She did not breathe for a second. When she began again, she spoke slowly. "By sacrificing a child and mixing its blood into the mortar. That would ensure the palace stood forever, protected by its victim."

"Build it up with blood and bone," I said.

"Blood and bone will keep the stone," Simon answered, as if by rote. "Dear God, Robert. Are you sure?"

"I have no evidence."

"You have awareness." I did not know what he meant, but he spoke with such certainty that I did not think to question. "Are you sure?"

"Yes," I said. "Yes, I am quite sure."

We were all silent for a moment. Miss Kay spoke first. "Who else knows?"

"Nobody," I said. "I realised when I was going home, less than half an hour ago. But that man… I suppose he followed me, but I stopped to eat and to watch the procession. Perhaps he has already communicated with his masters. Perhaps he is doing that now."

"Who are his masters?" Simon and Miss Kay spoke together, and exchanged brief, familiar smiles. Despite the tension in the room, it was perhaps the most relaxed expression I had ever seen Simon wear, and in truth, I resented that it was not for me.

"I don't know who they are," I said.

"Not Sarum," Miss Kay mused. "If he had known, the origin of the haunting would have been obvious to him. No, Sarum summoned us, and someone pricked up his ears. Kept an eye on us, and you, Mr. Caldwell. And, as soon as they feared you were coming close to the truth, made a determined effort to silence you."

"Robert is not easily silenced," Simon said.

"You could not find out the truth because the chosen victims were too young to speak," Miss Kay went on. "I could not because the protection was interwoven with the crime. The crime was committed to protect the house; discovery of the crime endangers the house. Hmm." She shook out her left hand, a little flick of the fingers, and I saw then that every nail on her left hand was the same: disturbingly long, black, polished to an oily sheen. "Allow me to think." She sat back, examining her crooked fingers.

Simon rose and pulled the bell. "You are exhausted, Robert. I will have a room made up for tonight. It is not safe for you to go home now. Tomorrow we will go to Hartley House."

A knock at the door, some time later, indicated that the room was ready. I followed Simon up a flight of stairs and along a passageway, looking around me, feeling the pain in my toes from that frantic run. "Do you own the whole house?"

"It belongs to Theodosia. Here." He opened a door. The room revealed was plain enough, with an iron-framed bed, a small fire just set and a ewer steaming with hot water, shelves piled with books, otherwise bare walls. It had the look of the rest of the house: a place that was inhabited but not lived in, a place used for food and work and sleep, desperately unlike a home.

"Thank you," I said.

"You should try to sleep. You must be exhausted. Be assured, the house is safe."

"Yes." I wanted him to stay with me. Of course he could not, of course he could risk nothing in his own home—which was Miss Kay's home. I could not consider that yet. But to have him so close, when I had been so frightened, and be unable to touch, even to ask for a comforting embrace…

I did not often repine about my situation under the law, but at that moment the injustice was thick in my throat. All I wanted was his warmth now, and I was afraid to ask for it.

I stared at him, silhouetted in the doorway, not coming in. He looked back at me, face unreadable in the dim light. Was he hesitating? Because he wanted to come in? Because he did not, and feared I might ask?

I had rendered myself feeble enough in his eyes and my own, crying out for help earlier. I did not think I could bear a rejection, and so I did not ask.

"Good night," I said. "Thank you."

"Don't…" He took a deep breath. "Good night, Robert."

He shut the door. I slept in chilly sheets alone.

Simon, Miss Kay and I came to the front door of Hartley House together. The butler betrayed no sign of agitation in his majestic request that we should follow to the Small Drawing-Room, and yet I thought there was perturbation in the house.

As we paced silently down a corridor, Simon and Miss Kay both inhaled sharply. I had just time to wonder what they had seen when I felt it myself, the faintest sensation of cold, like the memory of a wet cloth drawn over skin, and the weeping began once more. I gritted my teeth against the noise. Simon muttered, "Good."

"Why?"

"Berry hasn't done his work."

Miss Kay looked about to reply but at that moment a door ahead of us burst open and a woman rushed out. She was young, dressed in the most elegant manner possible for a lady whose shape still suggested recent motherhood, but her demeanour did not match the expense of her clothing. Her hands were clapped over her ears.

"Make it stop!" She shrieked the words into the room she had left. "I don't care! Make it *stop*!"

A young man came out after her: his grace the duke of Sarum. He cried, "Claudia!" after his wife as the duchess fled down the corridor, made to pursue her, then stopped and turned to Simon instead. Around us, the child's sobs rose higher.

"You must end this, Mr. Feximal. Today." Sarum's face was drawn with sleeplessness. "I have heard your representations, but this is not to be borne. I have my wife and child to consider, and Dr. Berry—"

"We know what he says," Miss Kay interrupted, with a bluntness that startled the young duke. He drew himself up, affronted, but she carried on, in much the same tone, "I imagine we are expected."

Sarum made a gesture of invitation, and we walked into the drawing-room.

It was a pretty room, bright and modern with walls papered in a chinoiserie style and delicate tables that looked as though they could scarcely bear the weight of a teacup. It was not a room that should have housed Dr. Berry, standing with his fat fingers smothering a porcelain teacup. He sat by the side of a well-dressed, tow-haired man of some forty years.

"Ah. The occultists," said this man, not rising from his seat or inviting us to sit. "Mr. Feximal, Miss Kay." He turned a cold eye on me. "This gentleman is not a scholar, nor is he in the employ of his grace. He has nothing to do with this affair. I insist he leave at once."

"Mr. Caldwell was brought in to this affair very comprehensively last night," said Simon. "Those that should leave are Dr. Berry and his grace."

"The devil I shall!" exclaimed that young man. "This is my house."

"You are not in a position to dictate terms, Mr. Feximal," said the seated man. "I am most unhappy with the conduct of this matter and the distress caused to their graces."

"May I be introduced?" I asked.

The man gave me a chilly look. "My name is Parker. I am employed to assist with difficult and distressing matters that require tact."

"Or silence?" I suggested, and Simon shot me a warning look.

"Or, as you say, silence." The word was unquestionably a threat. "I have already spoken with your employers, Mr. Caldwell. I will not tolerate—"

Miss Kay began to whistle. The sound was shocking from a woman, doubly so in a ducal drawing-room. We all looked round at her as the notes she whistled resolved into a tune.

London Bridge is falling down, falling down, falling down…

She kept whistling, reached the end of the verse, began again. The duke shifted uncomfortably. Simon stood stock-still, looking at Mr. Parker, who watched Miss Kay without comment. Dr. Berry looked at me.

We stood in silence. Miss Kay finished the second verse. There was a tiny pause. Mr. Parker opened his mouth to speak, and she began the tune once more.

"Do you intend to continue whistling indefinitely, madam?" enquired Mr. Parker coldly.

Miss Kay gave him a startlingly unpleasant smile. "Would you like me to sing the words?"

This time the silence was longer. Mr. Parker's face was expressionless but his eyes were calculating, running odds and probabilities.

"We will speak," Simon told him. "You may choose who hears what we have to say."

Mr. Parker considered that. Then he rose, took the duke by the arm, and steered the young man out, murmuring in a placatory manner. He closed the door on the ducal back and turned to Simon. "You have some claim to make. Get it out and have done."

Simon glanced at Miss Kay, who was examining her long gleaming fingernails, apparently lost in thought, and back at Mr. Parker.

"The architect who built this house, Glasport, murdered children." His voice was deep and even. The wailing had diminished as we spoke, but now I had a sudden sense of attention, as though something other had its eyes on me. "He killed them, mixed their blood with mortar and laid the foundation stone of this building with it."

The shriek was deafening. It was that most unrestrained sound of rage, the scream of a furious child, and it cut through the air so savagely that we all except Miss Kay flinched in different degrees. Which is to say that Dr. Berry's face worked slightly, Simon frowned, Mr. Parker jolted in his chair, and I ducked to the floor with both arms over my head.

"He murdered them to protect this house," Simon said loudly. "And afterwards, he hanged, as murderers should."

"Then what is your concern?" demanded Parker as another spectral shriek swept through the room.

"To tell their story," Simon said, and the noise dropped away on the instant, leaving a yawning sense of attentiveness. Something was listening. "To say aloud that their unlived lives were snatched for the benefit of others. To say that was wrong."

"We all make sacrifices, Mr. Feximal." Dr. Berry's smile was bland, malicious. "Do we not?"

"The architect sacrificed children," I put in angrily, since Simon did not answer. "Not himself."

"Oh, but he did," Mr. Parker said. "As Mr. Feximal reminds us, he hanged. He paid."

"And their graces of Sarum?" I demanded. "Two children died to assure the safety of their home!"

"You don't believe that the royal family should be safe?" Mr. Parker raised a brow.

"Not at the expense of innocent lives. Not at the expense of—"

"Betty Marks and her baby brother Toby." Miss Kay spoke dreamily. She was swaying slightly, eyes fixed on her fingernails. "Born to poverty. Sold to blood. Ignored, lost, forgotten."

"What a very great deal of fuss about two beggars," said Dr. Berry.

"Two *children*." I felt as though I were choking on the words. Simon remained silent. "Two children who had nothing but their lives, and even those were taken from them for the benefit of a palace?"

"You are blasphemous, Mr. Caldwell." Dr. Berry was smiling still. "Is it not written, 'For whosoever hath, to him shall be given, and he shall have more abundance: but whosoever hath not, from him shall be taken away even that he hath'?"

"The architect was a madman," Mr. Parker said, as I stared, speechless. "He committed a crime and paid the price. What more is there?"

"Justice," I said furiously. "You *knew* about this. I don't know who you are but you knew. Someone sent that man to kill me when I found out about the architect. Someone knew about this and hid it. Was it you?"

"Robert." Simon's voice rumbled, low and strained. I ignored him. The spectral tension was closing in around me, like a note too high or low to hear.

"Was this the first time?" I demanded, glaring at Mr. Parker's impassive features even as Dr. Berry took a menacing step towards me. "Are other great houses protected like this? If we asked around Balmoral—"

The children cried out. Not in pain or anguish, this time, just two startled voices. Simon gasped with effort, and Miss Kay staggered back. Dr. Berry gave a cry of fury, and there was a gurgle of laughter at the very edge of my senses as the presence in the air fled.

"There." Simon sounded a little raw. "The haunting is lifted."

"The infestation," Dr. Berry snarled. He looked thwarted.

"A neat job, Simon," Miss Kay said with mild approval. "Let us go."

She turned, and stopped, as Mr. Parker rose slowly. He was looking at me.

"Excuse me." His voice was level, and I felt a chill at its tone. "Mr. Caldwell made certain allegations just now that must not be repeated. Treasonous allegations that, should they be repeated, will earn Mr. Caldwell a very long spell at Her Majesty's pleasure."

"He will not repeat them," Simon said.

I was young, and outraged, and a man had tried to kill me, but it was the presumption of those words after that cold night alone—in *Miss Kay's* house—that pushed me over the edge of all sense. "I damned well shall!" I said. "I shall write this story, sir. I will not be silenced."

"Yes," said Mr. Parker. "You will."

"Enough. No, be quiet, Mr. Caldwell." Simon took a long stride forward so that he stood close to Mr. Parker. "The acts you order, or hide, or protect, are your acts, sir. You will pay their price in the end. Nothing goes unpaid."

"How wisely you speak, you who pander to devils. Have you any advice for me?" enquired Dr. Berry. His face was blotched red with anger.

"Stay away from us," Simon said.

"Your arm, Mr. Caldwell." Miss Kay looped her hand through the crook of my elbow, and dug her nails into the back of my hand with such force I was hard put not to cry out. "We have finished our task. Let us go."

I was seething as Simon and Miss Kay more or less frog-marched me down the street, away from that luxurious home, once more made pleasant for its pampered inhabitants. Simon glanced at me. "You may as well speak."

"How could you?" I demanded. "How could you walk out of there so?"

"The children are free."

"Parker knew about their murder. I am sure of it."

"So am I," Simon said. "He is ruthless, dedicated to his masters' service, and in a position of great and unaccountable power. You must not cross him."

I could not believe that a man of Simon's contained strength, his justice, should accede to this. "Even if he covers up murder? Orders it?"

"If he ordered a murder, it was of the architect," Simon said.

"Which I for one do not regret," Miss Kay put in.

"Mr. Parker is a dangerous man but not a stupid one. He will protect the reputation of the throne at all costs."

"And you will do the same?" I demanded, transported by anger and disappointment that Simon should be willing to take part in the concealment of such a crime. "You will be a party to this conspiracy?"

"Don't be a fool," said Miss Kay. "Do you imagine you can tell the nation that the royal palaces are built on blood sacrifice? Exhort the populace to rise up against the House of Hanover?"

"I am a loyal servant of the Queen," I said, stung.

"So is Mr. Parker, in his way," Simon said. "A wrong was done. The perpetrator is dead. The victims are freed. The story is *over*, Robert. You must not pursue this."

"No. It is not over. I shall write it. I shall not let this be concealed. And do not you dare tell me what to do!"

I turned on my heel and walked off. Simon called my name but I would not stop.

My heart was full with righteous anger and disgust for the cowardice that allowed wrongs to go unpunished. My head whirled with words that would inspire pity and outrage in my readers, that should ensure no such crime could be committed again, even if the storm I caused should shake the very foundations of the House of Hanover. Simon had given the children's spirits their freedom; I should bring them justice.

And perhaps I would have, but the next day, everything changed.

Silver

"You are dismissing me?" I repeated.

Mr. Lownie scowled. I would have said *scowled at me*, but he did not quite meet my eyes. He sat at his desk as though to deliver an official reprimand, I standing before him, but his knuckles were white on the pipe he clutched.

It was the seventh of November, the day after I had walked away from Simon. I had returned to the *Chronicle* to learn that my story had been spiked. That was no matter; it was no longer required. I left a note for Mr. Lownie to inform him that I had a story of far greater import for him, and settled down to write.

Naturally, it was the kind of thing that one should wish to discuss with one's editor, but he did not return to the office that day. I stayed until it was clear he would not return; went home (an unpleasantly nervous walk, starting at shadows, and an uncomfortable night hearing a murderer's tread in every creak on the stairs); and had come in to an office of sideways looks, whispers, and an order to present myself in the editor's private office at once.

Now this.

"I do not understand," I said. "How have I deserved dismissal? My stories—"

Mr. Lownie took refuge in his notebook. "I am informed that you collaborated with two journalists on rival newspapers to bribe the duke of Sarum's servant. That is gross misconduct."

"That's journalism!"

A muscle ticced under his mouth. "The Board of Directors considers it unethical behaviour."

"The Board?" I repeated. "How is the Board concerned?"

"The duke lodged a complaint." Mr. Lownie seemed to force the words out.

"And you're dismissing me for one complaint?" I said incredulously, before the import of his words dawned on me. "Did you say the duke complained? The duke himself? Not Mr. Parker?"

Mr. Lownie met my eyes at that. His were angry and fearful. He spoke in an intense mutter, much more like himself. "I don't know what you've meddled with, Caldwell, but there's the very devil to pay. I can't help you. There's no choice."

"You're dismissing me on Mr. Parker's orders? *You*, Mr. Lownie?" He had always prided himself on his designation as the most independent-minded editor on Fleet Street. He never backed down. "Damn it, sir, will you at least listen to my story first? Don't you want to know what I've discovered?"

"No!" That was almost a shout. "I will not hear it, I will not print it. I have a wife and family, you damned fool."

"You've been threatened?"

He took a deep breath, staring at the desk, then looked up. "I'm sorry, Caldwell. If you wish to resign, rather than be dismissed—"

"Yes, I do!"

"I accept your resignation. Clear your desk. Don't speak to your colleagues. You have poisoned your own well, don't poison theirs."

I did as bid. I collected my few possessions, snapped a curt, "Resigned," in response to questioning looks, and left the *Chronicle* building forever.

But I did not despair. Far from it. Mr. Lownie had been silenced, but other editors would listen. There were other posts at other newspapers. I could write as a free-lance scribe. *I have not yet begun to fight*, I thought, and my stride was defiant as I headed for home.

Three weeks later, I understood quite how wrong I had been.

No other newspaper would so much as interview me. I wrote to editors and received curt responses by return of post. I contacted friends and had cheerful assurances of help that, the next day, were retracted in shamefaced notes.

I had been blackballed on Fleet Street. Very well, I thought, and wrote to the Manchester Guardian and Glasgow Herald. The refusals came the next morning.

My attempts to find free-lance work bore no more fruit. The most innocuous stories were rejected—rejected, mind, not ignored or left on a desk by harassed editors, but firmly sent back as soon as they arrived. As though editors wanted to prove they had nothing to do with me.

Writing was my sole income. I had no savings, no family left, no means of support but my career. Caldwell Place was a bleak and mouldering mansion on worthless land, mortgaged to the hilt. None of this had concerned me greatly before. I was young, hardworking, without dependants, in good health. I had felt confident in my ability to secure my future, had recklessly spent all my meagre inheritance in the effort to make Caldwell Place more attractive to possible buyers. It had not mattered that my monthly stipend barely covered my expenses when I had a berth at the *Chronicle* and knew that next month's pay was forthcoming.

It mattered now.

It is surprising how fast a man can fall when there is nobody to extend a hand to him. I ate frugally, turned my cuffs and collars rather than send out washing, wore all my clothes in my rooms rather than deplete my little store of coals. I pawned my watch for ready money, and calculated my store of coins with a miser's eye because I was all too aware that the month's rent would deplete it entirely. I kept hope alive, spending penny after penny on paper and ink and stamps to write my pleas for employment, but after a fortnight I faced the fact. I should have to seek other work—as clerk, if I could find such a place with no experience, as labourer if I must. I would return to journalism when I could but for now, I should put my shoulder to the wheel and survive. I took to my bed that night cold and very hungry but defiant. Let the cards fall how they would, I should not be defeated.

The next day I received the letter from the bank.

The words swam in front of my eyes as I read. It did not seem possible, a sick, grotesque jest, but there it was, in black ink. The mortgages on Caldwell Place were to be called in. The bank would extend no further period of credit. Since the mortgages outstripped the value of the house, I was personally liable for a sum so impossible that I could barely breathe, and the bank would be grateful for its remittance within a period of twenty-eight days.

I laughed, then. Laughed, because otherwise I should weep. Straightened my dirty cuffs, arranged my necktie to disguise the grime of my collar, and stepped out of the door to go I knew not where, because I had nowhere to go.

As I write, at a distance of two decades spent in Simon's company, it seems extraordinary that I should not have fled to him. Even then, the temptation came to go to Fetter Lane to draw strength from his firm presence. I would pretend that all was well and speak of other things, I told myself, but I knew that I could not pretend, and so I did not go.

In truth, there was no reason he should help me. We had encountered each other but three times, shared a bed twice. That did not constitute a relationship on which I could call for aid. Worse: our last meeting had ended with me turning my back on him and refusing to accept a warning which my current situation proved to be all too prescient. Simon had tried to tell me, and I had not listened.

And I was ashamed. As a journalist I could hold up my head and call myself his equal. As a shabby, unwashed beggar, a man soon to face proceedings for bankruptcy, I was no man's equal. The shame of my plight was corrosive. I hated the pity in the eyes of old friends, hated more that men hurried by me on Fleet Street rather than exchange a word. Such is our fear of ill luck, we shun those touched by it in case it proves contagious.

Not that my case was ill luck. It was malice, and cold calculating vengeance, and my own obstinate self-righteous stupidity that had brought this upon me and I could call on nobody to assist me in my distress.

I walked the streets that day, cold and empty, turning possibilities in my head. There were none. My plan to seek other work might have allowed me to keep my rooms or feed myself, but I could never raise the sum demanded on that cursed inheritance.

I did not eat. It was a bitterly cold winter, and I should need every penny I had to pay for a roof over my head next month. Sleeping in doss-houses was a terrible thought, but I feared the icy streets more than that. Men died of cold in the London nights.

I lay empty that night, in a room I could not afford the coals to heat. When I left the house again, near midday, I was not even surprised when my landlady cast a practised eye over my shabby garb and advised me that she was not a charity, and that the rent was payable on the first of the month and not a day later.

I made her some assurance, I don't know what. I was dizzy with hunger now, having restricted my purchase of food to the bare minimum for days, but too afraid to spend my dwindling resources. I walked anyway, because although walking in the icy air would make me hungrier, staying any longer in my unheated room without movement would chill me to the bone.

I was so hungry. I was so cold.

As I set off with faltering steps down the streets to nowhere, a voice hailed me. "Mr. Caldwell!"

It was Dr. Berry.

I did not run. I could not have run, in any case, but he looked…different. The pale eyes behind the thick glasses beamed with fatherly concern. His bald head gave him a benevolent aspect, like a kindly friar. He spoke with paternal care to me, his whole being radiating his trustworthiness. And he had sought me out when I felt the loneliest man in London, and spoken to me by name, and for that alone I could have fallen upon him and wept.

I shook his hand instead. His plump fingers were cold and damp against my skin, but that was just the November air.

"My dear sir," he said, with concern. "You look half-starved. Are you quite well?"

"I have been…a little…"

"Goodness me. You must sit down. Here."

He grasped my arm and steered me into a little chop house that I had occasionally frequented. The warmth of the room almost overpowered me, and the smell: chops broiling, the savoury scent of meat as it browned on the griddle, that delightfully comforting odour of a steak-and-kidney pudding that promises such richness of gravy, such mouth-filling satisfaction of the suet crust. I could almost taste the glorious greasiness of those smells, and I fell onto the chair he offered me, senses awhirl. He tugged the coat off my shoulders, carefully draping it over the back of my chair.

"Coffee," he told the attendant. "And the bill of fare for luncheon, if you please."

"Sir, I cannot," I mumbled. *Cannot pay. Cannot afford this.*

"You are my guest, Mr. Caldwell. I insist. You must allow me this as some small redress for our first meeting." He smiled at me, pale lips stretching wide over his smoke-browned teeth. It had been wrong of me to find that so repulsive. He was a kindly man. "I was very brusque, which I regret. I can only apologise. I was greatly misinformed as to your character."

"Oh," I mumbled.

"Ah, coffee." Dr. Berry beamed at the waiter and examined the bill of fare as the man poured fragrant hot liquid into cups. I added cream and sugar, neither of which I normally take, with a heavy and trembling hand. "Will steak-and-kidney pudding suit your appetite, Mr. Caldwell? Very well then: two of those and quickly, please. My guest is hungry."

He turned to me once more as the waiter departed. "Yes, greatly misinformed. Let me be frank. I was misled by your association with the man Feximal."

"Mr. Feximal? Why?"

Dr. Berry's expression was pained. "I am a religious man, sir. Mr. Feximal is…" He shuddered slightly. "His beliefs are peculiar. His work is not done right. He has—I regret that I must say this—he has sympathy for evil."

My hands tightened on the steaming cup, still a little too hot to sip from, and I opened my mouth to protest. Not that I wished to disagree with Dr. Berry, far from it, but I knew what he said to be incorrect. Dr. Berry forestalled my argument with a plump finger. "I do not say he is an evil man, Mr. Caldwell, far from it. He is *misinformed*, sir. The hauntings that he and I are called to address are sent to trick us. Mr. Feximal has been played upon: bewildered, fooled and misled. Seduced by dark forces until his very natural sympathies have been distorted into doing evil's work. With the best intentions, of course, yet we all know where good intentions lead."

I was sure that was wrong. Or, at least, I thought it was wrong. I *believed* it was wrong because of my own instincts. But what if they were wrong? What if I too had been practised upon?

Suppose Simon was wrong. Suppose Dr. Berry was right.

"Mr. Caldwell." Dr. Berry's voice was compelling. "I believed you to be an ally of the man Feximal and his misguided quest to give succour to creatures of darkness that should be fought with all the weapons at our disposal. Clearly that is not true, else you would not be in such straits now. I see he has abandoned you utterly."

There had to be some answer to this, but I couldn't think of it, of anything but his eyes and the sound of his voice, and my hunger.

"I should like to help you, Mr. Caldwell." Dr. Berry took a cheroot from his cigarette case and struck a match. "I wonder if you should care to work for me."

"Work?" I lifted the cup to my lips, and at that moment my companion exhaled. The smoke that issued from his lips seemed to have an oddly acrid, choking scent. I put the cup down untasted and tried not to cough.

Dr. Berry's eyes gleamed behind the thick lenses of his spectacles. "If you were able to help me, Mr. Caldwell, if you could aid me in persuading Mr. Feximal to the light…"

"What do you mean?"

"He will not learn. He must be *made* to learn, and you can help me to do that. You can gain his trust, learn how to guide him, under my direction. It would be a true kindness. His very soul stands in peril, and if I must bring him to his knees to make him understand, I will do it. That is, after all, the position from which we pray." Dr. Berry smiled, a radiantly pure and benevolent smile. "There is right and wrong, and right will always triumph. Be on the side of right and you will be saved. Do you want to be saved?"

I could only nod. I did, I truly did, and now I could see Simon, with his fierce eyes, the pagan runes and strange ways, as the enemy of salvation.

A waft of savoury scent came to my nose. The waiter had arrived with our plates. He put them down, brimming with rich juices, each piled with cabbage and potatoes around the glorious mound of crust and meat.

I went to take up my fork and Dr. Berry's plump hand landed on mine, stopping me. I looked up and was caught anew by his pale gaze.

"Hungry?" His hand pressed mine down.

I could only nod.

"Poor?" His other hand was putting something on the table. A pile of shining coins, I saw in my peripheral vision, because I could not have looked away from him if I tried.

"I will feed you. I will pay you. And you will work for me. Whatever is required of you, at my direction. Will you do it?"

"Yes," I said, and felt the rasp of his smoky breath in my lungs.

His hand lifted. Mine closed, without my conscious volition, on the fork.

"Take this and eat it." Dr. Berry spoke the words like a benediction. Like a benevolent master.

I plunged the fork into the pudding. Gravy oozed and gleamed through the wound. I pushed the fork in, stabbed a chunk of tender flesh that dripped with dark red juices, lifted it to my lips. Put it in.

For a glorious instant I felt the richness on my tongue, filling my mouth, and then—

An unnatural taste, metallic and bitter. *Rotten*, I thought, and *Poisoned*, because it was so very wrong, and as I looked up from my plate I saw the gleam of coins and thought, *Silver*. It tasted of silver.

"What is it, Mr. Caldwell?"

Dr. Berry's eyes were very large behind his spectacles, their pale intensity fixed on me, and with that foul taste in my mouth cutting through the fog of his words, I saw him once more as he was. The lump of carrion that he fed me burned in my mouth like betrayal.

"Mr. Caldwell?"

Those yellowed drowned-man fingers reached for me, and I pushed my chair back, seized my coat, and fled. I ran outside, heedless of those I pushed past, spitting the contaminated flesh from my mouth as I ran, retching but too afraid to stop. I had little enough strength, but desperation can do much.

I did not care about my dirt or my shame. I did not care about asking help from a man who had no reason to give it. I was hopelessly frightened of Dr. Berry, terrified for my very soul, and I could only think of Simon.

I remember little of that headlong flight except its length. It was not much more than a mile, but that is a long way to a hungry, heartsore, frightened man. I was stumbling and shaking when I got there, making the motions of running though I was moving no faster than a walk, and I leaned against his door as I pulled the bell consumed with fear that he should not be there, that I should sit alone on the stone step, that Dr. Berry should pursue me here…

The door opened. His deep voice said, "Robert?" Then powerful arms held me up, and pulled me inside the house, and at last I was safe.

I was not permitted to tell my story for some time. A servant-woman, hideously disfigured by a cross-hatching of scars over an empty eye socket, brought steaming beef broth that revived me sufficiently to luxuriate in a hot bath and drive the chill from my bones. (The scent of meat juices caused me but a momentary queasiness, I was pleased to note.) Clean and clad scarecrow-like in Simon's flannel gown, I devoured a plateful of broiled fowl, seated at Simon's dining-table, as he sat with me and watched in silence.

My immediate physical wants supplied, I was able to look around the room. It was a gloomy space indeed, with heavy dark wood furnishings and thickly striped green wallpaper in the fashion of thirty years ago. It had once sported pictures, I could see from the brighter rectangles of unfaded colour; now there were none. Books and sheaves of paper were stacked on the table's end.

"Do you entertain much?" I asked. "Or Miss Kay?"

"Neither."

"It is a large house for two people," I observed. "It must take a deal of upkeep."

"Mmm."

"Your servant's eye—"

"I can see you are recovered, Robert." Simon put his elbows on the table and leaned forward. "Now, you will tell me what the devil happened, and how it is that you arrived in such a state of distress."

I pushed away my empty plate and began my tale. His face clouded over as I spoke of my blackballing, assuming a thunderous aspect. When I reached the part about the bank letter he said, "That was Parker too."

"Do you think so? I confess, the thought crossed my mind, but is it within his powers to influence a bank?"

"There is a great deal within his powers." Simon's voice was grim. "I blame myself for this. I should have warned you."

"You tried."

"I could have tried harder."

"I doubt I should have listened," I pointed out. "I am responsible for myself."

"You went into this blindfold," Simon said heavily. "I know Mr. Parker. His profession is the suppression of secrets, by all the means at his disposal."

"And yours is to bring secrets to light?"

"To bring the untold stories to an end. To free those trapped within them. That is my concern. Not to tell those stories to the world."

"No," I said. "I should apologise. I spoke poorly to you on our last meeting. I was unjust."

He waved that away. "Go on. The bank letter; and then what?" I grimaced, unwilling to tell, and he scowled. "Robert, you were alarmed. I saw that. And…you came to me." He hesitated, then added, low, "I wish you had done so earlier."

"These are my troubles. I could scarcely have brought my financial woes to you."

"You could," Simon said, astonishingly. "That is… I hope you consider me your friend."

Did I? *Friend* seemed such an inappropriately intimate word for one so intimidating. My friends were jolly, laughing, cheerful fellows. My friends did not endure agony and face terror to free trapped souls from pain.

"I should be proud to call you my friend," I said, and received one of those rare smiles. It seemed a little easier than before. Maybe he was getting used to the facial effort, I told myself, because it was easier to jest than to consider how very much I should have liked to lean on his friendship then.

Should have liked to. Could not.

"Then will you allow me the privilege of a friend, to assist in time of trouble?"

"I believe I already have," I pointed out, with a gesture at my unconventional garb. "And with gratitude."

"Unnecessary. And you did not come to me in that spirit. You were frightened. By what?"

I stared at my hands. "Dr. Berry," I admitted, and told him of that terrible luncheon.

It is not easy to repeat such things as Dr. Berry had said to a man's face, particularly not when that face can convey so much menace so effortlessly. Nor is it pleasant to admit one's own weakness to be such that one could betray a friend—a lover, even—for the sake of a plate of food.

I told it all. I could not meet his eyes as I did it, but I told him.

He heard me out in silence. At the end, he said, "You are a fortunate man."

"Am I?" It seemed, on the face of things, unlikely.

He shrugged. "You might have eaten."

"What would that have done?" I demanded. "Was the food poisoned?"

"Not in the sense you mean. I suspect the taste was your awareness of its import." He rapped his knuckles on the table. "Never take anything from Dr. Berry, Robert. Never."

"The only thing I would wish to take of him is my leave," I assured him. "You did not say what would have happened."

"No. Dr. Berry is a very dangerous man."

"He said much the same of you."

"He believes," Simon said, ignoring that. "He believes that his mission is right, and that everything he does is in service of his mission, therefore everything he does is right. I do not agree."

"Nor do I." I shuddered. "He sounds like an officer of the Spanish Inquisition. To what church does he belong?"

"Any self-respecting church would burn him at the stake." Simon's tone suggested he would be pleased to supply the tinderbox.

"I'm glad to know it. Why did he believe that I could be used against you?" I glanced at the closed door. "Is our…connexion discovered?"

"He would not have used kindness to you then. I suppose he saw a chance to exploit a friendship." Simon grimaced. "Outside my field, I have few to exploit."

I swallowed. "I'm sorry that I—that I—"

"Nonsense, Robert. Dr. Berry has defeated far stronger men than you," Simon said dismissively, and apparently without intending offence. "A question. I can only assume you have nowhere to go beyond the end of the month. No family?"

"None."

"Will you stay here?" He spoke with great brusqueness, not quite meeting my eyes. "Until this matter is resolved."

"Here?" I repeated.

"I dragged you into this. We have plenty of space. I should be happy to assist my friend in such a small way. Dr. Berry may know your direction, and I should not wish him to find you unprotected." Four unrelated arguments, hurried out one on top of the other. I might have drawn conclusions from that, had I thought about it, but I was torn between a strong disinclination to accept charity from one whose good opinion I valued, and an equally strong fear that I might return to my cold, clammy rooms alone and find Dr. Berry there.

I did not reply at once. He put out a hand to mine, but did not touch it. Such strong hands he had, the fingers a little thickened and the knuckles spread by boxing.

"Please," he said. "Accept my help. As your friend."

"I do not wish you to rescue me. I am no damsel in distress."

"Damn it, Robert, we all need help sometimes. I have asked for yours before now."

"Not like this."

He sighed heavily. "Let me make you a promise."

"What?" I said, startled.

"Accept my help now, and I swear to you, when the day comes that I need help, I shall ask for yours and accept it. Lord knows you have aided me already—"

"Not like this. I am—was—merely a journalist. If I have helped you in some small way, I am proud, but I can hardly repay—"

"Good God, will you be forever talking," said Miss Kay, coming into the room. "Why is Mr. Caldwell wearing your dressing gown, Simon?"

"Dr. Berry endeavoured to recruit him. And Mr. Parker's machinations—"

"Mr. Caldwell brought vengeance down on himself, did he? I thought he might." Miss Kay gave me a quick, penetrating look. "Dr. Berry?"

"I'm inclined to break his neck," Simon said.

"Is he still pursuing our scribbling friend here?"

"Probably." Simon glanced at me. "It would be safest to assume so."

"Then you shall stay with us for now," Miss Kay told me. "If Dr. Berry wants you then we should prevent him having you, on principle. I'll have Cornelia make up the room again. Meanwhile, Simon, for God's sake come and help me with this accursed text before I inadvertently call upon the great toad."

She departed in a swish of skirts. I said, "Call upon a toad?"

"I'm sure she won't," Simon assured me, rising. "And as Theodosia says, you are far better staying here. Let it be so."

As Miss Kay said, Miss Kay who owned the house where they lived together on first-name terms, and could call upon him as she wished. And of course God forfend that Dr. Berry should have his way, or that Simon should feel it necessary to comfort me now.

I had brought it all on myself, turned myself from an independent man to a vulnerable, helpless burden. No wonder I had lost his interest. I should doubtless be grateful that he was still prepared to be kind to me, rather than wishing for more.

I was not.

The next day, Simon and I went back to my rooms. He had assumed, as a matter of course, that he would accompany me. I could not quite bring myself to refuse or object, but I felt the sting of shame at my cowardice, and resented Simon for it accordingly.

My landlady was not in evidence. We went up the stairs, I opened the door to my rooms, and the acrid smell of smoke reached my nose.

"Ah, Mr. Caldwell." Dr. Berry was seated at my desk, reading through my papers. He did not turn. "Our conversation is not finished."

"Yes, it is," said Simon from behind me. Dr. Berry whipped round, eyes blazing fury, and Simon put me out of the way with a hand so firm that one might have called it a shove. I staggered sideways; he strode forward as Dr. Berry rose.

"Has the dog returned to his master's heel?" Dr. Berry asked me, ignoring Simon, an impressive feat given the man's bulk. "Do you choose the path of deception and delusion?"

"Begone, or I shall throw you down the stairs," Simon said. "Mr. Caldwell is not for your taking."

Dr. Berry's face tightened, but he doubtless heard the purpose that rang in Simon's voice. He stalked by, pausing to look at me.

"You are making a mistake," he murmured. "You will understand that soon. Come to me then, and you may yet win forgiveness."

"Get out, you carcass," Simon said ferociously, and Dr. Berry departed.

"God." I sat on the bed. "*God.*"

"Mmm." Simon was looking around. "Is this everything you have to take?"

"I suppose it is not much," I said, flushing.

Simon, who would probably not have noticed if Fetter Lane had been gutted by thieves in his absence, shrugged, pulled open the desk drawer, and riffled through the few papers within.

"Excuse me!" I rose with alacrity, and some offence.

Simon seemed not to notice my reaction. "Look for coins. Silver coins."

"Believe me, there is not so much as a copper to be found."

"I doubt that," Simon said grimly. "Look, and pack nothing until you have checked it. Where is your trunk?"

I had a steamer trunk, which I used as a chest. I pulled it away from the wall. Simon began to inspect it minutely. I, disturbed and mistrusting, began to pile up my papers. What was he talking about? Why had he delved into my private belongings with such disregard? And again, the nagging thought: what if Dr. Berry was correct?

My room stank of the smoke he had left behind. That smell was enough to make me think of the doctor with revulsion, but my uneasiness persisted. Simon was not my master. But Dr. Berry had said so. Did Simon think so?

My distress was overwhelming me, and I did not want Simon rooting through my possessions. I had little enough left to myself, and he had not the right. A sudden wave of resentment came over me and I turned to voice my objection, with an uncoordinated gesture. My hand hit the little porcelain pot that I used to store pencils, and sent it flying off my desk. It hit the floor and smashed.

The pot had been a relic of my mother, one of the very few precious things she had owned. The loss was one blow too much. I stared at the shards in disbelief, unable to find words, and saw something glint. "What the—"

"Don't touch it."

Simon was over by me. On the floor lay broken china, spilled pencils and a gleaming silver coin. The taste of metal was rank in my mouth once more.

"What is it?" I asked, although I think I already knew.

"Berry has not given up. Never take anything from him, or you will find yourself bought without knowing you were for sale. Even when foisted upon a victim, his relics have power." Simon took the coin up between finger and thumb, opened the window and hurled it out. "There will be more."

I sat on the bed and put my head in my hands as Simon went through my possessions with the impersonal efficiency of a Metropolitan Police detective, searching everything I owned. He found two more pieces of silver, which he treated in the same unceremonious manner, packed my meagre belongings up in the trunk as I stared at the wreckage of my life, and took the lion's share of the weight as we heaved it in silence down the stairs.

Back in Fetter Lane, the scarred servant brought us coffee. Simon sat opposite me in that dark, lifeless drawing-room, watching me as he sipped his drink, cup vanishing in those large, strong hands.

"Have you any plans for the future, Robert?"

"Bankruptcy," I said, with a tight smile. "The mortgages on Caldwell Place, if you recall? I will need to visit the bank, to make some arrangement…" As if I could bargain, with no income, not even my own address. I should have to throw myself on their mercy. The future yawned in front of me, an abyss rather than a path.

Simon wore his formidable scowl. "Rather than talking to the bank, I think you should speak to Mr. Parker."

"I have burned my boats there, I believe."

"You will not win his regard," Simon agreed. "However, he may agree to withdraw his persecution in return for your assurance of silence, and until he does I fear you will not meet with success with the bank, or anywhere else. God knows I respect your principles." I blinked, startled by the sudden feeling in his voice. "You were right to cry out against what was done there. It was shameful."

"But the powerful cannot be shamed, can they?" I said bitterly. "They see no wrong in their acts, or if they do, their answer is to silence their critics. They cannot be made to confront their actions."

Simon paused a moment. "May I come with you? To Mr. Parker?"

"This is my trouble."

"I know." Simon sounded weary. "Your troubles, your responsibilities, you do not want my aid. I understand that, but for God's sake, Robert, it is the privilege of a friend to extend a helping hand without it being struck away. And," he added, "I know where to find him, and you do not."

That was inarguable, if irritating, and within a short time we stood together in the front room of a discreet, well-appointed office outside Whitehall. The young man at the desk regarded me with a mildly contemptuous blankness that told me I would not have got far alone; he rose to his feet with alacrity for Simon's low growl. We were escorted to Mr. Parker's inner sanctum within a quarter of an hour.

He was seated behind a desk that was piled with dossiers and papers. Red sealing wax, thick vellum and engraved crests abounded.

"What do you want, Mr. Feximal?" he asked, without looking up.

"It is I who have the request," I said. "You have made your point, sir. You have exerted your power and destroyed my livelihood."

"I?" Mr. Parker spoke coldly, as if my accusation were arrant nonsense. He reached for another paper.

"You," Simon said. "Let us not play games. Go on, Mr. Caldwell."

I did not want to go on. This was appalling, and humiliating, and I saw no prospect of success. But what choice had I?

"You demanded my silence." I hated the weakness of my voice. "Well, you have it. I shall not speak of the…the allegations I made again. And therefore, I have come to ask you to call off your persecution."

"Really," said Mr. Parker.

"The bank. They have called in my mortgage—"

"Then you must pay it."

"I cannot," I said desperately. "I have no work, I have no means to survive. For God's sake, have you not done enough?"

"No." He looked up then. "No, I think not. Occasionally an example must be made, Mr. Caldwell. An example to those who interfere in matters that do not concern them, or who presume to dictate to their betters." His gaze swung from me to Simon. "Consider this a reminder, or a warning, and be grateful for my clemency. It could be worse. It could be *made* worse."

I could feel the blood draining from my head. "But—"

"No buts. Leave."

"Mr. Parker." Simon stepped forward, to the very edge of the desk. "I suggest you reconsider. Mr. Caldwell has conceded defeat. Your continued persecution is not duty, but malice."

"It is a lesson, Mr. Feximal. I suggest you heed it."

Simon's breath hissed. "You exceed your authority."

"On the contrary." Mr. Parker smiled without humour. "That is limitless."

Simon moved, lunging with one powerful arm. His big hand slammed down on Mr. Parker's wrist, clamping it to the desk.

"What the devil—!" Mr. Parker wrenched uselessly at the grip.

Simon ignored his protest. He was undoing his cuff with his free hand, and as I watched in astonishment, he pushed coat and shirt sleeves up, exposing his arm almost to the elbow.

My mouth dried. Mr. Parker swallowed convulsively.

The runes were moving down Simon's arm.

They curled and twisted. I could not read them, had no desire to. The writing was frantic, black and red scrawling over one another, jagged and skittering along his skin. Simon's face was tense and remote, his lips moving very slightly as if he recited something to himself.

"Let me go," Mr. Parker demanded, tugging at the hand that trapped his own, but Simon was leaning forward, and I knew from experience that his considerable weight was not easily shifted. "Let me go now, Feximal, or you will regret this!"

Simon reached with his free hand into the pocket of his coat and brought something out. Mr. Parker made a noise in his throat as he saw what it was. A small hand mirror.

The runes were past Simon's wrist now, crawling over and around the back of his hand, probing like the tendrils of some terrible weed. Mr. Parker pulled back hard, uselessly. I should not have wanted Simon holding my hand then either.

"Mr. Caldwell made a remark today," Simon said calmly. "He observed that the powerful cannot be made to confront their actions. He was incorrect." He put the mirror onto his wrist, so that its reflective surface faced Mr. Parker. "Read it."

Mr. Parker turned his face away, eyes clamped shut. Simon leaned forward. "Read it," he repeated in a low growl. "Or I shall read it to you."

Mr. Parker's eyes opened. They flickered as he scanned the text in the mirror, his pupils widening. God alone knows what he saw in there, what histories, what accusations silently screamed on Simon's skin, but he read for perhaps two minutes, until at last something dreadful came across his face and he turned away once more.

"You will regret this," he managed, voice thick.

"I regret working under your authority," Simon said. "You will not request my services again. And you will call off Mr. Caldwell's bank."

"He may bid his journalistic career farewell," gritted out Mr. Parker. "That is done with." His skin was grey and sweaty, and his eyes strained, but his voice retained at least an approximation of authority. I had to admire his nerve.

Simon glanced at me, then nodded. He pocketed the mirror and released Mr. Parker's hand. The runes went crawling back up Simon's arms as soon as he let go.

"Good," Simon said. "If we have this conversation again, it will be in public and it will not be resolved so easily. Come, Mr. Caldwell."

I followed him out. Mr. Parker did not move or speak, but as we closed the office door I heard a noise that might have been a gasp, or something else.

We set off back to Fetter Lane on foot, in silence. At last I asked, "Was that wise?"

"Necessary." Simon sounded very tired. "Theodosia would say it was overdue. It will be interesting to see how he responds. I trust he will take the warning, but..." He scowled. "It would put my mind at rest if you would stay with us for a while. It would be safer."

"I have nowhere else to go." Hardly an enthusiastic acceptance, but it had hardly been an enthusiastic invitation. Simon nodded without looking at me, and we walked on through the chilly air, neither speaking, back to Fetter Lane.

Cakes and Ale

I had nothing to do.

I could scarcely remember having nothing to do. I had been earning my own living since the age of sixteen, had only been in receipt of a salary rather than irregular payments in the last couple of years. I had worked every hour of the day, and taken my pleasures where I could in between. I had been busy. Now I was not.

We had no repercussions from the visit to Mr. Parker. Evidently he had decided to take his lesson, or possibly to have his revenge cold. The bank wrote to me a few days after our visit with an apology for their error and an assurance that the mortgages need not be paid back at once, which merely left me with no occupation, no salary and a ruined eyesore of a house to sell before it fell down around my ears.

There was no sign of Dr. Berry either. "Biding his time, I expect," said Miss Kay, unreassuringly. "He doesn't like to be found out." She and Simon agreed that I should stay in the house, and not roam London on my own. I knew them to be right, I had no desire to meet Dr. Berry or Mr. Parker's vengeance, but I was trapped, and resentful, and unhappy.

I wandered aimlessly around such of 166 Fetter Lane as I was permitted to enter. Most of it was closed off, and every room on the second floor locked tight, so the house resembled the lair of some excessively industrious Blackbeard. The crowded bookshelves contained, not novels or poetry, but tomes that I could not hope to understand and had no wish to read if I could. Leather-bound things with disturbing illustrations, bound holograph manuscripts whose cramped writing made my eyes water and my skin itch, any amount of Latin, Greek, Hebrew, and what I guessed to be Arabic. I had my own books, including a copy of the latest sensation novel, an adventure story entitled *The Prisoner of Zenda* that I had bought before my life had fallen to pieces, and its wild whirl of action occupied my imagination for some little time. Not enough. I found a *History of English Folklore* written in a manner that a layman might understand, and read it from cover to cover. It had pencil remarks scrawled in the margin at points, childish comments in childish hands which gave it the air of a most peculiar schoolbook, but it was all I could find.

Simon made no approach to me. Of course he did not, in his own home, with Miss Kay ever there poring over some ancient text, and the servant Cornelia moving silently around. He was busy. He was occupied. He was of some use to the world, and I was not.

But it was worse than that. He barely met my eye, could not speak to me as he had before. He had seemed to respect me; now he grunted reasons to leave the room, or conducted stilted conversations that avoided the subject of his work, which, as that has always been his main topic of discourse, left us with nothing to say. He certainly did not come to my bedroom, and I did not dare visit his for fear of whom I might find there.

Miss Kay did not sleep in his bedroom, or use his name, but what was I to conclude? For a man and woman to live together in such proximity meant only one thing, impossible though that seemed. Of course I knew that many married men, or men who owed women marriage, might also sport with men; I had had a few married lovers myself. But I did not think Simon was a man who would ignore or betray his responsibilities, and Miss Kay was not a woman that any sane man would betray. The thought of wooing her in the first place was terrifying, but I was hardly an expert.

In any case, whatever Simon was to her, he did not come to me, or look at me, or want me, and I had no idea what I was to think.

I wanted to say something. To meet his eye, or touch his hand, or ask him outright if I had lost his favour and what I might do to regain it. But I could not let go of the last shreds of my pride, or perhaps I could not bring myself to risk another humiliation.

I told myself in the early days that I must just bear it. I had nowhere else to go. But after three endless weeks, in which I had secured no work, earned no money, been uselessly dependent on the charity of a man who appeared to have not the slightest wish to have me in his grim and silent house, the discomfort of my situation had me casting around for almost any alternative.

My instinct was always to chase the story, to make people talk. Miss Kay was unforthcoming to a remarkable degree; Simon barely spoke; I decided the servant Cornelia might be of more use, and went to seek her in the kitchen. Perhaps, I thought, she was silent out of shame at her unsightly disfigurement, and might open up to a kindly word.

I attempted to speak to her. She ignored me, then she gestured irritably, and finally she made a cawing sound and opened her mouth to reveal the blackened, truncated root of what used to be a tongue.

At this point, I decided to leave Fetter Lane.

"I am going to Caldwell Place," I told Simon. "I must find a way to sell it, and if I cannot then I will…live in it, I suppose." Burn it bit by bit for firewood, perhaps. "I will surely be able to sell the contents. Some of the furniture isn't rotten yet, and the paintings—"

Something changed in his face at the reminder of the paintings, or rather of one particular one, that of the lustful ancestor whose restless spirit had brought us so briefly together. I felt myself flush. I had not meant to raise the spectre of our illicit lusts in this house—or anywhere else, come to that—but since our entire first acquaintance had consisted of fucking, it was difficult not to.

"I wonder if," I went on, not quite able to meet his eye, "I wonder if you might consider loaning me the railway fare. You know I am not in funds but I shall be able to repay—"

He was waving a hand at me, almost angrily. "Of course. You need not ask, but, Robert, must you…that is, you are welcome to stay."

"No. I cannot."

He stared down at me. "Then— Would you do me a service?"

"Yes," I said at once. God knew I owed him more than one.

"I have a summons to a house, Elphill Abbey. A troublesome haunting. It is up north, on the way to Caldwell Place. Would you accompany me?"

"To your destination?"

"On my task. It seems a complex little problem. It occurred to me that you might be of help."

I doubted that. Yes, I had connected certain facts when they were put under my nose, but that was scarcely qualification to assist a ghost-hunter. If I had learned anything at Fetter Lane, it was the extraordinary wealth of arcane knowledge wielded by both Simon and Miss Kay. This was not a matter of instinct and guesswork for them: it was a life's work of study. My nose for a story scarcely weighed in the balance.

But perhaps that was not what he wanted. Perhaps this was merely an excuse to resume our previous relations one more time, or one last time, away from this house and his home and Miss Kay.

I could not tell if the thought appealed or appalled.

"I shall certainly come if you want me." I cursed myself immediately, but Simon seemed not to notice my (for once) unintentional double meaning, or not to care. "If you think I can help, I mean. You know the limitations of my experience in these matters."

"All the same, I should appreciate your time, if you will give it."

"Then I shall," I said, because I had to, and went to pack.

I cannot say that the journey was comfortable. We travelled first class—despite his wretchedly uncomfortable home, Simon seemed not to struggle with funds—but found nothing to say to one another. There was much I wanted to say, much I wanted to ask, or to simply spill out and hear his deep voice in thoughtful response, but I could not.

I did not want his kindness, or his friendship. What I wanted was to be his lover, as I so briefly had been, but not if it meant betraying Miss Kay. She was nothing to me, but I did not want Simon to be that flawed, treacherous man. God knows I did not think him perfect, but I had thought him true. If he wanted me, if we might find a corner of secrecy at Elphill Abbey, I should let him have his desire, but I should think the less of him for it.

Unless he and Miss Kay were not together, but then in God's name why had he left me untouched, unglanced at, for weeks?

Impossible to ask, the more so because I wanted the answer painfully. I had learned to expect nothing from lovers beyond mutual pleasure, caution and a bare minimum of decency. That was safe, that was reliable. Excessive emotion brought danger in its wake, the risk of exposure, shame, gaol. Safer by far to shrug and move on. Not to ask, not to pursue, not to hope. Perhaps, not to trust.

So I did not speak of that, instead breaking a very long silence to ask, "What is the matter in this abbey?"

Simon seemed jolted out of his thoughts at my words. "See for yourself," he said, and handed me a letter. Easier than speaking, I supposed.

The letter was written in an educated hand, from one Mrs. Fontley, of Elphill Abbey. The house had, she wrote, recently become afflicted with a spirit of vexatious nature.

It opens everything, she wrote. *Chests and suitcases are found open, preserves have their lids removed, bottles are uncorked, and every door in the house stands ajar. The only area still untouched is the wine cellar, and my husband remains in a state of the gravest apprehension.*

I thought I might like Mrs. Fontley.

Naturally we assumed it was human mischief at work, she went on. *But all our efforts to trap the miscreant have merely succeeded in convincing us that our troubles are of supernatural origin. Will you aid us in bringing rest to a perturbed and most perturbing spirit?*

"She seems very calm," I observed.

"Remarkably so," Simon said. "Some people have an enviable ability to accept the world as it is and not to let it affect them." He rested his head on the seat back and added, lower, "Some people lie."

Mrs. Fontley gave no impression of being a liar. She was a bright-eyed woman of no more than thirty years, with two tow-headed children clinging to her skirts and a future addition to her family suggested in the roundness of her person. She greeted us in the hall of the beautiful old building with two hands and a welcoming smile. It was cold, as any old stone house would be, with the December night closing in around us, but a fire blazed, and greenery adorned the walls, branches of holly and pine giving a fresh scent to the air. It lacked ten days to Christmas still, but clearly this house was one that relished midwinter.

"Mr. Feximal. I am so grateful for your trouble. And Mr. Caldwell?" She extended a hand and a merry smile with it.

"My most valued colleague," Simon said, somewhat to my surprise. "Let us hear your problem."

If the lady found him lacking in social graces, as well she might, she did not show it. She nodded with ready acquiescence, directed a servant to take our bags and bring tea—there were several around, some clad in conventional black and white and some in a more sombre grey—and took us to a cosy, well-lit drawing-room. It was comfortably appointed with deep chairs and cushions, rendered warm by a blazing fire, and hazardous by a scattering of wheeled toys on the floor. It was as close to the perfection of domestic bliss as I had encountered, except that the drawers of the bureau, the case of the grandfather clock and the lid of an ancient carved chest all stood wide open.

"I do wish he wouldn't," Mrs. Fontley said, gesturing to us to sit and moving to close the various open doors and lids. "At least he doesn't open windows, in this weather. But really, it is terribly odd."

"The spirit opens…"

"Everything except the wine. Everything sealed in the larder. A year's preserves, ruined. I am *cross* about that." She gave an indicative frown. "We have given up on the ice box, not that we need it in this weather. If it has a door, or a lid, or a top, or a cork, he opens it."

"He?" I asked.

"Oh, I think it's a he." She considered. "I don't know why. I suppose because leaving everything open is such a *mannish* way to go on. And because he seems so cross."

"Are you afraid?" Simon asked.

She made a face. "I don't wish to be. It wouldn't be comfortable to be afraid in my own home, would it?"

"No," I said. "No, that is not comfortable."

"When did this begin?" Simon asked.

Mrs. Fontley launched into her tale without hesitation. "The first thing, I *think*—I cannot be sure—it happened in summer. We had a terribly hot dry spell. The soil here has a great deal of clay in it, and it was parched and deeply cracked. And one morning we got up, and the earth in the lichyard had burst."

"In the…?"

"Oh, the old graveyard. This was once an abbey, of course, with Romish monks. Long deconsecrated, and the Fontleys have changed it a great deal, but naturally the lichyard is sacred. Well, I say *sacred*. We let the children play there, just as my husband did as a boy, but I think that's *right*, you know. It's so very old, and I do think the sound of children laughing would hardly distress the sleepers there, would it? This is a happy house."

"And the graveyard soil?" I prompted.

"Burst," she repeated. "Scattered upwards as if…well, really…a trench…" She looked at her hands and up again. "As if something had climbed out of the earth."

A maid took us to the two adjacent rooms prepared for us. All the doors along the corridor stood open; the maid closed them without comment as she went. Another maid, in grey, slipped off ahead of us. The room given to me was comfortable indeed, decorated in a simple yet pleasing style with a fire blazing in the hearth, but every door and drawer stood open, and my coat lay on the floor before the wardrobe in a heap.

"Well, that's new," the maid said, picking it up. "If you're going to start making a mess, we'll have words!" That remark was addressed in loud tones to the empty air.

"You are not intimidated by the ghost?" I asked.

"Lord bless you, sir, if I was to run screaming at a few open doors, we *should* be in a pickle." She gave a comfortable chuckle, shut the various drawers, observed that she didn't know why she bothered, and left.

I was just unpacking my few accoutrements when Simon came in. "What do you think?"

"I don't know. The servants and the children seem unafraid, the atmosphere is comfortable. This is really the least alarming haunting I've encountered to date."

Simon scowled. "Or I. Yet the ghost manifests physically, and it is strong. That is great age or great distress. Normally I should recommend the family leave the house, yet there is no sense of threat. Why is there no threat?"

"What sort of thing is this? A boggart? What the Germans call a *poltergeist*?"

"You have been reading, I see." Simon sat on the bed. "The graveyard is disturbed, then nothing, then a few weeks later, every door and jar and closed object in the house is continually opened. It does not form a pattern." He frowned. "I wonder if Mrs. Fontley is concealing something."

"She seems entirely sincere." I couldn't bring myself to care. There was no tragedy here, no pain. A peculiar puzzle only, which meant that my mind was not occupied with anything more urgent than Simon sitting on a bed.

He looked so painfully out of place in this cosy room. His strange, remote air and that beak of a nose…he would have been at home here centuries ago, I thought, his deep-set eyes shadowed by a cowl, walking a path of prayer and penance. If I had lived then, it would have been as a merry monk, the kind who brewed strong ale and could not forget what was under his cassock. I wondered how I would have fared with Simon as my abbot. Poorly, I had little doubt.

He was watching me. "You have thought of something?"

"No. I honestly don't know what you expect of me, Simon. You know I am ignorant as a child in these matters."

"I expect nothing," he said with sudden force. "Curse it, Robert—"

I did not want an argument now. "I suggest we see what Mr. Fontley has to offer at dinner. And in the meantime, if you will excuse me, I must dress."

Dinner was informal, and very pleasant. The food was good, the company (with the exception of ever-taciturn Simon) excellent. Mr. Fontley was every bit as charming as his wife, a weather-beaten man of good birth but no pretensions. He ran his ancient home as a smallholding, rather than aspiring to society, was deeply content with his life, and seemed only mildly disturbed by the fact that it contained a ghost.

"Are you sure it's a haunting?" I asked the Fontleys directly. "You both seem very placid about the possibility."

The couple exchanged a smile. "Quite sure," Mr. Fontley said. "We took all the usual steps. Flour on the floor, strings and bells to trap a human actor. We shut everything and waited outside a closed room with no other door, only to find all the drawers open again five minutes later." He raised his hands. "I can only conclude it is a haunting. And really, a very tiresome one. I live in fear of the day that I find my wine cellar assailed by its work." The Fontleys chuckled. Evidently this was a long-standing and oft-repeated joke. They had served us a Burgundy of excellent vintage.

"Is it the cellar or the wine bottles that it avoids?" Simon asked. He was not smiling. Obviously.

"I don't know." Mrs. Fontley considered the question. "We have not lost any wine to my recollection…"

"Or ale, or my French brandy," Mr. Fontley added. "Perhaps our ghost is a teetotaller!" And he and Mrs. Fontley laughed together, a merry sound in the dark night.

The drawers and wardrobe doors were open and my coat once again on the floor when I returned to my room. I picked the coat up, wondering what it was that so offended the spirit. The Fontleys had been quite positive that the ghost did not throw things around. I speculated briefly on a natural explanation. Could it be one of the children in innocent mischief, or a light-fingered servant? Well, my coat would be unsatisfying to a thief, since I had not so much as a coin to steal…

Then I stopped, and I stood. I stood, holding the coat that the ghost did not want, feeling shudders crawl up my arms, and I had to force myself to put my hands into pocket after pocket, the sense of dread growing rather than dissipating each time I found one empty. At last I pushed my finger into the little pouch made to hold a fob watch, and touched cold metal.

I dropped the coat as though it were a poisonous snake. "Simon!"

He was in within seconds at my hoarse shout. "What?"

"My pocket. Christ, there's money in my pocket."

As cries of distress go, it was not perhaps the most coherent, but Simon has never lacked professional understanding. He picked up the coat, went over it with fingertip thoroughness and took out a single silver coin.

"The ghost didn't want it in the wardrobe," I said, numbly.

"I don't want it in the house," Simon said. "Open the window."

"It won't cause harm to anyone who finds it, will it?" I was ashamed I had not asked before.

"No. It was for you." I opened the window, and Simon pitched the damned thing out into the garden, with such force I half expected to hear something smash. "How did it get there? Have you met him?"

"I think he put it in my coat at the eating-house. I must have had it all this time. In Fetter Lane."

"Thank God you did not go out. I should not have wanted you wearing that garment more than you have. Damn the man."

I wrapped my arms round myself. After all Simon's care, to have brought Dr. Berry's foul touch with me into his home…

He saw my distress and put out a hand, but stopped before he quite touched me. "Come, Robert, it is gone now. Let us go to the other room while any influence dissipates."

I followed him meekly. I felt sickened at the realisation of Dr. Berry's clammy touch so close to me, but alongside that came a palpable sense of relief, as though some part of the burden I bore was lifting at last.

Simon's room was in the expected state of open doors and drawers. "Tiresome," I observed.

"But only tiresome." Simon shut the wardrobe door. He was in his shirtsleeves, coat and waistcoat removed, and the muscles of his powerful form were evident under the white linen. "I am very rarely called upon to deal with inconvenience. If the spirit were leaving trails of blood or terror…"

"You would feel much more at home," I completed, and saw his rare smile. I had not seen that at all these last weeks, and it made my heart hurt for my short-lived hopes. "Have you looked in a mirror?"

"Not yet. I was about to. Will you stay?"

Stay, and watch him strip half-naked. *And then what?* I wanted to cry out, to demand what it was he expected or wanted from me, or if it was nothing, then why I could not simply have gone to my mouldering house for a poor and solitary Christmas rather than stretch this out longer.

I wanted to *talk* to him, as I had not in weeks. I was not, now, quite sure why I had not.

"Of course," I said.

His cuffs were unfastened already. I shut the door behind me and locked it as he dealt with his buttons, then pulled off the linen and his undershirt in turn, looking away from me, into the mirror.

Good God, he was an impressive specimen in the candlelight. I was no great admirer of Eugen Sandow's bodybuilding school, and had always preferred lithe grace to brute strength, and a cheerful attitude to both. Yet Simon's hulking form, deep-chested and grim-faced, made the wanting clench in my belly, till it was all I could do not to go to my knees here and now. One last time. Could I not have one last time?

I made myself look away from that thick, powerful corded muscle, up to his face in the mirror, and as I did, I saw him watching me.

I did not know what my face had shown, but from his expression, I feared it was everything.

"Robert," he said hoarsely, and turned.

I backed away, because I wanted to move forward. He looked so powerful, and so helpless. "Simon, do not—"

"How have I offended you?" He sounded lost. "I have done my best to respect your position, not to impose upon you. I have tried—" He made a frustrated noise. "How am I to know what you want?"

"What *I* want? What about Miss Kay?" I blurted the words, reddening, but they had to be spoken.

"What about her?" he said, blankly.

"Well, are you—is she— You live in her house! What is your relationship with her?"

"May I remind you that her title is Miss." Simon's voice was close to a growl. "*Miss* Kay. If we had the connexion you suggest, her name would be Mrs. Feximal. Great Scott, Robert, you cannot have imagined—"

If I had flushed before I was scarlet now. "What else was I to think?" I demanded. "You live with her, you are scarcely conventional in your ways—"

Simon's expression was composed of bafflement and annoyance. "Robert, you are as aware of my preferences as any man alive. Of course I do not wish to…to marry Theodosia, and if I did, I should be disappointed, for I assure you she would not marry me."

"Then what do your domestic arrangements mean?"

"We were raised as sister and brother." He spoke as though I should have known, as though it were obvious that these two remote, strange, alarming beings should have played together as children, he with moving runes inscribed on his body; she with those extraordinary fingernails.

I opened my mouth. Simon held up a hand. "Listen. I don't know how to say this. You must know I have very little experience with intimacy. I have tried to offer you my…my friendship, I have tried not to force matters while you are in a position that grieves me and distresses you. I do not ask or wish you to come to me out of obligation, Robert." He was pushing out the words in a low tone, his whole posture betraying his discomfort. "But…I do not know how to ask for this… If you can only grant me friendship then I shall treasure it, but if you should, if you could want something more than friendship—"

"Excuse me," I broke in. "Do you mean to say that you have refused to look me in the eye or lay a finger on me for weeks from a sense of *chivalry*?"

"You have been in a vulnerable position, obliged to live in my house. I could scarcely abuse that." He looked away from me. "God knows I have wished to speak, but I hope you have not felt any burden of expectation—"

"Good Christ and his angels," I said with, I think, pardonable annoyance, and more or less jumped at him.

It is fortunate I am the smaller man, as I might have toppled him otherwise. He took my weight with a startled grunt, and I pulled his head down to mine, and then we were kissing, with a passion that set a slow tingle of pure joy burning through me. His lips were urgent, clumsy, and I recognised the look of startled happiness in his eyes because I could feel it in my own. I laughed against his mouth. His lips curved in return, and then he picked me up by the hips—God, he was strong—and I wrapped my legs around his waist and kissed him soundly.

"Dear God," he mumbled. "Robert."

"You should have said." I shut my eyes against the truth of that. "Damn it, Simon, you should have *said*." Or I should have asked. "How was I to know—"

"I did not dare."

"You, afraid?"

It was meant to be a tease, but he looked at me with those deep, dark, lonely eyes and said, "Yes."

I stilled. He let me slip back to the ground, against his body, pressed to his bare chest, and I cupped his noble head and pulled it down to kiss him with all the tenderness of which I was capable, cursing myself as I did so, then pulled back to speak.

"I do not like to be weak, Simon. I have not wished to be dependent on you, and I have thought less of myself for it. I should have realised…" Of course he would not treat my vulnerability with disdain. He had seen in it only more reason to treat me with care and consideration.

It had not occurred to him to ask if I wanted care and consideration.

"You are not weak," Simon said, voice low. "You are remarkable. And remarkably obstinate."

"And in remarkably urgent need," I told him. "Can we…?"

The door was locked, and we in a corridor with no other inhabitants. It had to be safe enough. Simon evidently agreed. He kissed me gently, then more urgently, and then pulled his mouth away to growl, "Clothes. Off. Now."

He was not—never would be—a sophisticated lover, but sincerity can do things sophistication cannot. He stripped off his trousers with haste, then moved to help me with mine, since I was apparently moving too slowly. He more or less threw me onto the bed on my back, and knelt over me, and I had to put out a hand to make him pause while I allowed myself to gaze on his thick torso, and the strange runes in red and black that curled around and over it.

"They're moving." I reached a tentative finger to his chest.

"Be damned to them." Simon grasped my wrist, pushed it back down to the bed over my head. I extended my other arm, so he held me pinned with one powerful hand, and licked my lips in a pointed manner. He rose to the invitation, shifting forward to bring his stand to my mouth. His strong calves squeezed my ribcage, his strong fist held me down, and I made noises of approval around his solid prick. Simon groaned in response, his weight pushing me into the mattress in a most satisfactory manner. I squirmed under him, for the pleasure of feeling entirely overpowered, and he dealt with that very effectually by reaching back with his free hand and taking a firm hold of my cock.

That won him a strangled cry. He tightened his grip, leaned in and murmured, "Is this what you want?"

I could not imagine how he expected me to respond, under the circumstances. I did my best to make affirmative noises. His thick member battered my lips and his thighs crushed my chest, and I spluttered and choked and thrust against up him with no more finesse than he, until he gave a deep, animal grunt and spent.

I gulped and gasped as he pulled back and lifted himself off me. He looked down at me, his face flushed and softened with pleasure, then he shifted off me without a word, moved down the bed and took me in his mouth.

"Simon!" I yelped.

He had never done that before. I had not imagined he would. Most men of similarly forceful habits would not have dreamed of so debasing themselves, at least in my experience. Yet he did, lips covering me, warm and tight. There was little skill to it, in truth, but great application, and such passionate need and care that I was momentarily overwhelmed. I felt his mouth slide against my skin, his tongue flick and curl tentatively, then he sucked on me and I could not hold back a soft cry. He did it again, and his hand came round to enclose my shaft. Too hard, too firm, the sensation well-nigh intolerable, and I came far too soon, stifling a sound of something between pleasure and dismay.

He moved up the bed to hold me afterwards, and we lay together, skin to skin, in warm content.

"Will you come home?" he asked at last. No preamble, naturally.

I stared up at the ceiling. "Simon, I must have employment. I cannot live as your dependent."

"You will find something," he said, with more faith than reason. "But surely you stand more chance in London than at Caldwell Place."

That was inarguable. And I did not want to leave London. I did not want to leave him, and the green joy that grew in me as we lay with our fingers entangled, my head on his shoulder. Still, I needed purpose.

"I don't know," I said. "Let me think."

He nodded, lips brushing my hair, and we lay together in fragile happiness, until my drowsiness made it necessary for me to return to my room, lest we be discovered in the morning. I dressed, reluctantly, and was grateful I had bothered, because a grey-clad maid was drifting down the corridor as I left his room.

We roamed the house the next day. It was bright, cold and clear, and we were happy together. Mrs. Fontley smiled at us both. She would doubtless have lost her cheerful demeanour had she known the nature of her guests, but all she knew was that we were in her house and content, and that pleased her. The children charged around us, shyness forgotten, playing complicated and incoherent games. We explored room after room, doors and drawers gaping in each one, found nothing, and went down to the untouched wine cellar. It was cold there, not with the eldritch chill that I had felt in Caldwell Place's haunting, but with the entirely earthly cold of a damp underground space in winter. I shivered, and Simon put his arm over my shoulder to pull me close. It seemed entirely natural to him, and Mrs. Fontley did not so much as comment.

The cellar led to another where ale was stored. They brewed their own, of course. My grandfather on my mother's side had been a cooper, and I held up my lantern to look around with an inherited professional interest. Barrels were stacked all around, some great old things. The light of my oil lamp glinted off a brass plate on one great hogshead.

"Brewed to mark the birth of Henry Fontley, 1890," I read. "Your son?"

"That's right. A family tradition, to brew a cask ale for the eldest boy that will keep until his twenty-fifth birthday. It was done for my husband, and it will be done for Henry's son, no doubt." She smiled as she spoke, thinking of another generation of happy tow-headed children to come, and I smiled back.

Christ, to think of that as I write these words. To know that Henry Fontley would be dead before he reached twenty-five, his last sight the mud and slaughter of Flanders fields, his ale undrunk and turning to vinegar in his grieving parents' cellar.

But he was a laughing little boy then, and none of us knew what was coming to the world, so we smiled in thought of a future that would never be.

I looked around a little more at the untouched casks as Simon searched with an expression of mild frustration, his strange senses evidently detecting nothing out of the ordinary.

"What's this?" I enquired.

Mrs. Fontley looked over my shoulder at the ancient barrel. It was nothing of great note, except that it stood alone on a shelf, and it was very old, its wood dark with age and dirt.

"An ancient ale indeed," Simon observed. "Why that one, Robert?"

It had caught my eye, that was all. "Mere curiosity."

"Ever curious." Simon leaned forward, touched a finger to the cask, and stilled. I had seen that stillness before, the alertness of a hunting dog. Mrs. Fontley glanced at me with wide-eyed excitement. I put a finger to my lips, not wishing to distract him and hoping that no strange results would ensue in front of our hostess.

Simon's head went back, and he pulled his hand away and up. He resembled some painting of an ancient philosopher in the chiaroscuro style. "What is it?" demanded Mrs. Fontley breathlessly.

"I don't know," Simon said. "Tell me about the barrel."

Mrs. Fontley admitted ignorance, but fled to fetch her husband, which gave us a few moments alone. Simon contemplated me in the flickering light, eyes deep in shadow but still expressing puzzlement. "How did you know?"

"I don't know anything," I told him patiently. "What did you find?"

"Nothing I can identify yet." He put his oil lamp down. "Come here."

"What?" I asked, assuming it was some professional query, and was quite taken aback when he took the opportunity to kiss me with startling thoroughness. I may have yelped. He pushed his hands into my hair, holding me so roughly that he squeezed the breath from my body, and we had reason to be grateful for the stone steps that warned us of our hosts' return, and for the darkness that concealed flushed faces.

"Oh, the brother's barrel," said Mr. Fontley when his wife indicated the cask.

"Brother?"

"I don't know, that was what my father called it. Perhaps a younger brother's aged ale? It's always been here. There was a tradition my father used to carry on—"

"—which you do not," Simon finished.

"Well, no, as it happens, I don't. I had quite forgot it." Mr. Fontley looked a little awkward. "It was one of those tasks for the man of the house. My father died unexpectedly when I was fifteen and things were difficult for a while and I dare say I left a great deal undone." His wife squeezed his arm, and he threw her an affectionate look. "I must admit, I haven't thought of the brother's barrel in years. You don't suppose it's linked to our problem?"

"What was the tradition you failed to observe?"

"To fill it up." Mr. Fontley spread his hands. "We had to add a cup of ale through the spout every year, to prevent evaporation, you see. We do that with the aged ales for the boys, but the brother's ale would be undrinkable now in any case. The barrel is centuries old." He tapped the cask lightly. It made a hollow noise. "Dried up, I think, or very low. What a pity."

"Yes," Simon said. "Do you have a history of the house?"

They did of course. The old building was an antiquarian's dream and the Fontleys respected their past. Mr. Fontley produced a history written in 1796, which I took upstairs, and settled to read on Simon's bed. (Some ghost-hunters of greater social grace than Simon may mix with their employers after dinner. I have found it easiest to remove him from company altogether.)

He paced around the room a little as I read, shutting the various drawers that stood open, then began to take off his coat.

"Is that a suggestion?" I enquired.

He gave me a look of rebuke, mostly. "We omitted to look at the runes last night."

"How careless of us. You know, the writing is far from frantic, considering how active the ghost seems to be," I observed as he stripped off his undershirt. "Could this be human deception, practised upon the Fontleys after all?"

"Possibly. But you had something in the cellar."

I grimaced at the book, turned the page. "Did I? Simon, I think you overestimate my…whatever ability you believe I have. I am not like you, I am not educated in these matters, I have no occult powers. Really, I just notice things."

"You have a nose for a story," Simon said obstinately. "Look at this."

I got up to peer into the mirror at the scrawled, cramped hand repeating itself on his torso. *De me, de me, de me…*

"Latin?"

"Church Latin, by the hand. It means, 'Let me out'. That is all it says. Let me out."

"Let me out," I repeated. "So, our ghost may have died in confinement?"

"Perhaps, though I wonder if it is a case of reading down."

"What's that?" I asked, even as the memory of the folklore book came to me. "No, wait, I recall. That is when ghosts are forced into a container, a bottle or some such, by means of people reading the Bible aloud?"

Simon gave me a nod of approval. I felt an entirely disproportionate glow of satisfaction. "Any sacred text will do, and I once saw it done with Dickens. It is the relentless reading in a spirit of faith that enforces the ghost. And a ghost can be bound into anything. A shoe, a hollow stone, a cat…"

"A barrel of ale?"

"Precisely. If he was bound into the ale and kept there while the barrel was full—"

"And as the ale evaporated this summer he was freed to cause mischief." I snapped my fingers. "Is that why he does not open bottles of wine or casks of ale? He has had enough of strong drink?"

"Or fears to be trapped in an open cask again. Perhaps. But why open everything else? And why does he still ask to be freed?"

"And why confine him in the first place?" I added.

Simon came to sit on the bed by me. Bare skin, warm and close. He took the history of the house from my hands and closed it. "Do something for me, Robert."

I brushed my fingers over his chest, over a dark nipple, watched him shudder. "With the greatest pleasure."

He grasped my exploring hand, stopping it in its tracks through the sparse, wiry hair. "Not that. Well, not yet," he amended, almost with embarrassment, and handed the book back. "Open it."

"It *was* open. You just shut it."

"And now I want you to open it."

"The exciting life of an occultist," I muttered. "Very well, if you insist." I let the book drop open in my hands. "Like that?"

"Mmm. What does it say?"

I examined the page. It discussed an early stage in the house's life, when it was still an abbey. Medieval ecclesiastical history. I stifled a sigh, scanned the close-set type and let out an oath.

"What is it?" Simon sounded entirely unsurprised.

"How did you do that?"

"I did nothing. What have you found?"

"*Tragic Tale of Ill Advised Indulgence and Mistak'n Death*," I read. "A monk of the abbey in the sixteenth century, one Humphrey, drank an entire bottle of the abbot's peach brandy and collapsed. He was pronounced dead, given the appropriate rites and interred. Strange noises came from the crypt over the next few days…"

"Buried alive," Simon said. "Yes?"

"I fear so. They opened the coffin after about a week, and found his body fresh, lips gnawed and scratches on the inside of the lid. Good Lord, what a terrible thing."

To awake from a drunken stupor in God knew what state of painful thirst and hellish head. To find yourself encased in wood, to kick and scream uselessly, to endure the awful dawning realisation over a space of days that there would be no rescue, no alleviation, no escape…

"Robert." Simon's arms were around me. "Ssh, Robert. I am here."

"Thirsty," I managed. He poured me a glass of water from the pitcher by the bed, and I gulped it down, breathing deeply, telling myself it was but my imagination. It *was* imagination; mine had always been vivid. Still, I leaned against him and took comfort from his strength and solidity.

"I take it we have found the brother of the barrel," Simon observed, once I was recovered. He picked up the book and flipped to the next page. "And…yes. The ghost walked, we are told, and was laid by the efforts of the saintly abbot. By reading down into a barrel of ale, I will speculate. Doubtless that seemed appropriate. And while the ale lasted, so did his imprisonment."

"Is that why he opens things? To escape?" Simon nodded. I shuddered. "Nobody noticed he was alive when they interred him, nobody remembered him when he was dead. Shut in and forgotten, twice over. Poor Humphrey."

"The perils of overindulgence." Simon's bare arm was around me, his bare chest pressed to my back. "Thank you, Robert. If we know his story, we can end this."

"Why thank me?" I demanded. "How did that happen?"

"It's called *sortes*. A form of divination, seeking guidance in books, by the operation of chance. I thought you might have the knack."

"I do not have any such thing. I have never in my life just opened a book and found what I needed. I should have been a rather more successful journalist with that up my sleeve."

Simon gave a huff of amusement. His breath was warm on my neck. "Indeed. I do not suggest you have gifts of divination, Robert. More that you are…open. To influences, to impressions, to the story. And if a story needs to be told…" He indicated his own inscribed skin. "It will reach for a teller."

"I have a nose for a story, true—"

"Indeed you do. And some senses can be made more acute—noses sharpened, as it were—when one is touched by the supernatural."

I had been very thoroughly touched by the supernatural, of course. The thought appalled. "Do you mean to say that my reprehensible ancestor has given me some sort of spiritual clap?"

Simon actually laughed. Threw back his head and laughed, deep and resonating, so that I could not but laugh too in my pleasure at his amusement.

"My God, Robert. Come back with me."

"I—what?"

"To London." He tightened his grip, arms enclosing me with such solid power that I felt quite unmanned. "Work with me. You have a gift for it. So much empathy, so much instinct. I have use for you."

"Use?"

"Need," he muttered. I could feel his lips against my neck, head resting against mine as he held me. "God damn it, I need you. I can *breathe* around you, Robert. I need air, and I need you, and in much the same measure. Come home. Stay."

Air, he said, and here I was, barely able to inhale with those words squeezing the breath from my lungs.

"What about Miss Kay?" I managed. "Is there not a danger she will suspect us?"

"Theodosia might remark it if I laid you over the dining-room table at suppertime. But only to request that we did not spill her soup. She is not concerned with such things." He kissed my ear. "She would like me to be happy, and she finds you amusing."

"Oh, good."

"Then you will come."

"I have not said so," I pointed out. "I am a journalist, not a ghost-hunter, and I have not at all decided that I wish to change my profession, even if change is being forced upon me. It seems," I added plaintively, "that all sorts of things are being forced upon me these days."

"Is that a hint?" Simon rumbled in my ear, and set about persuading me of his case.

He was most persuasive.

The next day, Simon and I and the Fontleys stood in the icy air of the lichyard, over a spot that had been torn earth, and Simon murmured inaudible words. It was not a ceremony of any recognised kind and he was no priest. But he told the story of the dead, took it out into the light once more, assured the spirit it had been remembered, and assisted it to let go its clutch on this world.

"I'm so grateful," Mrs. Fontley told us, giving us each her hand. "Poor Humphrey, I feel so sorry for him. I wish he could have stayed, but he wasn't happy. And I am relieved for my next year's preserves and the wine cellar, of course."

"You wish he could have stayed," Simon repeated.

"With the others." Mrs. Fontley laughed merrily. "Oh dear, you must think I'm odd. But we have so many of them here and most seem content. Well, they don't make any fuss. The grey people, I don't know if you noticed?"

"They're ghosts? The grey people are *ghosts*? But—"

"It's a very old house," Mrs. Fontley said. "Anyone who wishes to stay is most welcome to our hospitality. And I do think they are quite happy, as I hope you have been. Thank you so much Mr. Feximal, Mr. Caldwell. Merry Christmas to you both."

"Merry Christmas," I replied faintly, and we went upon our way.

Devils on Horseback

By the New Year I had taken my place by Simon's side. I threw myself into arcane studies, in order to earn my keep and underpin the instincts which I had, reluctantly, to accept I possessed. I settled into the strange house on Fetter Lane with Miss Kay (who has never to this day remarked on the fact that Simon and I share a bedroom) and the mute Cornelia. I even managed to rid myself of Caldwell Place, and wished the buyers joy of it.

After a couple of months, I wrote up my first of Simon's stories and sent it to *The Strand Magazine*. I need not rehearse its popular success or the clamour for more that followed. Miss Kay read it out to Simon, adding a withering commentary at which I had to laugh while I winced. Simon merely said, "Good God, Robert," but in truth I think he was pleased by his portrayal. Even if he had not been, I doubt he would have objected. Writing satisfied me, so he was content.

I was a writer once more, and a ghost-hunter's companion, and very soon a part of London's occult hinterland.

Those who knew London of the 1890s will recall the importance of the clubs. There were clubs for braying young oafs of good family, and for upper servants on a spree, for Navy or Army, for the universities and the professions, for political beliefs and sporting habits, artistic inclinations and personal tastes, too. If one wished to describe a good, likeable, pleasant fellow, one would simply call him *clubbable*.

Simon, needless to say, was not clubbable. He *was* a member of the Diogenes Club, to which he had been nominated by one of his more peculiar acquaintances, a Government man whose intellectual capacity was matched only by his physical corpulence. This establishment gathered the least sociable men in London under one roof where conversation was strictly forbidden, and was thus Simon's place of first resort. I did not consider application (I suspect Simon would have blackballed me himself), preferring the undistinguished Stratton Club, where the penny-a-line crowd gathered to talk shop, and the atmosphere was as raucous as the Diogenes was monastic. But we both belonged to the Remnant.

Its exterior was not welcoming—an undistinguished red-brick house on the corner of Lincoln's Inn Fields—but then, it did not wish to attract passers-by. The Remnant was the occultists' club. Here was the biggest library of arcane texts in the British Isles, including some volumes that were locked in cages, and not for fear of thieves. Here gathered the students of shadows, the men and women (for the Remnant admitted both) who had plunged deep into the world beneath the world, and been irrevocably stained. Here one might find Dr. Silence, with his faithful hound by his side; Thomas Carnacki, always ready to tell a story (at length); the formidable Beatrice Phan, with her ever-friendly face, forgiving little and forgetting nothing; and on one memorable occasion Dr. Nikola himself, who held the room spellbound with his stories, fascinated even Miss Kay with his dark mesmeric gaze, and left with a rare compendium of Tibetan magic concealed under his coat.

One did not find Dr. Berry there. His skills as an occultist were unquestioned, but the club committee had indicated that his room was preferred to his company.

"Considering the personalities that *are* welcome here," I remarked to Mrs. Phan, "it is a testament to Dr. Berry that he has made himself intolerable."

"It isn't his manner that we object to," she assured me. "It is his methods."

We were in the Remnant one misty day in late autumn 1895. I had been Simon's partner, acknowledged in work and secretly in his bed, for some ten months, and it had been a busy time, as readers of my first published Casebook will recall. We had recently concluded the loathsome business of the black swine of Hampstead and had treated ourselves to an excellent dinner as reward, and we were comfortably seated with a glass of port when the Fat Man came in.

(You may ask why I do not name the Fat Man even in an account written after his death. The answer is simple: he had my word that I would never name him in my stories, published or unpublished, and I cannot persuade myself he would not wreak vengeance on faithlessness from beyond the grave.)

The Fat Man was not a habitué of the Remnant. He was not a habitué of anywhere but the Diogenes, since he was too corpulent to move easily: one felt he should have some sort of small wheelbarrow to support his belly. His ponderous entrance attracted several casual glances and a few sharp ones from those who recognised him: Carnacki, Simon, myself.

"Mr. Feximal," he wheezed. "A moment, please. And a chair."

We took him to one of the many little studies with which the Remnant was well supplied. Never was there such a club for secret meetings: most of the rooms seated no more than six, and all the walls were thick and doors soundproofed. This occasionally meant that screams went unheard until too late, but that was seen as a tolerable disadvantage.

The Fat Man seated himself in a large armchair that creaked under his bulk, accepted a glass of sherry, folded his hands on his belly and peered at us. He had the shrewdest, most intelligent eyes I have ever seen.

"Tell me," he began without preamble. "Are you familiar with the story of the dandy-dogs?"

"A Wild Hunt legend, from the south part of the country. One of many."

"In the mists of time, those unspecified bad old days of yore, a parson named Dando kept the parish of St Germans in Cornwall," the Fat Man began, in the tone of one determined to tell a story. "Dando was known for his indulgences in the sins of the flesh: eating, drinking, and the darker vices. He was popular with his parishioners, for he saw no need to condemn them for their sins when he was so busily committing his own, but he had one vice that was hard for his neighbours to forgive, and that was hunting. He led the chase across cornfields and cottage gardens without regard for the labour and profit he destroyed, and he went so far as to call out horse and hound on the Sabbath, without regard for the holiness of the day."

Simon exhaled hard and leaned back with his arms crossed, eyelids drooping. (This should be taken as an indication of his respect for the Fat Man's authority; I have seen him simply get up and leave the room when he felt a story's length exceeded its interest.)

The Fat Man ignored him. "Dando, then, rode with his riotous companions, drinking strong wines and taking the Lord's name in vain in his excitement, until at last the Devil claimed his own." He waved a hand. "The usual thing. A well-dressed stranger, an intemperate exchange. The stranger seized Dando's spoils of the chase; the enraged parson proclaimed that he would get his property back if he had to follow the stranger into Hell. 'So thou shalt,' the stranger said, and lifted Dando bodily onto his own steed. Horse, riders and hounds galloped headlong into the Lynher, disappearing beneath the waters in a blaze of fire which caused the river to boil for a moment. The wicked priest was never seen again, although he is said to ride the skies of Cornwall on stormy nights, accompanied by his pack of spectral hounds."

"I trust he *has* been seen again," Simon said. "Else I cannot imagine why you have subjected us to this rigmarole."

"Indeed. Yes, Dando rides out once more. Or something like him."

"Reports of the Wild Hunt generally prove to be wild geese," I offered. "I take it something more tangible has happened."

"There have been sightings. An elderly parson, dressed in antique clothes and of full habit"—the Fat Man made an expressive gesture at his own bulk—"was seen riding a great black horse, a spectral pack of hounds in full cry at his heels."

"Seen where?" Simon asked.

"First, through the skies over the local hostelry, past midnight. Then, past an isolated cottage inhabited by a nervous widow." The Fat Man gave a mirthless smile. "Then right down the market street of St Germans at twilight."

I whistled. "Witnesses?"

"At least fifty, neither drunken nor nervous. Or, at least, not nervous *before* the manifestation of a ghostly hunt through the marketplace. And then..." He grimaced. "Matters became more serious. The local parson, by all accounts a decent man, if excessively stern with his parishioners, went for a ride on the moors. His horse, a sluggish and elderly beast, returned alone, sweating and terrified, as though it had galloped itself to exhaustion. The parson's body was found in the river some miles away."

"Which river?" I asked, at once with Simon's "How did he die?"

"The Lynher, where Dando met his fate. He drowned—no evidence of hellfire—but his visage was transfigured with terror, it is said. Of course, this might be mere chance. But there is no question of the next. One Mathew Tregow was outside a public house with five friends. They all attest that the Hunt came upon them—'swooped down out of nowhere'—that the horseman, laughing wildly, pointed his whip at Tregow, that the dogs set after him. The man ran. The huntsman, on his black steed, caught up. The horse rose into the air, with the struggling man clutched in the rider's grip, and disappeared from view. His body was found in the middle of a plain, shattered and broken, as though it had fallen from a great height."

Simon scowled. "Serious indeed. But what is it to you?"

The Fat Man exhaled. "One of St Germans' most notable residents is Lord Westerbury."

Simon glanced to me. He had abandoned any effort to pay attention to politics, now that I could supply him with information on demand.

"He fought in Afghanistan as General Winton, who ordered the Kabul massacre," I said. "On his return to England he was given a title but no office. His past was a little too controversial, and his political ambitions a little too, uh, ambitious. He retired to the country a few years ago where he has become a political host."

"Indeed," said the Fat Man. "Lord Westerbury was given no place in the halls of power so he has built his own. He invites various men of high standing to Penmadown House, his Cornish property, for…conversation."

Simon looked blank. "Conversation?"

"Plotting," I supplied. "If there is a party leader to be dislodged, or a MP to be lured across the floor, or a vote in the House to be swayed, Penmadown House offers a comfortable setting for conspiracy."

"Stratton Club scribblers' gossip," the Fat Man said. "I could not confirm any such thing. However, when the pheasant shooting begins in just two days, Penmadown House will accommodate, among others, the Chief Secretary to the Treasury and four Members of Parliament, each of whom can deliver a number of votes in the House. And a murderous ghost rides the moors."

"Perhaps the party should be rearranged, then."

"It will not be." The Fat Man sounded grim. "Lord Salisbury's premiership is at stake; so is Lord Westerbury's reputation as a broker of power. There is a rebellion growing against Salisbury's conduct of the wars, but it is very early days. The malcontents cannot afford to give any ground. And if Westerbury calls the party off against their will, he will not be trusted again."

"So you require the Hunt stopped before any of the assembled worthies become its prey," Simon said. "Very well. Is anyone else on this?"

"Dr. Berry has left for Cornwall already."

Simon's jaw set. "Then we shall not. I do not work with Berry, as well you know."

"I fear I must request it."

"No."

The Fat Man's grey eyes were steely. "Mr. Feximal, this is a matter of national importance. The lives of notable men may depend on your assistance."

"They risk their lives by choice," Simon snapped. "Is this anything more than a struggle for power? Can you tell me there is principle at stake?" The Fat Man raised a scornful brow, but he did not disagree; Simon went on. "The lives of many people depend on my work, sir, and all of them are important, if only to themselves. Your men may take their chances."

"They are important to the nation," the Fat Man said. There was a note in his voice I did not like.

"I am not the nation," Simon retorted, heedless. "And Berry is a competent occultist. Trust him to do the task, or if you do not, call him off."

"Unfortunately, Dr. Berry was engaged by Mr. Parker—"

"Then Mr. Parker can call him off," Simon interrupted impatiently. "Must I repeat myself?"

The Fat Man's nostrils flared a little. "Mr. Feximal. You will go to St Germans and put an end to whatever is happening there, *alongside* Dr. Berry. That is an order."

The Fat Man held a government position which I will not specify. He was the spider at the centre of a very great web, operating not quite within the bounds of Whitehall, making use of individuals with unusual talents. He had made use of us before, but always as a matter of request, never as of right. He *had* no right.

Simon's fist was clenched on the arm of his chair. "You do not give me orders. Remove Berry from the scene, or send Carnacki, or tell Lord Westerbury to cancel his party, I don't give a curse which. All are within your powers."

"Yes." The Fat Man leaned forward. "*Everything* is within my powers."

Simon's face set. "Your meaning?"

"I wish this party to proceed. I wish to know what Dr. Berry does. You will tell me."

"Absolutely not." Simon stood. "I do not involve myself in political manoeuvring, and I shall not play your games. Come, Robert."

I stood. Simon took a stride towards the door. The Fat Man leaned back in his chair and said, "Any male person who, in public or private, commits, or is a party to the commission of—"

"What?"

"—or procures, or attempts to procure the commission by any male person of any act of gross indecency with another male person—"

Simon swung back round to him, face darkening. I grabbed his arm.

"—shall be guilty of a misdemeanour, and being convicted thereof, shall be liable at the discretion of the Court to be imprisoned for any term not exceeding two years, with or without hard labour."

"That is indeed the law," I said, as calmly as I could. "What is its application here?"

"Very few men are above the law," the Fat Man said. "Not even Mr. Parker, and certainly not you, Mr. Feximal, with your friend here." I felt the swell of Simon's bicep, dug in my fingers more urgently. "Your domestic arrangements do not interest me. What concerns me is to know Mr. Parker's orders, as expressed in Dr. Berry's actions. I wish you to go, and go you shall."

Simon was rigid in my grip. I told the Fat Man, "We shall discuss it," and dragged him out. It took an effort.

St Germans is a small village not far from the Tamar estuary. It sits atop a height, a gathering of picturesque white-painted houses clinging to steep grey lanes, doubtless very pretty in summer, but this was an autumn evening. The sea winds whipped at our coattails and howled round our ears. The people looked afraid.

The village offered just one hostelry, the George and Dragon. I procured us a large shared room, pleasingly enough. I do dislike the creeping along corridors necessitated by separate bedrooms. Not that Simon was in a mood for bedroom activities. He had been in a spitting rage since we had spoken to the Fat Man, and I could hardly blame him.

It was my fault. Simon had lived a mostly celibate life before he met me, his few encounters hurried and nameless. I, on the other hand, while discreet, had happily taken part in the entertainments London offered to men of our persuasion. I attended the Gilded Lily, had been often found on Cleveland Street and in the Alhambra, and had—I blush to confess it—enhanced my income in the early days by supplying erotic writings to some of Holywell Street's more specialist pornographers. (I was considered to have quite the knack for it.) If the Fat Man had been looking for Simon's weak spot, I was it, and it would probably have been a matter of hours rather than days for him to find that out.

Simon's ill humour did not derive from that. He never spoke a word of blame or accusation to me on that subject nor, I truly believe, thought one. But he was furious at the Fat Man's blackmail, furious to be made a puppet in a game he did not wish to play, and enraged beyond measure that I should encounter the loathsome Dr. Berry once more. He had not wanted me to come with him at all, but I had insisted, with all the force at my disposal.

"You must not go out alone," he said now, sitting heavily on one of the beds to test it. It had a solid wooden frame and barely protested. "Berry is a malicious creature and not to be trusted."

"I don't intend to." I slung my Gladstone bag on the other bed, stripped off my coat, relishing the warmth of a fire that had clearly been blazing all day, and came to sit by him. "And the Fat Man does not trust him either. What purpose do you think he has here, if not to put an end to this haunting?"

"I don't know or care," Simon snapped. "My intention is to end this as quickly as possible and return home. I shall not report back on Dr. Berry; I am not a Government spy."

No, of course he was not, which meant that I would have to take that role or risk the Fat Man's displeasure. I suppressed a sigh. "It is too late to visit Lord Westerbury tonight. Shall we dine here and see what we can glean from the locals?"

Simon nodded then, as I made to rise, grasped my arm. "A moment. Will you promise me caution?"

"I am always cautious," I pointed out. "I am far too cowardly not to be."

"Don't jest. I am concerned, Robert. I don't like this business. I suspect we are pawns in a game played by two masters."

"Well, that is obvious. The Fat Man could have sent any ghost-hunter in the country, and chose the one who most dislikes Dr. Berry. Therefore our role is to provoke him, or to mistrust him, or both. Neither should be hard to do."

"As long as you mistrust him above all else," Simon said firmly.

Simon had been very careful to keep me apart from the repulsive doctor, refusing any cases that might bring us into contact. I knew very well that this was his mistrust of Dr. Berry rather than me, and felt no resentment. Simon might fear that I would be the victim of Berry's powers; I was absolutely terrified by the prospect.

"If I should see Berry without you present, all he will see of me is a clean pair of heels," I assured him. "I have to ask, though, Simon. If we are fighting this proxy war, however reluctantly… Do you think Berry might know of our connexion?"

Simon shrugged. "What the Fat Man can find out, so can Mr. Parker."

"Curse them all. Should I go back down and demand separate rooms?"

"No. I don't want you on your own."

I raised a brow. "You think I'm in danger of attack?"

Simon gave my arm a forceful tug which, given that he is as strong as an ox, left me sprawling face-down over his lap. "Not from Berry."

I squirmed a bit, for the look of the thing, and then quite sincerely, as his hand ran over my thigh, down, up, delving between my legs, cupping my balls with a pressure that declared him in charge. I whimpered. Simon shifted me bodily so my rapidly hardening cock was trapped against his powerful thigh, and continued his work, rubbing at me through the fabric of my clothing, until I was writhing in earnest, aroused and imprisoned.

I thought he might throw me on the bed to have his way (which was also very much my way, needless to say). He did not. I felt his other hand move to unfasten my trousers, drag them and my drawers down, push my shirttails out of the way. He paused, while I lay quivering, waiting, and then I felt his fingers brush my skin, the very lightest stroke. Over a buttock, down a thigh, up again, a gentle fingertip exploration, taking his time, while all I could do was wait upon his pleasure.

"Simon," I gasped.

"Sssh."

I moved against him, an inelegant thrust driven by the need for friction against my prick, and he slapped my arse, light but firm. "Stay still."

"I don't want to stay still," I complained.

"Then turn over." Simon hoisted me up bodily, turning me over, so I lay across his lap, face up, his legs wide to support me. I stared up at him, his dark, intent eyes fixed on my body with utter absorption, his little frown of concentration as he went about pleasuring me with all the dedication he put into ridding the world of roaming spirits, and I felt my heart contract.

"Robert." One hand was playing between my legs, stroking and pressing in the way he knew I liked, his fingers probing just enough to tantalise. The other palm skimmed over the skin of my prick, and I gasped and jerked like a landed fish. Entirely caught. He repeated the movement, pressing and pleasing me, rhythmic and steady. "My Robert."

"All yours," I whispered.

His hand closed round my cock, thumbing the top. "I will not let you fall."

I made a faint sort of noise, and he smiled down at me then with such a look in his eyes. Such a fond affection.

Such love.

"My own," he said softly, and I came in his hand with a soft cry, pulsing and straining upwards towards him, wanting nothing more than his touch.

I gasped for breath after, feeling the tremors of pleasure running through me. Simon mopped the mess with a pocket handkerchief, scooped me up in his strong arms and kissed me. I dropped my arms round his shoulders and opened my mouth to his, weak with pleasure, and with the trembling sensation of the naked truth that lay between us.

The Victorian age was known for its sentiment, but Simon was not sentimental. Deeply passionate, under the granite exterior, and profoundly compassionate too, but he kept those fires concealed. Expressing his feelings was a matter of torture for him, and he had no idea what to do with such expressions from others. I would have told him I loved him a dozen times a day, if he had wished to hear it; I should have showered him with love tokens, if he would have taken them with anything but discomfort.

He did not, he never would. That was not his way. But I pulled my mouth from his, and smiled, and he nodded and kissed me again, and I was entirely content.

I should have preferred to spend the evening wrapped around him in that narrow bed, but there was work to be done. We made our way downstairs, and had an excellent meal of mutton pie followed by a kind of crumbly cheese with a rind made of nettle leaves, the whole washed down with good local ale. I was in a very positive frame of mind as we came into the crowded public saloon.

Simon led the way through the door. Heads turned. Weather-beaten, watchful faces stilled. All talk ceased. There was a long still moment and then a purposeful scrape of wood against stone as a burly man pushed back his chair and stood.

I supposed it was too much to hope that this was mere rustic shyness.

"So," said the man, speaking to the landlord, as he sidled behind the bar, rather than to us. I shall not attempt a full reproduction of his Cornish burr on the page, for fear of becoming incomprehensible. "E be ghost-hunter, do ee?"

"Aye," the landlord muttered. "Now, Jem—"

"Another one of 'em? Well." Jem took a step forward. Simon took a step to meet him, consciously or unconsciously taking a pugilistic stance.

I had no doubt of who would win a fair fight, or even a reasonably unfair one, but there were twenty men in the room. I stepped round Simon and said, "When you say *another*, sir, who do you mean? What other ghost-hunter?"

A few glances, a little hesitation, then one of them muttered, almost reluctantly, "Doctor."

"Dr. Silence? Oh good heavens, not Dr. Berry?" I asked with, I hoped, suitable dismay.

More looks exchanged. "Aye." Jem hooked his thumbs behind his braces. "Know 'e, do you, zur?"

"We are—acquainted with him," I said carefully. "But *not* associates. I am surprised to learn this. Had you any inkling he was here?" I asked Simon, who gave me a look that suggested he had no inclination to play-act. This was as well, since he was incapable of it, but the disgust in his expression did good service. I could see the men settling, a few pint-pots picked up. "My name is Robert Caldwell and this is Mr. Simon Feximal," I added, addressing myself to the room at large. "We would be most interested to learn anything about the recent events, if anyone should be willing to talk to us. Ah, landlord?" I motioned meaningfully to the bar, and within a very few minutes we were comfortably settled with no fewer than four eyewitnesses to the apparition at the market, and one man who had seen the abduction of the atheist Mathew Tregow.

It was all very much as the Fat Man had told us. A single huntsman on a great black steed, and the hounds of hell following after.

"Dressed in the old way," one man assured us, "and a fine fat fellow, too. I'd say bright-coloured clothes and red in the face, but 'e were…" He groped for a word. "Shadowy."

"Aye," his fellow agreed. "As if 'e were covered in cobweb. Grey, like."

They agreed that the horse was huge and black. Suggestions of flaming eyes and nostrils were raised by the crowd around us, but discounted by the eyewitnesses. Nor did they agree on the dogs.

"Pack o'smoke," said one of the market witnesses. "Grey dogs, all flowing into each other. Couldn't count 'em. And the *eyes*."

"Fiery!" said someone from the crowd.

"Black as the pit," retorted the witness, with some irritation. "No light. No white. No flames either, Bill Penney." The previous speaker looked abashed. "Just great black—"

"Holes," said a second eyewitness flatly. "They was holes, not eyes."

"Yes," Simon said. "I expect they were."

His tone was heavy. The men around us glanced nervously at one another.

Simon asked a few further questions, then moved on to the abduction of Mathew Tregow.

"Yelling, the dogs were, full throat." The witness was eager to speak, but not from a desire for attention, as I gathered. He wanted to rid himself of what he had seen, expel it in words. I knew that desire. "Horse hooves beating on the turf and the cry of dogs, then the horn sounding."

"Did the huntsman raise a cry?"

"No. Just the horn and the dogs and the hooves, and that were enough. That and Mathew screaming."

"And the horse rose into the air." Simon's deep voice made anything sound reasonable.

"Aye, it did, with Mathew calling for help and struggling. We ran after ee, zur, but—"

"Be glad you did not catch him. You would have done no good." Simon sat back, brows knitting in thought.

"Tregow and the parson," I said, since his part of the proceedings seemed to be over. "Had they anything in common?"

The answer to that was a comprehensive *no*. Parson Adams had been an ascetic, profoundly religious man, morally upright and unbending, but charitable to the point that he gave away most of his church stipend to needy parishioners, and made himself loathsome to his less generous neighbours by demanding they did the same. The rich man and the eye of the needle had come up frequently in his sermons.

Tregow, on the other hand, was a miner of little education, a drunkard, a womaniser with three children outside the benefit of marriage. He ranted about politics in his cups, cried for revolution, and was an open atheist who refused to attend Sunday service.

These were the two men that Dando and his dogs had hunted, and nobody had an inkling why they had been chosen.

Simon had retreated into thought, which left me to pursue our other unwanted duty. "Dr. Berry. I trust he is not staying here?"

"Thank the Lord, no, zur," a sunbrowned young fellow said. "No, he be at Penmadown this time."

"Staying with Lord Westerbury?"

"Aye, sir, and welcome to bide there." There was a mutter of agreement. Dr. Berry's personal charisma had clearly not improved. It made one wonder why Lord Westerbury had accepted such a guest at such a time; I could only conclude that the general, who boasted such a magnificent fighting pedigree, was afraid.

We went to Penmadown House the next day to seek audience with Lord Westerbury. It was a great grey stone mansion on a rise of bleak, scrubby ground. The wind was knifelike, spattering us with rain that came in horizontal drifts. I am informed that Cornwall is lovely in the summer.

Lord Westerbury had evidently been advised to expect us. We were shown into his study, which was adorned by souvenirs of the wars: regimental photographs, flags, rifles and the like. No Afghan rugs or artefacts, though. One might conclude he did not wish to recall his time there.

He was a compact man of medium height, in his sixties, hair clipped short around the dome of his bare scalp. I could imagine him barking orders on the ramparts of some sunbaked fortress as easily as I could picture him in a smoke-wreathed room, manoeuvring the pieces on the political chessboard. A formidable man, but undoubtedly a frightened one.

At least part of what frightened him was evident from the fact that a footman discreetly followed us to the study door, and I glimpsed him taking station outside before Lord Westerbury closed it.

"So, Dr. Berry is staying here," I observed, to see his reaction.

He glanced at the door. "Yes. I understand you do not generally work together."

"No. Our methods are not his."

Lord Westerbury's straight-backed posture did not relax, precisely, but I had no doubt he was relieved. "I have not encountered the supernatural before. I do not know what methods an occultist might use."

"That depends on the manifestation," Simon said. "Have you seen the Hunt?"

Lord Westerbury shook his head. "I have heard it, I believe, though it might of course be merely—"

"—wild geese—" Simon and I murmured along with him.

"—but I cannot ignore the reports of my neighbours, or the man Tregow's fate."

"Yet you do not cancel your house party, though it starts tomorrow," Simon observed.

"My guests are my business. That is not your concern." Lord Westerbury spoke with instant authority.

"Indeed not," Simon said. "It may be the concern of any of your guests who ride the moors, though. Tell me, do you know of any link between Tregow and Parson Adams?"

"You cannot imagine I was personally acquainted with Tregow," Westerbury said stiffly. "I am told he was an atheistical radical of the worst kind. Adams was a man of great, indeed excessive rectitude. I am not aware of any link between them except that both were fanatics of their causes." He snorted. "One might almost say, their shared cause. The parson insisted that every man of more than moderate means should open his purse for the feckless to help themselves at will. Tregow went a step further. He proposed to steal my possessions and have me dynamited, the blackguard."

"Was this a practical proposal or merely a theoretical aim?" I asked.

Lord Westbury waved his hand dismissively. "Oh, wild talk and drink. The man was a wastrel. Does it matter now?"

"The question is whether the hunter chose his targets at random or for a reason," Simon said. "It seems to me you disliked both men, Lord Westerbury."

"I did, but Dando would hardly have shared my reasons, would he? Who knows why a hunting parson three centuries dead would take a grudge, hey?"

"Mmm," I said. "You believe it is Dando, then, the old legend returned to earth?"

"Is there any doubt? Dr. Berry speaks of the phantom as Dando."

"When did he come?" I asked. "Dr. Berry, I mean. How long has he stayed with you?"

"Three days now." It sounded as if that were quite long enough.

"And he came down at your request?"

"Well, he contacted me," Lord Westerbury said. "He offered his services. Had I known that Whitehall would send its own man, I should have waited. If you feel that, now you are here, it might be a case of too many cooks…" He let that trail off invitingly, evidently hoping that Simon would recommend the doctor's dismissal.

"I will speak to him." Simon glanced at me. "Perhaps I could do that while my colleague asks you for the further information we require."

It would have been foolish for me to argue. Simon was more than capable of dealing with Berry by himself, after all. Still, I felt a twinge of shame at my relief.

Lord Westerbury had a servant take Simon to Dr. Berry, then turned back to me. "You have further questions, sir?"

"I do. Please accept my assurance that nothing said will go further than the walls of this room—"

"Can I accept that?" Lord Westerbury's voice had a ring of command. "You are a journalist, Mr. Caldwell. That is not a breed known for discretion."

"I was a journalist; now I am Mr. Feximal's colleague, and he would not thank me for betraying a confidence or letting down a client. Talking of letting down clients, sir, why do you not postpone your party?"

It was a gamble, which had a very real risk of ending with my unceremonious exit from the house, and for a moment I thought that would be the result. Then Lord Westerbury glanced at the door once more and said, "I suppose if you are to deal with this business…"

"In strictest confidence, your lordship," I assured him.

"Then I shall tell you this much: some of my guests need an opportunity to discuss matters of importance away from the bustle of London. Where nobody can interfere with the conversation or apply pressure to the participants. I pride myself on…*facilitating* such discussions. I learned a great deal about negotiation in the Army, Mr. Caldwell. Location and isolation, that's the trick."

Sending cavalry into an unarmed crowd had been highly effective too. I did not mention that. "And I assume these discussions are urgent. Can you not find another location?"

"This house is very well suited," Lord Westerbury said with a frown.

"Do you have another property, at all?"

"I do not."

In other words, he wanted to hold on to the glory. A different location would mean a different host. Lord Westerbury was not a man who let go of what he had.

"Tell me, sir," I said. "Who else wants you to give your money away?"

"I beg your pardon?"

"Parson Adams made speeches from the pulpit, exhorting you to give what you have to the poor. Tregow was the loudest voice for redistribution of wealth. You clearly felt a personal attack in both cases, and now they are both dead. I must wonder, sir, about the link between the two."

I thought he might have an apoplexy. His face went slowly red, he swelled with fury as he took in my meaning, and I found myself on the doorstep in the rain some five minutes afterwards.

"I see you have made yourself unpopular," Simon observed when he joined me, a very wet and cold quarter hour later.

"I did, but it was worth it."

"Tell me as we walk."

"Where are we going?"

"The moor, of course."

"Of course," I said with resignation, glad I had worn good boots. We set off along a path that was both muddy and stony, the chill wind pushing at my hat and flapping my coattails. "What a charming day for exercise. Well, what seems clear is that Dando killed the two locals most disliked by Lord Westerbury, and that this fact had not occurred to him. He didn't notice when you made the implication, and his reaction when I spelled it out was of genuine outrage. It had not occurred to him that he was a beneficiary of their deaths."

"Someone else might have been also," Simon observed.

"Perhaps, but as we learned last night—as *I* learned, you weren't listening—there are no other very wealthy men in the area. No. It strikes me that Dando's acts might be in the nature of…how can I put it…a carrot used as a stick."

"That would be an ineffective weapon."

"You know perfectly well what I mean. A threat: *I can kill.* But an inducement: *I can kill your enemies.*"

Simon scowled, hunching his shoulders against a flurry of rain. "You have something in mind."

"Politics. I don't believe that Dando's return just happened to coincide with a conspiracy to overthrow the Prime Minister. Or that he just happened to target two people who irritated a power broker of immense standing. Or that Dr. Berry just happened to offer his services."

"He claims he did," Simon said. "He insists he heard about the haunting through the usual channels, and was moved to give his aid."

"What a charitable man he is. Did you ask him if Mr. Parker sent him?"

"No. He would have asked why, and I felt sure you would think it best not to mention the Fat Man. I am acquiring cunning from you," Simon added, with an air of mild self-satisfaction.

"Well done. So, assuming the Fat Man is correct—"

"He has yet to be wrong, in my experience."

"—Mr. Parker sent Dr. Berry here and Dr. Berry wishes to conceal that. Did he say when he came down?"

"Three days ago."

"Isn't that odd," I remarked. "Because the men at the George and Dragon spoke of 'this time'. Dr. Berry was here before."

"And chose not to mention that."

We had climbed a rise as we talked and now stood on some little height, staring over a view that, in more clement weather, would have been astounding. Around us stretched the greys and greens of scrubgrass, heather, moss and lichened granite. Penmadown Wood was behind us; ahead was only moorland.

"The very definition of a blasted heath," I said with a shiver.

"You are a city creature." Simon took a huge breath of the very cold air. "This is cleansing."

"It's freezing. Simon, is it possible Dando was summoned to do someone's bidding? Could someone mean to use him, or it, to control Lord Westerbury?"

Simon made a face of revulsion. "Politics. But I must assume the Fat Man sent us here for a reason… No. No, not us, of course, but *you*. A journalist, a political animal with his nose in all sorts of corners. That is why he selected me over any other ghost-hunter, is it not? Because I have you."

"I think so." I could not tell if the icy sensation down my back was the dripping of water off the brim of my hat and down my collar, or not. "He directed our thoughts towards conspiracy, even stated that Mr. Parker is not above the law."

Simon glowered. "What does this mean?"

"Mr. Parker operates by influence," I said, thinking it through. "Lord Westerbury is becoming a rival. Mr. Parker wants either to control or to remove him, but he is wealthy, well connected, no hints of scandal, not easily intimidated. So let us say Mr. Parker commands Dr. Berry to raise a ghost—can he?"

"Any fool can. The trick is to control it."

"Dr. Berry raises the spirit. If Lord Westerbury cancels the planned gathering, his position of influence is badly compromised. If he does not, then presumably he will be given the choice: to oppose Mr. Parker, with two dead men as a delicate hint as to the consequences, or to take those dead men as a gift from his master. Am I too cynical? Is this beyond what Mr. Parker would do?"

"Very little is," Simon said grimly. "He has always regarded the world beneath the world as a resource to be used. And Dr. Berry can help him use it."

The wind whipped and tugged at our coats. I clapped a hand to my hat, staring out at the bleak prospect. "What can we do?"

"Test the theory. Find if this is a summoning; if it is, find the summoner, and end it, before there are more deaths."

"And let the Fat Man deal with Mr. Parker?"

"I think so. We can only do our part, Robert."

Rain splattered my face, and I turned my back to the driving wind. "Can you—?" I gestured at his chest.

"I doubt it. If Dando is present in this world, his spirit will not cry out. And in any case a ghost so old…"

He made a face. I recalled his contact with the ancient butterfly bishop, and said, hastily, "No, you must not. But what, then?"

"I could wish to have Theodosia here," Simon muttered. "She is the great expert. But…" He hefted his small black Gladstone bag. "I dare say I can do something."

"You are going to summon Dando?" I enquired, not very enthusiastically.

"Of course not." He knelt on the sodden ground, ferreting in his bag. "I shall enact a *quaero vestigiis*, a search for footprints, as it were. Have you seen this before?" He slipped something out of a velvet case and handed it to me. It was a stone or glass disc, I could not tell which, absolutely black. It was polished to a smoothness that made it feel almost unreal to my fingers, as though it were not there at all, and when I looked into it, despite the high sheen, I could see no reflection. I tilted it, staring into the depths.

"Don't play the fool," Simon said, whisking it from my fingers.

"What is it?"

"Obsidian. A scrying-glass. This is a little difficult, and I do not use it unless I must." He squatted, balancing the thing on his broad thighs, and began to murmur under his breath. As he spoke, he flicked the cork from a flask with his thumb, and poured the contents out onto the disc: a fine grey powder. One might have expected that to be whipped away by the wind. It was not. It formed a heap, instead, one that slowly spread outwards over the smooth surface.

Simon took out a penknife and sliced into the tip of his little finger, a deep enough cut that the blood welled at once and ran freely. He circled his hand over the scrying-glass, still whispering. The blood dripped onto the dust and…sank in. Not as water soaks into earth, but falling, as though the polished blackness was suddenly a tunnel, a hole that led very far down indeed.

I looked at his face. He was staring into the pit he held, and what he saw I do not know, but the veins stood in rigid relief against his pallid skin.

When I looked back at the obsidian disc, it was a smooth surface once more, clean of blood or dust. Just black.

"Now." Simon's voice rasped. "*Ostende mihi.*" Show me.

The glass clouded, as though it had been breathed on, but not on the surface. Underneath, rather, as if something had exhaled from the other side.

Then there were pictures, forming in miniature on the surface, with perfect clarity.

"Seen through a glass, darkly," I whispered, and Simon gave me a short nod.

I saw a small figure in emptiness. On the moor, I realised. A man, crouched at his work, and a big black horse tethered by him, tossing its head, shifting in discomfort.

"He's in pentacle," Simon murmured. "Is the horse a sacrifice, or a steed?"

"I can't see his face," I said. "Is it—"

"No names."

The picture became larger, as though our vantage point were coming nearer to its subject. The man was indeed within a large pentacle, made of heaped earth and stone, with pale sticks delineating its shape. Bones, I realised. There were unmoving huddled shapes at each point. Dead animals.

"Foxes," Simon said. "Clever."

The man finished his close work in the pentacle. He tilted his head back to the sky, eyes shut, mouth moving and we both said, "*Ah,*" confirmation rather than realisation.

Dr. Berry.

His chant was silent in the scrying-glass, but I could feel it gathering strength, I knew that around him the light was being sucked from the air. The glass seemed to vibrate. Its surface clouded again, a roiling fog. The tethered horse reared, front legs striking the air, and Simon gasped, "*Desistite!*"

The surface of the glass cleared instantly, and now—for the first time, I realised—the rain began to leave droplets on it. Simon rocked backwards, and if I had not taken his weight, I think he must have fallen. His little finger looked white and shrivelled, as though it had lost a great deal of blood.

"Are you all right?" I asked, pointlessly. He did not reply, but he leaned against me for just a few seconds, breathing deeply, before he straightened up and moved to return the scrying-glass to its velvet bag. "You didn't want to see Dando come?"

"The glasses have a tendency to break under stress," Simon said. "And are damned expensive to replace. I think there can be no doubt, Robert. We need to see Dr. Berry again."

We tramped back down the hill, sodden and chilled, only to learn that Lord Westerbury and Dr. Berry had already left Penmadown House.

"Gone to moors," the footman repeated, quavering a little in the face of Simon's ferocious questioning. "Up to Lanjore Hill."

"Where is that?" Simon demanded. "Damnation, this is urgent!"

The footman pointed us to the footpath, informing us that it was no more than a mile, and added that his master had taken the carriage.

"Let us hurry." Simon set off at a spanking pace that made it clear he would not hear further enquiries about his health.

"You think we alarmed Berry?" I asked, half running to keep up.

"As like as not. In any case, the political guests arrive tomorrow. Berry had to make his offer soon."

I nodded in agreement, so as to save my breath, and hurried at his heels.

The footpath led us upwards. It split at one point, without signposts, as is apparently compulsory for country roads. Simon paused, eyes distant, then sucked in a breath as though he had been struck, clenching his arms around himself for a brief moment.

"Simon?"

"He is coming."

"You mean Dr. Berry?" I said hopefully.

"No."

We more or less ran up the steeper path, slipping and stumbling and gasping. It was raining in earnest now, coming across us in grey waves, and the sky growing darker. I wiped my wet hair from my eyes as we crested the hill and saw the men we sought.

Lord Westerbury, that fierce soldier and accomplished politician, was on his knees in the mud, huddled in white-faced terror. Dr. Berry stood before him, pointing out at the sky. He was brandishing a fox's brush, the white-tipped fur sodden and bedraggled, and I could hear him shouting. The words were unclear, but I recognised the tone. Oh, I recognised it, and the marrow went from my bones at the sound.

"Berry!" Simon roared.

Dr. Berry swung round, startled, and his face changed as he saw us. He hissed, a serpent sound that carried over the wind and rain, and Simon gave a wordless growl in response.

I had no desire to get between them. I ducked sideways, edging round a few paces to get a clear sight of Lord Westerbury. The terrified plea in his eyes as he looked to me, this man who had commanded troops and supervised a massacre…

I glanced at Berry. He was advancing on Simon, shouting, so I ran to the old soldier.

"Can you move?"

"That man," Westerbury wheezed. "He said, if I didn't… He said…"

"We need to leave this hill." I tugged at his arm. "Get up. Get *up*. The Hunt is coming."

"Jesu help me," Westerbury whispered. "Lord save me."

I could hear it now, in the sky, the baying of hounds, a dreadful clamour several notes deeper than the sound of geese, and above it, the brassy blast of a hunting horn. I put my hands under Westerbury's armpits and heaved, but he was immovable, as heavy and unwieldy as a corpse, every bit of sense he had left focused on the skies, and the darkness that swept towards us, and the Hunt.

Dr. Berry was screaming at Simon, words lost in the howling wind. Simon, face granite as the hill we stood on, stared out at the oncoming storm.

Too late to run. Nowhere to hide on this bleak hill, except behind Simon, and he was busy. I locked my knees and planted a hand on Westerbury's shoulder—I hoped he took it as reassurance; in fact, I needed the support—and faced what came.

The hunting horn rang out again. Hoofbeats thundered towards us, sounding on nothing. The black horse, sweating and frothing, landed on the hill and reared up with a neigh that sounded like a shriek. Beads of rain shone on the coarse black hairs of its coat, and as it went back down to four legs, I concluded that, gallop through the air though it had, it was real.

Dogs flowed like water around it, and the part of me that never ceases to observe noted that the men had been accurate eyewitnesses. *Pack of smoke*, they had called the dogs, and that was right. They were indeterminate shapes, solidifying into dog form if you stared at one closely, until it melted back into the mass. Only the eyes were clear, those holes into the world beneath, and I did not want to look at those.

If the horse was real and the dogs were not, God alone knows what the rider was. A stout, florid, elderly man of the John Bull sort, the kind whose raucous jollity was but a thin veneer over cruel temper. His eyes gave that away, gleaming with malevolence. I should have said he was red-faced and wearing a bright huntsman's coat, except that I seemed to see him through shadows.

Westerbury whimpered helplessly. I could not blame him.

Berry was chanting. Simon's voice rose over him, addressing the huntsman. "Go. Leave this place or be sent howling. Begone!"

"You will do my commands," Berry called, equally loud. "I summoned you, I freed you, I gave you your steed, and *you will ride.*" He went back to his chant, a dreadful penetrating whisper, and I heard Simon's deep tones pronounce the strange resonant syllables of the Saaamaaa Ritual.

He's using the Sixth Line, I thought, with the strange abstraction that terror brings. *I expect we're going to die, then.*

Dando gave a roar of fury, mouth opening wide to reveal not teeth or tongue but a deep, dark hole. Berry shrieked his own incantation, challenging Simon's, and if Simon's words sounded like bronze gongs, Berry's were retched up, wet and fleshy sounds. The two did not go together at all, not at all. They seemed to snarl and tangle in one another, the sounds dragging at my ear. The air smelled of tin.

"You are my creature!" Berry cried. "Take your prey!" He pointed at Simon with the hand that held the bedraggled foxtail. The horseman's head turned, sighting, and the dogs stopped their endless movement and stiffened as one, ready to pounce.

Simon was shouting the syllables of the Ritual, feet wide, braced against all comers, as he would always be until he found the opponent he could not defeat, but I feared he had found it now. The Ritual commanded creatures from the world beneath, and Dando, on his flesh and blood horse, was all too firmly *here.*

The horseman stiffened in his saddle, pointing down at Simon, and raised the horn to his lips. Dr. Berry watched, spectacles glistening with rain, mouth stretched in a terrible smile.

He was not even looking at me when I collided with him.

As I have mentioned, I am not a large man, but surprise can do a great deal, and so can the prospect of one's lover dying in front of one's eyes. I hit Berry from the side as I had learned in long-ago games of rugby at school, sending him lurching, and as he staggered, I snatched the fox's tail from his hand.

Dando's head snapped round, to me. Berry lunged at me, and I leapt backwards, stumbling on a loose stone underfoot. I flung out my arms to keep myself upright, the wind cracked like a whip, and the brush was snatched from my hand, tumbling upwards into the sky, vanishing in an instant.

Dando turned his head again, slowly this time, back to Dr. Berry.

The doctor's mouth worked. I expected that look of terrible certainty to settle on his face again, but it did not. He took a step back, another. He was shaking.

The horse came forward a slow, deliberate pace, and to my horror, Simon took a long stride to stand in front of it, arms out. "*Run*, damn you!" he bellowed—at Berry, not at me—and shouted words at the horseman that were sucked into nothing.

The air was hot now, so hot that raindrops were evaporating with little sizzles. The horse advanced another step, its breath ruffling Simon's hair, and I grabbed his arm, and pulled with all my weight.

Simon stumbled sideways. Berry screamed, thin and desperate, the kind of airless semi-sound that is all one can make in a nightmare. He turned then, turned to run, and the dogs flowed forward to surround him.

It would have been kinder if the dogs had torn him to pieces, instead of holding him. It would have been kinder, even, had Dando ridden forward quickly, instead of step by slow step.

Simon strained against me. I had my arms round his neck, my legs wrapped round one of his, holding him back with everything I had.

Dando reached down and plucked up Dr. Berry by the shoulder. The doctor screamed once more, and this time he could scream, and we could hear it. The horse took one pace forward, then broke into a trot. Its muscles bunched, and it leapt from the ground, the dogs baying at its heels. Dr. Berry dangled from Dando's hold, legs kicking like a child's puppet, as the Wild Hunt took to the sky. Then it was gone, horse, dogs, rider and captive, with a single shriek left ringing in our ears.

I released my grip on Simon and slid down his body to the ground. The wet, muddy, solid ground on which perfectly normal icy rain was falling. I tipped my head back to the sky and breathed hard.

After a moment I realised that Simon was sitting by me.

"If you are expecting remorse, you shall not have it," I said. "He was not worth your life."

"I could not merely watch." That might have been a rebuke, but it sounded very like an apology.

"I thought it was going to kill you." I am not ashamed that my voice broke on the words.

Simon pulled me close. "Come, no harm done. To us, at least."

"Easy to say." I wiped water irritably from my cheeks. It was raining particularly heavily. "You persist in plunging us into these situations without the slightest consideration for the consequences to me or yourself. I do not know why I tolerate you."

"Nor do I but I hope you will continue." His arm tightened a little, in lieu of a kiss, then he released me. "Lord Westerbury needs help." He rose, tugging me up with him, and we walked over to the fallen man on the empty, rainswept hilltop.

Lord Westerbury did not recover. I do not know if it was the influence Dr. Berry had exerted—we found handfuls of silver coins in his lordship's pockets—or the sights he had seen, but he was struck dumb and mindless from then on. He died a few months later, the last victim of Dando and his dogs.

We gave our information and speculations to the Fat Man. I cannot say what happened in the back corridors where strange business is discussed in whispers, but Mr. Parker was removed from his obscure, powerful office shortly afterwards, and his fall was as steep as his ambitions had been lofty. Unwanted servants of the state are usually retired with honours to compensate for their lost position; Mr. Parker was stripped of power, influence and credit at once. He and the Fat Man had fought a savage Whitehall war, and the victor was not merciful.

The Fat Man was grateful to us, I think. Simon did not give a damn for his gratitude and resigned from the Diogenes Club forthwith.

"I say, Feximal," Carnacki remarked one evening at the Remnant, as we sat in the members' lounge, quietly reading. "I haven't seen Berry in a while. Do you know what's become of him?"

Simon dislikes having his attention taken from a book. "Dragged to hell," he said, turning the page. "Screaming."

"Was he, now?" Carnacki did not sound unduly surprised. "Well, I'll be damned. Or rather, I suppose, he will."

There was a general chuckle at that—our profession does not lend itself to delicacy of feeling—and such was Dr. Berry's obituary among his peers.

An Eye for an Eye

London is foul in the summer. The great Mr. Bazalgette, whose system of sewers turned London from an open cesspool to a breathable metropolis, is in my view the patron saint of our city, yet even his remarkable ingenuity could not make the place tolerable in the sweltering August of 1897. It was hot, we had not had rain in too long, and the city stank: of horse manure, of drains, of sweaty unwashed humanity, foul clothes, tanneries, workshops, smoke, filth of every description, dry stone, dust, and two thousand years of human habitation in which it had not burned to the ground nearly often enough.

A year and a half, more or less, had passed since Dr. Berry's demise and Mr. Parker's fall. Parker had been succeeded by a remarkably bright young man named Ranjit Singh, a distant relative of the deposed Maharajah Duleep Singh who was such great friends with our Queen. Mr. Singh, later Sir Ranjit, quickly achieved the same unaccountable power as his predecessor, but used it with a great deal more charm. He was at this time deploying that charm in an effort to woo Simon back to the Government work that he steadfastly declined.

"Mr. Feximal is unforgiving," Mr. Singh observed to me after a particularly brusque refusal. "I suppose Mr. Parker was not forgivable?"

"He was not." Nor had the Fat Man's blackmail been easy to swallow, but I did not mention that. I cherished a faint hope that he might not share the power he held over us. "It is one thing to work for Whitehall, quite another to be made a catspaw in political manoeuvring."

Mr. Singh grimaced. "May I speak frankly, Mr. Caldwell?"

"By all means," I said, wondering what manipulation would follow. Men with royal relatives and cut-glass Oxford accents do not speak frankly to unimportant scribblers.

"Mr. Parker had occult ambitions. He dreamed of commanding the power used by Dr. Berry and Mr. Feximal and the rest. I do not. I have no desire to swim in your dark waters, Mr. Caldwell, still less to poach there, and I should not dream of infringing upon any occultist's independence. You might tell Mr. Feximal that, and ask him to reconsider."

I did tell Simon. His response was curt in the extreme, and I was forced to communicate to Mr. Singh that we could not entertain further Whitehall approaches.

It was no matter; we had plenty of work. On this hot summer day of 1897, we had but recently concluded the dramatic case of corpse theft from the church at St James Garlickhythe (the church's resident mummy had become animated, and hungry), and were treating ourselves to a richly deserved lazy morning. Simon, who always woke before I, had aroused me very thoroughly, and after a brief period of exhausted recovery, we were taking breakfast in the morning-room. It was near on ten of the clock and already warm.

As we finished our meal, sharing the last of the pot of tea, Cornelia came in.

I have not written a great deal of Simon's scarred and tongueless servant; her story is not mine to give. (I will say, because some things should be told, that Miss Kay had avenged Cornelia's tongue and eye on those who had taken them, and that her vengeance was comprehensive and far-reaching.) She ran our strange household, and paid no mind to either the occult or the unlawful goings-on, and I think, or I hope, she was as content as might be.

She clapped her hands in the way that she used on the rare occasions that she wanted our attention. Simon glanced up from the newspaper at once—I think he probably treated her with more courtesy than he did anyone else on earth, certainly more than he did me—and enquired, "What is it?"

She handed him a piece of paper. Some of the dumb use hand signals to communicate; she felt herself too old to learn, and was not talkative.

"Your friend wishes to consult us," Simon read. He kept his voice neutral, which was a kindness, since I knew just how much he had been looking forward to a little peace. "Of course. Make an appointment—" Cornelia jabbed a finger at the floor. "She's downstairs? Very well, show her in. And more tea, please."

"I suppose we have to," I observed reluctantly, once Cornelia had left us. "I do think you need a rest, dear fellow, you look tired."

"Nonsense," Simon said. "I am not at all tired and if we can deal with this business quickly, I shall take pleasure in proving to you just how much energy I have."

"Well, if you're up to it," I said, with a hint of doubt, and received a glowering look over the newspaper that promised the most delightful retribution.

Sadly—or fortunately, since in truth I was not up to another bout myself quite yet—we heard footsteps on the stair, and a moment later, Cornelia came in with a pot of tea, and ushered in a woman.

"Mr. Feximal?" she asked, looking from me to Simon as we both stood. He indicated himself, and she bobbed a curtsey. "Thank you for seeing me, sir. I'm grateful."

"Take a chair, Mrs—?"

"Robey." She seated herself in the chair I held out, with some relief. She was a full-figured woman, aged perhaps sixty. A lady of colour, with dark eyes and skin, and hair as grey as Simon's, under a bonnet that was old but obviously cared for with infinite pains, and adorned with a fresh

Michaelmas daisy. Her dress was equally worn. One of the deserving poor, I concluded; a lady who made every penny work for its keep and would rather go hungry than present a dirty face to the world.

"What's the problem?" Simon asked.

"Well, sir…" She glanced up at Cornelia, obviously hesitant, fingers twining in her skirt. Near her purse, I would have wagered.

"*Pro bono*," Simon said, with just a touch of impatience.

"What Mr. Feximal means," I put in, "is that if Cornelia has brought you to us then we will give you every assistance for her sake. You may speak freely. In every sense."

She gave me a look of gratitude. "Thank you kindly. I won't deny, that eases my mind. Well, sir, you asked my problem, and it is this: my grandson has a sweetheart. A good girl, but, well, a tosher's daughter."

I could imagine that this impeccably clean lady would object to a connexion with a family of toshers. They were a strange and secretive community, the men and women who skulked through the sewers and along the banks of the grey and greasy Thames searching for coins and valuables in the mire, and though I understood they set themselves apart with pride, they were an object of revulsion to most.

What I could not imagine was why this was a problem for Simon. He obviously also suspected that he was being asked to act as some kind of marriage bureau, and his expression was sufficiently incredulous that the lady went on hastily. "That's not my problem for you, sir, of course. No. What it is, well, the girl has vanished."

"Vanished?"

"Gone. There one evening, gone the next. Nor hide nor hair since Monday night."

"It's Wednesday morning," Simon said flatly.

"That is to say, have you any reason for concern as yet?" I interpreted. "And any reason to suspect this is a case for Mr. Feximal's particular skills?"

She shifted in her chair. "You see, Peggy—that's her name, Peggy Flowers—she's a piebald one. Of the toshers. A piebald girl."

"What is a piebald girl?" Simon asked.

Now she looked very uncomfortable indeed. "That's the problem, sir. I don't know if I can say."

Simon exhaled through his nose. I hurried to intervene. The lady might be circumlocutory but her whole posture indicated genuine distress. "By piebald, do you mean her appearance?" A quick nod, relieved, as though she felt she could agree without speech. "Her skin? She's a mulatto? Or disfigured in some way?" A shake, no. I had no idea what she was getting at. "Her hair is particoloured?"

Behind the chair, Cornelia touched a finger to her one eye.

"Her eyes," I said, and saw the relief on Mrs. Robey's face. This might seem like a parlour guessing game, but it was clearly real to her. "She has strange-coloured eyes? No? Then…different. Her eyes are different colours."

"Blue like the sky, grey like the river. Left grey, right blue. That's a piebald girl."

The detail had caught Simon's attention, I saw. "And what do you mean, gone?"

"Not come home. Nobody's seen her. And the toshers aren't telling us anything. Skip, my grandson, he's been to old Mr. Sweetly, asking for help, but they're doing naught. Peggy vanished, and none of the toshers looking for her and… I think they're afraid."

"Of someone?" I asked.

"Of something," Simon said.

"*Something* is right, sir." Her voice dropped to a mutter. "Something that comes in dark corners, something we oughtn't see, much less touch. Something claiming its own. And I'll swear Peggy's a good girl, sir, a God-fearing girl, baptised like a Christian, but she's piebald and she's gone, and I'm frightened for her, that's the truth. I'm frightened."

If I were asked to name my least favourite type of case, excluding those that threaten life, limb and immortal soul, I should probably name those where the first task is to find out what the story is. A witness out of whom the account must be pried is a deeply tiresome thing. Yet it was clear that Mrs. Robey's reticence was not due to notions of manners or modesty. There was something of which she could not speak. So we told her to take us to someone who could.

We accompanied her to Bermondsey, that scabrous district south of the river, opposite the great, cold presence of the Tower. The wharves were, as always, dank and sodden; the river was low. Bent figures combed the banks, ducking in and out of boats, clambering over pilings and into the unspeakable outlets of drains. God knows what it was like before the sewers. It stank now, and it did not stink less as we plunged into a maze of narrow back streets where teetering houses leaned together until they blotted out the sun, where half-clothed pinch-faced children squalled, and slatternly women sat on doorsteps and called coarse things to grimy men.

I have seen many things that bewilder the senses. Sometimes I think that the depth of poverty in the greatest and wealthiest city on earth is the most astounding of all.

We followed our guide into a house by Bermondsey Wall. It was small and dark, bare of everything but hooks on the walls for clothing, settles and chairs and a rough table. A room for many people to share. It was swept and tidy, so far as it might be, but there is no escaping the plain fact that it reeked. As we stepped inside, the smell of human excrement, and rot, and rats, and dead things, and every variety of foulness was such that I gagged, and thought for a moment I might disgrace myself and shame my hosts as my stomach rebelled. I glanced at Simon and realised he was breathing shallowly through his mouth.

"Well, it takes some gettin' used ter," our hostess said, observing our distress, no matter how we tried to hide it. "But this is a tosher's 'ouse, an' toshers will stink."

She was perhaps forty years, though hardship ages a face, a generation younger than Mrs. Robey, who she had greeted without warmth, eyes flickering to us. Her hair was greying, her skin lined, and she had one grey eye and one blue.

She did not seem to appreciate two well-dressed gentlemen coming to her door.

"This is Mr. Feximal," Mrs. Robey said. "He's going to find Peggy. Sir, this is Molly Flowers."

"Peggy's mother?" I had my answer in her face, the widening eyes, the hope and fear briefly betrayed, then clamped down upon.

"How'll he do that?" She spoke vituperatively, in reaction to her own feelings, I would hazard. "How'll a fine gentleman know our ways? How—"

"I hope, because you will speak to us," I said, and she turned on me.

"Speak? Oh, my eye! As if speaking wasn't what got my Peggy took, and my ma killed!" Hands on hips, now, in the classic posture of the Cockney female readying herself for battle. Before I could respond the door banged open, and a young fellow hurried in. He was dressed like a shopkeeper's man, sleeves rolled up to reveal admirably muscular forearms, and his brown skin and tight-curled hair suggested a relationship to Mrs. Robey that was confirmed by his cry.

"Grandma, did you get the gentleman?"

There was a moment's babel as Mrs. Flowers wrathfully demanded what the young man knew about this impertinence, Mrs. Robey attempted to put her grandson abreast of the situation, and Simon enquired, with some impatience, whether his assistance was required or not. It all stopped abruptly, at a very heavy thump from upstairs.

"*And* that's himself disturbed," Mrs. Flowers snapped. "I blame you, Martha Robey."

"Let the gentlemen talk to him, Ma." Skip darted forward and took her hand. It would, I thought, be a strong woman who could resist the plea on that handsome face. "For Peggy. Please, now. I want my Peg back, and so do you. Come, what's to be lost?"

"You got no idea," Mrs. Flowers said, through set teeth. "None. Go up if you must but I'll none of it." She marched over to a chair, sat, and threw her apron over her head.

Mrs. Robey glanced at her, then gestured, urging her grandson to take us upstairs. As he indicated the way, my last sight of Mrs. Flowers was her apron-muffled shoulders shaking with silent sobs, while Mrs. Robey put a comforting arm around her.

I closed the door, leaving us in a little, dank, dark space at the bottom of rickety stairs. "Before we proceed…"

"You want to know what's going on." The young man nodded earnestly. "I'm Skip Robey. Peggy's my intended, but she's gone missing. There's a matter of tosher business, here, sirs. You understand?"

"No," Simon said.

"It's not to be spoken of." Skip's hand balled to a fist. "We shouldn't have. But, you see, the old man—" He indicated upstairs. "He wanted Peg to take up with a tosher, because she's piebald. And *my* ma thought I could do better than a toshing girl, and when she got it in her head that old Jerry Sweetly thought I wasn't good enough for Peg, well, she got her hump up too. So Peg told her. About being piebald, you see. She shouldn't have spoken but she wanted my ma to understand what Pa Sweetly meant. And two days later, she was gone."

This Romeo-and-Juliet business was hardly our responsibility, but Skip was a good-looking youth, and concern for his sweetheart was writ clear on his face. I am doubtless a sentimentalist, but I did not like to imagine those features distorted by grief and loss.

Simon is not a sentimentalist in any way, but he is profoundly chivalrous. No matter how tiresome he found love affairs, or the painstaking wringing-out of information from those who ought to give it in a prompt and logical fashion, he would not ignore a missing girl.

"What do you think has happened to her?" he asked.

"I'd have said man." Skip's face tightened, unconsciously assuming a belligerent aspect. "I'd have said, some villain… But the toshers fear worse. You have to talk to Pa Sweetly, he'll tell you more than I can. Sir?"

"Yes?"

"Will you find her?" Skip had eyes of a remarkable brown, an intense deep chestnut warmth. They were full of pleading. "My Peg? Please?"

"We'll do our best," I said. "But we need information."

He nodded. "Yes, sir. Thank you. I'll take you up."

Mr. Jeremiah Sweetly lay in the corner of a little room. The luxury of separate bedrooms was unknown here; judging by the pallets and truckle beds, there might be six or seven adults sleeping in this space, and probably all of them toshers who spent the days combing the sewers and riverbanks. The stench was like a blow. Thank God it was summer and the small window was propped open; all the manners in the world could not have prevented me clapping a handkerchief to my mouth if there had been no fresh air at all.

He was a wizened and wrinkled man, stained an unpleasant yellow with ingrained dirt and grease. A white scar that looked very like a human bite mark stood out on his scrawny neck. He would be stooped if he stood, no doubt, after years bent over to examine the flotsam of London's waste, but currently he was bedbound, and racked by a rattling wet cough that shook his frame.

"Pa Sweetly," Skip said. "These gentlemen are going to help find Peggy."

Mr. Sweetly fixed us with a glance, bright and sharp. "No, boy. This is toshers' business. We'll 'ave no peelers 'ere."

"We are not of the police," I said. "This is Simon Feximal, and—"

Mr. Sweetly broke out in a fit of coughing that, I will admit, slightly alarmed me. One would not have been surprised to see him spit up a chunk of lung.

"Feximal?" he wheezed, eyes damp with the exertion. "The ghost-hunter?"

"And my companion, Robert Caldwell."

Mr. Sweetly drew a breath. "As writes the books? In my house? Why, my girl—Peg—" A slight quiver on his face at the name. "She's read 'em to me, twice over. Well, now. Mr. Caldwell and Mr. Feximal. I don't suppose you'd be wishful to shake a tosher's hand?"

Simon's impatience with convention in our highly conventional era has often proved a difficulty, or an embarrassment. In this case, it did not. He was already stepping forward to take the old man's wavering hand, with no appearance of hesitation or condescension. I could do no less, although I must admit to reflections on where Mr. Sweetly's hand had been, and the necessity of washing my own as soon as possible.

"Get the gentlemen chairs," Mr. Sweetly ordered Skip, who cast around and produced a couple of rickety stools. "Your idea, was it, boy, to ask Mr. Simon Feximal's aid?"

"Grandma's," Skip said. I liked him the more for not taking the credit.

"Sharp woman, Martha Robey. Fine woman too, in her day, very fine. Now get along, boy, this ain't for your ears."

Skip glanced at us, whether checking on our comfort or the old man's I could not say, and left the room. We took our stools by the sickbed.

"Now," Simon said. "Your granddaughter, Peggy Flowers, is missing. And she is what you call a piebald girl. One eye grey, one blue. And you believe that her disappearance is not the work of man?"

"Oh, not man." Mr. Sweetly shook his head. His wrinkled hand came up to touch the scar on his neck. "Not man at all."

"And nobody may speak of these matters. You believe Peggy was, what, taken because she spoke?"

"Mustn't speak," Mr. Sweetly muttered. "Brings ill luck. Asking for trouble. I should know."

"What ill luck had you?"

"Plenty of luck, but not in love. My first, she died in childbed. My second, she gave me six brats, one piebald. Good woman, she was, but fell off a wharf and a barge crushed her. God rest her soul."

I murmured agreement. Simon observed, "It seems to me they had the ill luck, not you."

"Aye, but I didn't talk, did I? I caused offense another way, never mind what but I had to pay for that, see. I did well enough, though. Kept my nippers fed and clothed, and grandchilders too. I had the luck and I never talked. But still she took my Peggy." Mr. Sweetly's voice quavered on that, gnarled hands clutching the threadbare sheets.

"You made a bargain," Simon said. "And you believe the entity with which you bargained has now taken your granddaughter. Because she's a piebald girl, which brings her under this entity's authority?"

Simon was, it must be said, extremely good at his work. Mr. Sweetly was nodding, expression hopeful.

"Can you tell me why you think a piebald girl ought to marry a tosher?" I asked.

"Her nippers won't drown," Mr. Sweetly said. "No son of a piebald girl'll die by drowning, and that's a fine thing for a tosher to know. It's hard in the drains, see. You're under the earth, in the tunnels. You don't hear the rain starting, don't hear naught but the splashing of your feet, and *her* folk rustling around you, maybe the echoes of yer own voice. It can be cats and dogs above, and you don't know. But the rain's pouring down through the drains and pipes, into the sewers, and then, of a sudden you hears all the water coming at once. That's when a tosher hopes *she*'s watching, see. That's when it's good to know you can't drown."

Simon glanced at me, back to Mr. Sweetly. "Can you tell me anything about *her*?" He gave the word the same stress as the old man had.

"No. No."

"She," Simon said thoughtfully. "And her folk in the sewers…"

I looked around, sharply. Simon glanced at me. "What?"

"Nothing." I had, in fact, heard a faint scuttle, the sound of vermin. Hardly surprising, in this house or this part of London, but never pleasant.

Simon was regarding me with narrowed eyes. I felt a well-founded sense of apprehension. "Ask your question, Robert."

"What question?"

"The one you want to ask."

I ought to be used to this by now, yet it always came with a sense of wrongness. I settled myself more firmly on the stool. "Mr. Sweetly. How did you get your scar?"

He may have answered. I never heard.

Usually what Simon calls my *awareness*, that sense of a story that was sharpened by the touch of a ghost, comes as fleeting visions. Fancies, impressions, random thoughts and feelings. I had become used to those over the last years.

This was something else. What I saw then, what I felt—

A boy, or young man, or something in between. Fifteen or so, a handsome youth with a wickedly charming smile, and a woman pulling him by the hand, giggling, through the darkness. They pass a man with a lantern of the sort used fifty years ago, and her eyes shine briefly, flat and blank in the light. Then they are inside some echoing space, crashing down together onto a heap of rags. Dust in my nose, dark in my eyes. The grunts and groans of intimacy, his urgency and hers, his hands on her breasts, he at worship between her legs, which do not bend quite as one would expect. He does not see her toes, with their long, crooked nails, or claws. Both of them are crying out with increasing volume, and around them, in the shadows and the edges, black bead eyes glint. Pink claws scrabble, naked tails stiffen into rigidity. The boy throws his head back in climax, drops it down, and her white, white teeth sink into his neck.

I opened my eyes with a gasp. Mr. Sweetly was staring at me with some alarm. "Sir?"

"You, uh, you made love to a woman," I said. I felt a little shaky. "In a rag warehouse. She bit you."

He gaped. "I never told you that. I never told anyone that."

"I think *she* just told me." I wiped a hand over my face. My fingers were trembling, and there was sweat on my top lip. "The rat woman."

"The Queen." Mr. Sweetly mouthed rather than spoke the word, relief and fear warring on his face.

Simon was scowling. "And this lady demands silence of you, but Robert was permitted to see her secrets. I think we need to look for Miss Flowers. Urgently."

That was easier said than done. Simon and I are not the police. We have no resources, no "Fetter Lane Irregulars" or troop of loyal street urchins to be our eyes and ears. And there was no calling on Simon's skin.

"At least that means she's not dead," I observed.

"Yet," Simon said.

We were standing by the river. The tide was going out, leaving its cargo of grease and filth along the dirty strands. Mr. Sweetly, galvanised now, had insisted on being carried downstairs (a task Simon had performed without flinching) and had sent out a summons for toshers. He would direct his men—sons, grandsons, cousins and friends—to search for the missing girl. Nobody in my hearing had observed that the decision might have come too late.

I rested my forearms on a rotten paling, looking out at the wide stretch of water, its waves flashing blinding white reflections over its grey-blue swell. Over the river, the foursquare shape of the Tower. We avoided going near there, for Simon's sake. Too many stories, too many deaths.

"What can we do?" I asked him. "We can hardly contact the police, with no witness prepared to speak. But if Miss Flowers has been abducted, rather than the victim of supernatural interference, how are we to help?"

"I don't know." Simon's hands were knotted together, betraying tension. "We must, though."

"Because it's Cornelia's case?"

"And because a young lady may well be in serious trouble. But also… Tell me again what you saw."

I went over it, giving my impressions in detail, watched his frown deepen. "Do you know what we are dealing with? Who is this woman?"

"I doubt she is a woman in any sense that we use the word. I suspect this is a *dea civitatis*."

I called upon my schoolboy Latin. "Goddess of the city?"

"Indeed."

"That sounds ominous."

"Well, 'god' is a loose term," Simon said dismissively. "If you would prefer to say 'spirit'…"

"I should, yes. Considerably."

"A spirit of the city, then. The tosher's life is dark and dangerous. They turn to one another, make their community and buttress it with stories, and you know the power stories hold."

"But this is a story that can't be told," I objected. "Except…they all knew it, or knew of it, didn't they?"

"Sacramental secrecy. Not quite the same as the real thing. The— let us use the name—the Rat Queen serves as a local deity to the toshers. Luck and fertility. She is taken with a handsome young man; he does her service for a single night; from then on he has good fortune in his work. Many dangerous occupations have such stories." Simon smiled at my expression. "There are all kinds of gods."

"Good Lord. Do you suppose there is one for our sort?"

"Perhaps, were you a tosher, you would have encountered a Rat King instead," Simon said. "It would be a foolish rodent who did not select you."

I looked up at him, startled. He was looking out over the vista of the grey Thames, but he unclasped his fingers to place one hand lightly on mine.

"Simon?"

"When Robey spoke of his sweetheart, I could only think, if you were taken from me like that." Simon's voice was low. "If I did not know what had become of you. If I lost you."

Considering how often I had seen him risk his own life, this statement rendered me briefly speechless. But that was Simon. Ever concerned for my well-being, so rarely thinking about what I might feel, the obtuse, awkward fellow that he is. But his hand was warm on mine, in public too, and the emotion raw in his voice.

"I'm very hard to lose," I assured him.

"You stick like a burr." Simon's hand tightened on mine. "Let us find Robey's young lady and go home."

"Where you will be the Rat King to my tosher?" I suggested. It was innuendo for the sake of it, but I had a blink of awareness again, the physicality of that long-past coupling, that sent my blood southwards, and suddenly the prospect of Simon playing god in the bedroom was decidedly compelling.

"What are you thinking about?" he asked, a laugh in his voice, and a huskiness too.

"How very much I want you. This morning seems a long time back." I had woken to his caresses, one hand on my prick, the other exerting pressure on my hip that pushed me to my back. He had worked me till I pleaded and babbled, then climbed over me, hands on my shoulders, driving me into the mattress with his weight, eyes intent on mine. I imagined him biting me, leaving a mark on my neck forever, a brand of ownership, and I shuddered at the thought.

His hand was pressing mine down, hard, his fingers spreading the bones of my hand wide as he had spread my body so often. That force, that weight, that need. "If I could bend you over this rail," he said, low and husky. "I should take you here and now, and make you cry out to the whole of London."

I could imagine it, and I was painfully hard at the thought. I had no doubt he was too, though our only contact was the touch of hands. I could hear the rasp in his breath.

So often we worked at night in solitary places, where the risk might have been worth taking. I should have let him do it, let him ride me, all need and no care, and muffled my cries against his skin. Should have thrilled to have him slake his lust and leave me unfulfilled and aching with arousal for the rest of the night till at last he deigned to allow me relief…

But, of course, it was broad daylight in a crowded area. Of course it blasted well was.

"Damn it," I said, somewhat strangulated, and Simon grunted frustrated agreement. We stood together for a long moment, breathing deeply, and he relaxed his hold, though still he did not move his hand.

"There are things we must do," he said at last, reluctantly. "Work."

"Indeed." I forced my rebellious thoughts back to the path of duty. "There are, I suppose, three possibilities. That the girl has met with an accident, that this is foul play unrelated to her birth, or that it is foul play because of her birth."

Simon nodded. "In the first two cases, we have nothing to offer and the family must rely upon the police or their own resources, as they now are. But it seems highly unlikely that you had such a powerful reaction for no reason. I think we must work on the assumption that Miss Flowers has been abducted because she is a piebald girl."

"But why? What is to be gained?"

Mr. Sweetly had told us a little more of the piebald girls, feeling as though he had been given permission. After a young man had done his service to the Rat Queen, his human partner would bear him a piebald girl, one only. Their hearing and night sight were exceptional, Mr. Sweetly asserted, and none of their offspring could drown; there was nothing else to mark them out save that each would bear one piebald girl among her own children. It was not a great deal to go on.

"And they are not the Rat Queen's children," I mused. "Not by blood."

"But there is influence there, still. Do rats take care of their young?"

"Good Lord, Simon, how do you expect me to know that?"

He shrugged. "You are a fount of unlikely information. I don't know, and I am greatly afraid that time is pressing. I think the best course is to consult Theodosia."

I was very rarely privileged to see Miss Kay at work. She was a deeply solitary woman, who found other people tiresome and draining. She and Simon were capable of sitting in the parlour for hours without exchanging a single word, and considering that a relaxing evening well spent. I tended to flee to my club on those nights. Her affection for Simon was unquestionable, but I am quite sure it was a relief to her when I came upon the scene and she could pursue her studies alone.

Studies, rather than cases. She was an academic occultist, if I may so put it, where Simon was more the practical kind. Yet when she applied her knowledge, the results were terrifying.

We were in the drawing-room, seated on the floor. Simon was stripped to the waist, with a couple of mirrors strategically positioned around him. This process was not intended to summon spirits in his way, but if messages came, they would be read. We had other things too: a set of bone dice with uneven sides she used for casting lots, a detailed map of London, a slate and pencil. The rug had been taken back to reveal the floorboards, upon which she had chalked two intersecting lines, the simple form augmented with strange sigils. She sat at point east, Simon at west, I at south, each with a candle before us. The north point was occupied by a cage containing a large brown rat, and a lock of dirty-blond hair secured by a ribbon lay at the cross-point of the compass, in the centre of the device. It was Peggy's hair, a keepsake reluctantly handed over by Skip Robey.

Miss Kay consulted a huge tome bound in some sort of dry-looking leather that I felt a strong desire not to touch, and put the book down. She lit the candles and began to murmur.

It comes to my nose. I suppose I am fortunate; one poor fellow of my acquaintance is afflicted in the stomach, and has to keep a chamberpot to hand during occult summonings. It takes Simon across the skin, of course, Miss Kay through her left hand—she does not complain, but her fingers curl into claws, the bones showing white. But I have it in the nose.

The smell first. God knows what the candles are made of; I have read human fat, and never asked in case that should be true. The smell is cloying, sticky, contaminating. It gets inside your breath and stays there. I was vividly conscious of the handkerchief in my pocket, and my urgent desire to use it.

Then the pressure. It comes to the bridge of my nose, along the sinuses, spreading outwards to ring my eye sockets, down to my teeth. It builds, as though the air is becoming heavier and thicker. It feels harder to breathe, and I do not wish to breathe because the air *tastes*, now, tastes of sour spice and old dry skin, and when I inhale I can feel it curling into my lungs like fog.

Miss Kay speaks on and the pressure builds. My eyes seem to darken a little, and now it feels as though there are thumbs pressing on my eyeballs. Not painful, but it would not take a great deal for it to become painful.

The runes are wild on Simon's skin, writing over themselves in jagged haste. I do not look at the mirrors, have no desire to read them. I want to be able to touch his skin again without fear.

The world dwindles to a point. There is nothing but Miss Kay's voice and candlelight, and the smell of spice, and the summoning has only just begun and lasted forever, and then—

Then at once, all around us, the air *listens*.

Simon inhaled sharply. Miss Kay said, "*Ah.*" In the cage, the rat stretched slowly and deliberately up onto its haunches.

"Peggy Flowers." Miss Kay spoke to the emptiness. "Piebald girl. The Rat Queen's child."

Pressure, remorseless, behind my eyes. I could taste rot in my mouth. Rot and the sump.

"Peggy Flowers. Margaret Ann Flowers. Where?" Her eyes were intent on nothing, or something I couldn't see and didn't want to.

She leaned forward and put her hand down over the lock of Peggy's hair.

Simon gasped. I bit my tongue. The rat screamed, high and childlike.

Miss Kay bent over her flattened hand, staring into the deep pools of space at the end of her fingers. With her other hand she groped for the slate, took up the pencil. The rat was thrashing in the cage, convulsing, so hard it was lifted off the ground by its jerks. The pencil screeched on the slate, the stench of burning hair crept into my nose, the rat wailed, higher and higher. I wanted to clap my hands to my ears, to get up and run. Simon's teeth were drawn back from his lips, and the scratchmark juddery writing on his skin looked like nothing so much as rodent tracks. Miss Kay jerked her hand away, leaving nothing but a smouldering ribbon behind, and—it stopped.

It had to be closed, of course, whatever gateway she had opened. She performed that duty as I sat nursing my painful tongue and making my tense muscles relax. Simon's head was bowed. The rat lay in its cage, very still.

"It's dead," Simon said at last.

Miss Kay inspected the beast. "So it is. Looks like its back broke."

Simon raised a brow: *What the devil?* Miss Kay opened her palms in silent answer: *I've no idea.* There was a burn mark on her skin where the hair had been.

"I have impressions. Give me an hour." She left the room without ceremony. Simon grasped my hand, pulling me upright, and led me to the bedroom in silence. I followed, feeling as though I had been cudgelled. That always happened, and the only sensible thing was to lie down and rest, perhaps have a restoring nap.

Be damned to sense.

I pulled Simon's head to mine, kissed him hard. There was blood in his mouth too.

"Robert," he whispered, and lifted me off my feet, pinning me against the wall. I wrapped my legs around him, drove my mouth and my hips against his. The need of earlier was back, and stronger.

"Now," I said. "*Now.*"

He was stripped to the waist already, I only in shirtsleeves and braces. It was the work of seconds to pull clothing out of the way—not off, no time for that—and then he grabbed me by the shoulders, spun me round, pushed me so I was bent face-first over the metal end of the bed frame.

No words, no preparation. He snatched up the oil, spilling it in his haste, slicked himself, took hold of my hips, and I could have come then, could have spent in that moment from sheer raw need.

He fucked me, rough and relentless, gripping my hip and shoulder to hold me where he wanted. I closed my eyes and pictured the wide grey river, the summer sun, and imagined that Simon was fucking me in the open, in the face of all the world, because nothing mattered except that he should take his pleasure with me. I clutched the counterpane and felt the rough wet wood of the palings under my fingers, inhaled the smell of sea salt and river rot on the air, felt him move inside me with the steady, unstoppable force of the tide. He wasn't touching my prick, had no need; the blood pounded to the point of pain. He hauled me up, buried his face in the curve of my neck, bit down hard on the flesh there, and I came, spilling into the Thames itself like a sacrifice, sobbing his name.

We stood there, bent over the bed in our room in Fetter Lane, both gasping. At last Simon very carefully traced the bite mark on my neck with his finger. "Hell and damnation."

"Did you feel it?" I asked, unnecessarily. "The river?"

Simon let out a long, hissing sigh that raised the hairs on my back. "Curse it."

"It wasn't your fault."

"It was my teeth." He kissed the mark. "I beg your pardon, Robert. Are you all right?"

I nodded, and he scooped me up, laid me carefully on the bed, and lay with me in his arms, his lips to my hair. Comfort and strength. I needed it then. So did he, I imagine.

"I should prefer that our work did not meddle with our play," I said at last, striving for a light tone. There was still a faint scent of sewers in my nose, but I felt dirtied beyond that. "And I should strongly prefer that our time together was not shanghaied by some cut-price Cockney deity."

Simon gave a snort of amusement, and we lay together in silence until it was time to dress, and to see what Miss Kay had for us.

She had a location. Under the earth, dark and dank. Stonework, not brickwork. A flat ceiling, not round. A ditch, within the cave—"writhing", she said, without explanation. Close to the river.

And Peggy was alive. Of that she was sure.

We went back to Bermondsey, the three of us. It was close to seven o'clock in the evening now, golden light streaming over the foetid Thames, air warm as bathwater and damned near as wet.

Jeremiah Sweetly sat like a general in his cramped house, with a gang of toshers about him. Despite the heat they wore long coats with huge pockets for the spoils, the tails stained beyond description. They looked like the refuse of London, but they carried themselves proudly.

I introduced myself and Simon to the mass of men, and Miss Kay to them all, explaining briefly that she had some sense of where Peggy was, but their knowledge of London's guts was required to identify the place. There was, perhaps, a little scepticism in the murmurs with which I was greeted, but Mr. Sweetly held up a hand with authority and all fell silent.

"Mr. Caldwell." He tapped the white bite mark at the side of his neck, mirrored by the red mark on my own. "She?"

I shrugged. He nodded. "You listen to him, boys. *She*'s given her favour."

That was all that was required. They listened when Miss Kay spoke, with intelligent respect that would have done credit to men of higher standing, and gathered round a table on which Simon spread a plan of the sewers. I stepped back. I had nothing to contribute to the discussion, and frankly, I was uncomfortable. The bite burned on my neck. I did not want to draw further attention to it, did not want questions as to who and how and when. And it was hot as hell in this cramped, stinking space full of men. I stepped outside.

The street was little better but at least there was air. I leaned against the wall, feeling wretchedly uncomfortable and dizzy. Nauseated too; my stomach roiled. Christ, I was going to vomit, and no surprise after the day's filth.

I was sick and, as I looked about me, I was afraid.

People. There were so many of them. They clumped through the narrow streets, shoes echoing on the ground, careless of where they trod, with their young clutching at their skirts or crying for food. So many.

So many vermin.

Dangerous vermin, too. Intelligence in their eyes, and malice, and greed. They wanted to eat everything, consume everything, spoil and destroy. The city floated on a tide of their shit.

And they would kill me if they saw me. Me, with my lover's bite on my neck, my mark of Cain. If they knew, if they suspected, if I ever allowed myself to emerge from the shadows, no matter my hunger, then the trap would be waiting for me, sharp jaws gaping.

I needed shadows.

I was walking then, without conscious volition, heading I knew not where. I threaded through a maze of passages, ducking under the low beams of little covered alleys with the bite throbbing on my neck and the sickness churning in my belly. I found a set of grey stone stairs, and went down, and through a gate whose rusty hinges screamed, and along a passageway that was wet underfoot even in this summer, the stench of piss in my nose. Mindlessly, urgently, following a need to be underground, through doors that stood open for no reason, until quite suddenly one shut behind me with a slam, and I turned back to look at it as I blinked myself awake.

"Oh fuckery," said a man's voice. "It's Caldwell!"

I jerked around, bewildered, and took in my surroundings.

A room under the earth, stone-walled and stone-ceilinged, lit by oil lamps that cast as much shadow as light. The floor ended before it reached the wall, in some sort of wide, deep gutter, or sump, full of liquid that gleamed oily black, and heaved oddly as I watched it. The place of Miss Kay's vision.

A cage. All too like the one we had used for the rat, but it was big enough to contain a large dog, or a small human, and it did. A young woman with dark blonde hair was curled up in it, unmoving.

A stone table in the centre of the room. Candles at each corner, and ropes attached to iron rings. A knife on it, shining pale metal. The word that came to my mind was "altar". At one end I saw a rat, on its back, unpleasantly splayed out with what looked like pins through its pink claws. It could not move but its tail twitched urgently.

A caged woman, a tortured beast, and in front of them, moving in a half circle to surround me, one from behind where he had bolted the door, three men, in black robes, cowled like monks.

I did not, then, feel optimistic.

I cleared my throat. "I believe you have the advantage of me." Someone chuckled, not pleasantly. "I take it the lady is Peggy Flowers." She didn't move at her name. I wondered if she lived. "And as you know me, you doubtless know that Mr. Feximal and Miss Kay will not be long after me."

Two of the men shifted, and one muttered an oath. The third did not flinch. "Well, we knew there was interference. It had to be someone, and if it is Feximal I am glad of it."

His colleagues didn't seem to share that view. "He's a damned great bruiser—" one began, and the other said, "But that *woman*—"

"Quiet, you vacillating fools!" snapped the leader, and I realised I knew the voice.

"Mr. *Parker*?"

He snatched the cowl back from his head. He appeared decidedly older than at our last meeting, though not quite three years had passed: older, thinner, angrier. His eyes were shadowed so dark they seemed painted, or bruised. He looked as though he did not sleep.

"You," he snarled. "You and that accursed brute. What he did to me— Get him down." It was an order, but the other men did not stir. Parker cursed them. "Get him down! Or do you want to wait for Feximal?" he shouted, and then they moved.

I fought as best I could, but there was in truth little I could do. Simon could give a good account of himself against three, but I am no pugilist. In a humiliatingly, frighteningly short space they had me on my back on their altar, two easily overcoming my unavailing struggles while Parker secured my wrists and ankles. I bucked uselessly, but all it did was tighten the bond.

"What do you propose to do?" I demanded. "Sacrifice me to the Rat Queen?"

Parker gave a barking laugh. "Good God, no. We're going to sacrifice her."

"What?"

He leaned over me. The silver knife was in his hand, and he ran the tip down my cheek and up, under my eye. It was almost ticklish.

"We trapped her in the trollop there, but she reached for you before we were done. So we're going to have to kill you. And then we'll kill her, and the rat, and take what she has." He spoke as if it were quite reasonable. Government business. "I will command the rats. I will have an army of eyes, I will know everything. I will have power once more." He snarled those words, lips drawn back. "And I will have my revenge."

The Fat Man had made a mistake, I realised; he had played the wrong game, or with the wrong opponent. One could destroy a Whitehall enemy simply by removing him from the board. But this fallen piece had armed himself and returned.

Mr. Parker had seen the scale of power occultists wielded, and he wanted that for himself. A power nobody could take from him. A defence against what Simon had done to him in his office, three years ago, for my sake.

In the great sewer that was London, Mr. Parker intended to become the Rat King.

I strained against my bonds, looking around with desperation. There were sigils traced on the walls in drying blood. I prayed it was rat, although Mr. Parker was welcome to have used his own.

The other two men were murmuring intently, syllables that buzzed unpleasantly in my ear. The rat, splayed at the end of the altar between my pinioned ankles, scrabbled and squealed. Mr. Parker traced the point of the silver blade over the bite mark on my neck, his expression thoughtful.

"Who gave you this?" he murmured. "Or, no, do you know, I think I can guess. Is that how the Fat Man calls Feximal to heel? Are you his weakness? Oh, I shall enjoy this. I shall take you from him, and then I shall *end* him."

I cursed him, in language I should be ashamed to repeat. There was little else to be done.

I cannot convey my state of mind then. I was afraid, needless to say, brutally afraid of what was to come. I am not a brave man, not a fighter. I use words, and when they are powerless, so am I. But there was something alien snarling in my mind, a heedless defiance for its own sake that said, *You are the stronger, I cannot win, but still I shall bite you if I can.*

She reached for you, he had said.

The chanting rose, in pitch and volume. Mr. Parker tilted his head back, mouth moving in a parody of prayer. I could hear his whisper. "Eyes, give me eyes. I shall take first his eyes, then hers, until you give me yours. I will have them all. I will see everything."

An army of eyes. That was what the rats would give him, the rats that infested the whole city, hiding in crevices and cracks and under tables, in drains and alleys, on window ledges and under stones, and watching everything with their bright black button eyes.

Rats had seen me walking like an opium-eater, mindlessly called. Rats had followed me through the maze of narrow passages. Rats knew where I was, and where Simon was too.

I bent my mind to the bite on my neck. Not the cold stone at my back or the rough rope at my wrists, or the three men who stood around me, their incantation rising to an unmistakable climax. Just the bite, the Rat Queen's mark.

Bring me luck, I thought. *Even better, bring me Simon.*

Parker moved the knife over my face. Positioned it beneath my eye socket. Put his other hand on my head, hard, to hold it still. Dug the point in.

Everyone screamed. I; the rat on the altar; the woman in the cage. He moved the knife, searingly, and it dawned on me through the pain that he intended to cut a pattern.

He shifted the knife again, gouging a chunk of flesh—I felt it lift—and there was a tremendous knock on the door.

Parker's head went up, hand stilling, eyes wide with shock. The welling blood began to run down my cheek.

The pounding came again, and I bellowed, with all my strength, "Simon! I'm here!"

A thud, as if a heavy man had set his shoulder to the door. One of the acolytes swore; the other said, high-pitched, "Oh Christ, it's Feximal, I'll wager it's Feximal, what will we do?"

"Kill him," Parker snapped.

"With what?" yelped the robed man. "Did anyone bring a pistol?"

"He won't kill you if you let me go," I said, as the door shook on its hinges with the force being applied. It hurt like the very devil to speak.

The cowled men were evidently no more convinced by my words than I was. Parker snarled, wordless, then raised his arm once more, holding the knife high, ready to plunge it into my breast, as the door gave up the unequal struggle and crashed inwards in a shower of broken wood and groaning metal.

Simon and Skip Robey half fell into the room. Simon's grim features were lit with unholy rage, and as he took in the scene, his face darkened in a way that made the two acolytes step back.

"Oh sweet Lord," Skip whispered. "Peg? Peggy!"

"Move a muscle and I'll kill him." Mr. Parker's eyes were intent on Simon's. The knife was above my heart.

"You put her in a cage." Skip looked from Parker to Peggy, slumped and motionless. His voice rang with incredulous fury. "A *cage*. You—"

"Don't move," Parker repeated.

"Be fucked!" Skip bolted forward, grabbing for the cage bars as if he intended to pull it apart by main force. "Peggy!"

Parker's hand wavered, but he must have known Simon was the greater threat, and if he killed me he would have no leverage at all. God knows what thwarted anger he felt then, but his face smoothed into the serene mask of the civil servant as he spoke.

"If you want your dainty scribbler intact, Mr. Feximal, you would do well to negotiate with me. His life depends on your obedience to my terms."

Simon was poised on the balls of his feet. He looked huge. He looked ready to kill with his bare hands, to break Parker's neck and be damned to the consequences, but he managed to speak through stiff lips. "I agree. Whatever your terms, I agree."

I think I had not fully known his love for me till then.

Parker's face lit with triumph. There was a splintering noise from the cage. I twisted my neck to see. Skip cried, "Peg!" And Peggy Flowers, piebald girl, shot out of confinement like—there are no other words—like a rat from a trap.

She moved with boneless fluidity, knocking Skip out of the way, accelerating in one leap, and hit Mr. Parker from behind. The knife flew out of his hand as he was thrown forward across me, and her weight landed on his, crushing the breath out of me until she wrenched him to the floor. Then there was simply screaming. Skip and Simon, as one, turned on the two cowled acolytes, avenging their fears with savage blows, as Peggy ripped at Parker with claws and teeth.

"Simon!" I shouted, seeing his man drop and Skip still demolishing his opponent, and I jerked my head towards Peggy.

I did not want those young lovers tainted. If I had seen Simon with those blank black eyes and bloody sharp-toothed mouth, I might have been able to forget it again; I feared Skip would not. And at some point, or so I prayed, Peggy would come back to herself, and she should not have to do it with a death on her conscience. She had endured enough already. Whereas, for us, one more would hardly make a difference.

Simon took my meaning. He reached down, separated Peggy and Parker by main force, and picked Parker up off the ground by his lapels. He looked at me, splayed and helpless on the altar. He looked around. Then he walked over to the drain, dragging the gasping, bleeding man with him, and dropped him in.

There was a huge splash. Parker cried out in shock. Then he screamed.

Simon was slicing through the bonds at my wrists with the silver knife. I sat up as they fell away, and stared with disbelief at Mr. Parker, as the inky water thrashed and boiled and moved like thick black ribbons that entangled him and dragged him down.

"Oh Lord, sir, that's eels in there." Skip's eyes were wide with horror. "Eels. Hadn't we better— Sir, he doesn't stand a chance."

"Good," Simon said, and moved to cut my ankles free.

"The rat," I managed, tearing my eyes from the heaving waters of the drain. Parker had gone under now. "Let it go."

Simon glanced down at the tortured rat, then, carefully, pulled out the pins. The beast leapt onto all fours, an acrobatic movement, with no sign of the pain it must have endured. It did not attempt to bite; rather, it stared at us, unblinking, and gave me what I can only call a regal nod.

"Thank you," I managed.

With a skitter of claws and tail, it was gone into the darkness. Skip knelt on the floor, whispering to his sweetheart. Simon took me in his arms as I sat on that accursed table, my head on his shoulder, and I felt the tremors run through him as he held me close.

The bite mark on my neck did not scar, and I was pleased to see it fade. Supernatural luck is occasionally welcome, but I have no desire to bear more marks. The scar beneath my eye, a teardrop shape too deep ever to heal, is quite bad enough.

The two surviving members of Mr. Parker's little cult included one fellow I had met several times at the Remnant, and rather got on with. I must say, that was something of a blow. Simon discouraged them both from pursuing occult studies, repeating any of Parker's implications about us, or ever coming to his notice in any way. His discouragement was so thorough that they both emigrated.

Peggy Flowers suffered no lasting ill effects from her experience. She did not remember attacking Parker, and if Skip had watched her do it, he did not let it trouble him long. We were proud to attend their wedding three months later; seven months after that, Peggy brought Eugene Simon Robey into the world. Gene is eighteen now, a strong and decent young man, serving on a battlecruiser in the North Atlantic. I pray that the family legend is true. I pray he cannot drown.

But then, little Joanie Robey was born with one grey eye and one blue, strikingly pale against her tawny skin, so it seems the Queen still watches her people.

The Writing on the Wall

I am an author of some little fame now, among those who enjoy sensational yellowback fiction at least. (Fiction. Ha. I recall a review in the *Criterion* that observed, "While Mr. Caldwell's talents as a wordsmith are only moderate, his grotesque imagination knows no bounds." Considering that I had concealed the worst of the horrors rather than dwelling on them, I felt that to be a somewhat unkind cut.) Yet, when I look back at my published works, the Casebooks that tell of our first few years together, they seem to me nothing but a patchwork of holes. Yes, they recount the earlier cases on which I worked with Simon, when I deepened my knowledge of the mysteries and secrets that run under the polished surface of our age. But so much is missing. I could not write of our lives together, as mutual affection and desire ripened into a deep and passionate companionship. I could not write of his vulnerabilities.

I suppose it is not easy to imagine Simon as a vulnerable man. Most people would sooner say *intimidating*, or *ill-tempered*, or *terrifying*, and I should not argue, but dear God, if you knew the pressures he was under. If you knew the risks he ran, the price he paid. If you knew what price *I* have had to pay…

I have never told this before.

I am afraid to tell it now.

I will not go over the case again. It was the matter that I have written up for public consumption in my third published Casebook as "The Lavender Girls": a haunting that left men dead, asphyxiated, with the cloying stench of flowers around them. It was a terrible and complex case, where the vengeful ghosts had been victims of the men they had killed, and the spiritual pressure had been nigh intolerable. Simon was forced to use the Second Line of the Saaamaaa Ritual, and he does not speak those inhuman syllables lightly. The scent of lavender sickens me still.

What I did not put in the published work, what I had to hide as a matter of course, was our personal relations at that time.

It had been a period of intense pressure. We had had two or three cases on the go at a time for several months, often involving late nights (the occult, endlessly supplied with dark deeds at midnight, really is no profession for a man who likes his sleep) and it had taken something of a toll on our intimacy. We had been together for some four years at that point, and naturally the savage need of the first months had worn off. We could make love at a slower pace; we did not feel the same urgent compulsion as we reached for one another; and we were tired.

Nevertheless…

For a few weeks now, Simon had worn nightclothes to bed. Flannel pyjamas, in fact. It had struck me as odd at the time, since it was summer and the nights warm. I asked him if he was well. He grunted.

He did not look well, in truth. His skin had a pallor I did not quite like; his eyes were reddened and ringed with sleeplessness, and I had observed him flinch, just once or twice, when he moved. He looked to be in pain.

So he wore flannel pyjamas to bed and was not inclined to fuck. Had, indeed, declined my suggestions and removed my questing hands on grounds of exhaustion, on the few occasions I found him in bed, because that was the other new habit he had developed that month. He would tell me he would join me in bed shortly, then delay for half an hour, so that with the best will in the world I was nigh-on asleep before he came into the room. And he rose before I woke. That was not new; he was a habitual (if ill-tempered) early riser, but previously he would at least sometimes reach for a book and stay until I awoke, or even shake me into consciousness for a bit of morning glory. Not now.

But we were busy, and he was under pressure. I did not think a great deal of it at first. Not until the case of the lavender girls.

As I have said, it was a hard one. The ghosts of the murdered men cried out; the ghosts of the women they had abused cried louder. Or so Simon told me, because he did not invite me to look with him in the mirror when he examined the runes on his skin. He found other tasks for me, or vanished on some pretext, and told me what the messages from the world beneath our world had said.

Three days into the case, we came home late after some fifteen hours on our feet chasing up leads, human and inhuman, that went nowhere. Cornelia and Miss Kay had both retired for the night. Simon made the usual noises that he would close up the house and follow me to bed.

"No," I said. "You are exhausted. I shall do it, you go up. And Simon: I want you to stay in bed tomorrow morning."

"We are too busy," he said brusquely. He looked drained, the grey stubble on his chin dark against his unusual pallor.

"We are not too busy to sleep, and we are not too busy for one another. You may be inclined to martyrdom but I am not. For heaven's sake, Simon—"

I reached for him as I spoke. He stepped back.

I blinked, not precisely hurt, because it seemed more inexplicable than hurtful in that moment. Simon might be tired, but he did not avoid my touch.

"Simon?"

"I shall go to bed." He turned as he spoke, not meeting my eyes.

I stared after him. It seemed wrong—it *was* wrong. In another man it would have suggested guilt, perhaps, even a heart inclining elsewhere. I did not believe that of Simon, and frankly, if I had, I couldn't imagine where he would have found the time. But he had avoided my touch and turned from me.

I closed up the house, locked the door, came upstairs to the bedroom we had shared for four years now…

He was not there. His pyjamas and dressing gown were gone.

I looked around, bewildered. Went out to the corridor. "Simon?"

The door to the next room, the spare bedroom, opened a crack. "I am restless tonight. You need sleep. I shall stay here."

"What? But—"

He closed the door.

I could not understand. Was he ill? Had I offended him? Even at the worst of times, even in exhaustion, we took strength from one another. "With you I can breathe," he had told me so often, and I could feel its truth in the relaxation of his powerful body when he lay with me.

Why did he not want me now?

I wanted to hammer on the door of the spare bedroom and demand answers, but I was tired too, so tired that in my confusion and distress I felt tears prick at my eyes. I had no intention of enacting a sentimental drama while we were both exhausted. I would go to my solitary bed, I decided; I should allow him to avoid me, if he must, until this case was concluded; and then I should insist on knowing what the devil he was playing at before we embarked on any other work.

So I resolved, at least, but sleep did not come easily. How could it, when I lay alone in a solitary bed, and did not know why my lover had separated himself from me?

We put an end to the case the next day. As I have said, Simon was forced to use the Ritual to dispel the thing that smelled of lavender. He spoke down the ghosts of the girls, and—angrily, reluctantly, harshly—those of the men who had been their murderers and their victims. He concluded the story, standing square-shouldered in a room that seemed empty to human eyes, and sent the spirits on their way, and then—

You must understand: he was so strong. A heavyweight boxer, who daily relieved his tensions in the ring so that his body was a thick mass of muscle. In four years he had never had so much as a cold. I had seen him injured, of course; I had seen him shot through the upper arm, only to reach for his assailant with his uninjured limb and wreak retribution.

So you may imagine my feelings as he spoke the last words that freed the spirits, then let out a gasp, and folded, hunching into himself, knees bending, his great powerful body toppling to the floor.

"Simon!" I was at his side in an instant. "Simon, what is it? What has happened?"

"Nothing." His face was a terrible shade of grey-white, and sweaty, like a man in shock. "Leave me."

"Rubbish," I snapped. "What the devil is wrong?"

Simon's face was drawn with pain. He knelt on the floor, huddled in his coat, wincing. His jaw was set, cords standing along his neck, lips white, and his arms were held oddly, around but not touching his chest, wrists crossed in front of his body.

"*Nothing,*" he snarled again.

"Is it your chest that hurts? Let me see." I reached out a hand and he jerked up his arms in defence.

It was not a blow. Nothing like that. For one thing his wrists were still crossed; for another, if Simon had hit me I should have been left in no doubt of it. But I had reached to him, and he had knocked my hand away to stop my touch.

We stared at one another. His dark eyes were wide with shock and strain.

"Simon," I said. "I will see. You *will* show me."

I thought for a moment he might refuse. But then, with an angry turn of his head, he moved his arms away from his chest. He did no more. I took the lapels of his coat, moved them carefully aside. I unbuttoned his waistcoat.

There was blood seeping through his shirt. Not just in one place but in lines. It was almost as if he had been slashed by some great beast's paw, and I stared in bewildered horror for a moment before the far worse truth dawned on me.

"Christ." I fumbled at the buttons of his shirt with clumsy fingers, as I had so often, but not like this. God, not like this. I pulled the cloth apart.

The scrawled writing on his skin. Red and black. Mostly red. And as I watched, as the unreadable script formed, blood beaded at its corners and oozed along its lines, the whorls and points becoming gleaming red stars on his skin. A long rune wrote itself like a slow razor slash across his chest, and I saw his face tighten with pain.

"Why is that happening?" I whispered.

He shook his head.

"How long— That's why you would not sleep with me these last nights. Isn't it? Curse you, Simon!"

"You think I wanted you to see this?"

"Why the devil should I not? How can I help you if I don't know—"

"You can't." He spoke with unutterable weariness, and it silenced me. "You cannot help me, Robert. In truth, I am fortunate to have had so long."

"What do you mean?" I asked through dry lips. "Damn it, what do you mean?"

"I am not made to bear this." Simon put a hand on my shoulder and leaned on me to rise. He was very, very heavy at that moment. "No man is. Let us go."

At home, we repaired to our bedroom in silence.

"Undress," I said.

Simon stripped himself with weary movements. It was a distressing sight. The runes moved on his skin, the usual gentle murmur, but now they had left traces: thin scab lines all over him, holding the shapes of the inscrutable alphabet in dried blood.

"Dear God," I said. "Why did they do that? Why are they not bleeding now?"

Simon sat on the bed, heavily. "You know as well as I that when one is touched by the occult, it leaves marks. I have been more than touched. The messages have been coming through my skin for so long. It could hardly fail to leave a trace."

I could imagine it. As though a man were to write, day after day, on the same sheet of paper. Sooner or later the inscription would begin to wear its way through. The paper would tear, first at the heaviest strokes of the pen, soon enough at the lightest touch.

I watched the runes scribbling themselves over him like an infection.

"It's going to get worse, isn't it?" It was barely a question.

"Probably. Yes."

"Can you stop it? Stop the runes?"

Simon smiled without mirth. "Do you imagine I should have them now if I could?"

"Yes," I said. "I imagine—I *know* that you would go on bearing these messages as long as you were able, because they are what help you do your work. You, turn your back on lost souls for such a small thing as your own comfort? I doubt it, Simon, and I ask you again, *can you stop it?*"

Simon looked at me, dark eyes unblinking for a couple of seconds, then reached out an arm. I came to his side, holding him with reluctant care. I should have preferred to cling, to cry out my sickening fear and demand his comfort, but one must be a man.

"I don't know," he said quietly. "I don't know."

"How did you get them?"

I had asked before, of course, and never had an answer. I had respected his privacy in days past. Damned if I was doing that again.

I pushed him back and sideways, urging him to lie on the bed. I lay by his side, still dressed, my arm over him, head on his broad chest with those hateful narrow scab lines scratching across it. I could not see his face that way, and I asked again, "How, Simon?"

A long pause.

"There is an occultist," he said at last. "His name is Karswell. A remarkable scholar. He dedicated many years of his life to studying the world beneath the world. Attempting to see below and beyond. You understand me." He put his arm round me, almost absently. "He wanted more sight than man is entitled to, and studied the twin branches of necromancy and divination. Neither are safe studies, as you know."

I did know. Occasionally, when one looks into the pit, the pit looks back. Sometimes it winks.

"Karswell is a cautious fellow. Once he felt ready to move from theoretical studies to practical experiments, he made sure to carry them out on others."

"Others," I repeated.

"Children. He bought several. The first experiments failed. But eventually—well, either he refined his work or he found a subject attuned to it. He bought an eight-year-old boy, sharpened his pens, and began to write the runes."

"Sweet Jesus."

"The black ink was the first set." Simon sounded very remote. "That was done with a pen fashioned from an obsidian blade used for sacrifice. The red ink was put on by a bone pen. The ink—" He exhaled hard. "It took five years, in all, and it was—painful."

I wanted to kill this Karswell. I wanted him dead. I have not often wished death on any man, but I should have killed him then, with my own hands.

"He experimented on his own child at that time," Simon went on. "More of his inks. He is an expert in ink. Feeding it into the nails of her left hand, to form the looking-surface for divination. Theodosia cried herself to sleep every night, curled over her hand. And then, during the day he educated us. I believe his initial intention was that we should be living conduits for his sight into the world of the dead and the world of the future. Merely exist for the convenience of his vision. But we proved resilient, and as he said, he could not see any reason we should not become useful, at least until our bodies ceased to tolerate what had been done to them."

"Simon…" My voice cracked.

"Karswell did not consider Theodosia's work more than a partial success," Simon went on. "Her sight into present events is deep but intermittent, not always clear, and she has no vision of the future. Eventually he decided to repeat the work on her other hand, with a different formula. It would have left her unable to use either hand without agony, but she would fulfil her purpose." I could feel the anger, old and deep, roiling low in his chest.

"What happened?" I asked.

Simon shrugged. "We grew."

"You…?"

"Theodosia was old enough to reject any remaining filial duty to her father. I was fifteen years old, close on the height I am now, and boxing regularly. And though Karswell is a powerful occultist and a dangerous, ill-willed man, he is physically negligible. I pinned him to the wall by his neck, she told him what she had put in his coffee, and we resigned from his service."

"Good," I said, with some force. "I wish you'd killed him."

Simon shrugged, his powerful shoulders lifting my head with the motion. "I have enough on my conscience."

"So what then?"

"We, ah, made a bargain. Karswell would move out and leave us in possession of the house in return for the antidote. He was not feeling very well by then. We evicted him on the spot, packed up such of his possessions as Theodosia chose not to keep, and took the house for our own. He attempted retaliation more than once, but…we gave him reason to believe that we would reciprocate."

I tried to imagine it. Simon as a sturdy young man, dark-haired and earnest. Miss Kay—I could not picture her as a girl at all. It did not surprise me to learn that she was capable of poisoning her own father; I could only be sorry she had shown mercy.

"In the end Karswell came to accept that he had lost his control of us, that it would never be regained. He retreated to a country property to pursue other studies. We stayed in Fetter Lane."

My jaw hung open. "Those things happened to you here? In our *house*? Why in God's name do you still live here? How can you bear it? What he did to you…" No wonder its atmosphere was so chilling, no wonder neither of them had ever made it a home.

"We take what he did to us wherever we go," Simon said. "And at least there's no rent to pay."

I stared, speechless. He cupped his hand over my head, stroking my hair. "It's all right, Robert."

"It is not. It is damned well not. Why did you never tell me this?"

He let out a long breath that shook a little. "Because you have been such a comfort to me. You cannot know how much. And I did not want to cause you pain."

"I may scream," I said. "Blast you, Simon, when will you stop trying to protect me? You can bear all this, but you don't think I can bear to hear about it? For God's sake, man." I propped myself up with an elbow on his chest, glaring down. "You believe your own publicity."

"I beg your pardon?"

"I may be nothing more than your chronicler, your humble assistant, your John Watson to the world, but I expect better than that between ourselves. I am not your subordinate partner."

He exhaled hard. "No, you are not, and nor are you here to carry my burdens. Damn it, have I not tainted you enough with the life you lead because of me?"

"Because of *me*," I snarled back. "I chose this path, Simon. I've been at your side for four years now, God help me. I have taken a life, I have faced creatures the likes of which I had not known existed, I have never ever run, or left you alone, and still you persist in this bloody patronising indulgence of my supposed weakness as though I were some fainting damsel—"

"You did faint," Simon observed.

"That was three years ago!" I shouted. "There was a rotting corpse walking towards me! Anyone might have fainted under the circumstances, and why you must bring that up—"

Simon silenced me by the crude but expedient means of a hand over my mouth. I made a noise of outrage.

"You may well be angry," he said. "But you're wrong."

I jerked my head away from his hand. "About what?"

"I don't think you're weak, Robert. I think you are…light. Light and warmth. And this—" He gestured at his torso, the gently moving runes. "This is very cold and very dark, and it has been swallowing me slowly for a long time. I don't want it to touch you. I need you as you are. Not to protect you, or not only that, but to protect me. Without you, I think I would be lost already."

"Oh." The anger sluiced away, leaving me stranded.

"What I expect is this," he said levelly. "I think the communications have become too strong, taken too much toll on my body. I think they will become worse, until the damage is not reparable. And I do not think there is anything to be done. That is the truth, Robert, and I wish it were not so."

The runes, moving, gouging into his skin. What was once written in ink now carved in flesh. I had a vivid picture, quite suddenly, of Simon wrapped in bandages, and the blood seeping through.

"No," I said. "There must be something we can do. We could go somewhere without spirits—"

"There is no such place. They clamour to tell their stories. And they must be told."

"For Christ's sake, Simon, have you not done enough? Have you not done your duty to the dead by now?"

"No." Voice flat. "That's the price of the runes. I didn't choose to pay it, but nevertheless I must. Do you imagine I have never tried to flee this before? Do you think, as a boy, I *wanted* to see the dead shrieking on my skin? Believe me, no matter how bad it is to have them, to ignore them is worse. If I do not go to them, they come to me."

"It's not right," I said, feebly. "It's not fair. Why are you not angry? Why aren't you fighting?"

"Because I have always known this would happen," Simon said. "Karswell explained it when he etched them."

I stared at him, beyond speech.

"I have expected it," Simon went on. "What I did not expect was you. The last years. A reason to want to grow old, instead of—this." He grimaced. "I had resigned myself a long time ago, had thought I should not repine when it came to me, but you have shaken my purpose. I'm sorry, Robert."

I scrambled up to take his face in my hands. "We will find something. We will talk to someone. Miss Kay. Dr. Nikola, if I must. *Someone* will have an idea. And—and if we cannot then I shall be here. You know that."

"Yes," Simon said. "I know. I should not mind this so much, if you were not here."

"One day—" I began, and my throat closed.

I had intended to say, *One day I shall teach you how to phrase a compliment so it does not become an insult.* I had said that to him on several occasions. Now it hit me with stunning force that *one day* might never come. Would never come. That I would lose my stubborn, irascible, ill-tempered, catastrophically blunt Simon to the curse written on his skin.

He read the realisation in my eyes, I suppose, because he pulled me down to him then, lips meeting mine with unusual care, and we kissed as though it were a sacred act. A sacrifice to the shadow that loomed over us.

I was unspeakably afraid.

"There's damn all I can do about it, so stop asking."

"There must be something!" I snapped.

I had not expected Miss Kay to solve the problem for us, naturally. She was reserved, unemotional and formidable, and entirely lacking in the nurturing qualities that are supposed to be part of woman's nature, but she would have set fire to the whole world for Simon's benefit, without a qualm. (Although this says as much for her attitude to the human race as it does her affection for Simon.) If she had had any answers, she would have put them into practice long ago. Still, I had hoped.

She paced about the drawing-room, skirts rustling with every angry step. "I thought this might take longer. He's so strong. But it was inevitable. It *is* inevitable."

"Can you not—" I gestured at her left hand, curled into itself as usual. Her palm was scarred with a lifetime of pressure from those long, hard, polished nails.

"See what is coming? Yes, I see." She made a face. "You don't wish to know what I see. The plain fact is this: what Karswell did to Simon, to us, cannot be undone. We have tried. It cannot be removed, or outrun, or mended."

"Explain to me," I said. It was just the two of us in the drawing-room, she and I. Earlier that day Simon had been accosted on the street by a beggar who was so vividly haunted by his past sins that even I could taste it. Simon had spoken to him, long and intent, and lifted some intangible thing from his shoulders as he did it. The exchange had left the beggar with relief and hope in his eyes, and Simon with a series of deep gouges across his chest. Cornelia was bandaging him upstairs as we spoke. "Why did this man, Karswell, have to write on Simon? On a person, I mean?"

"Life," Miss Kay said succinctly. "Divination can be practised by many means but always at the cost of life, one way or another. An animal is sacrificed and the entrails read. A crystal is drenched in blood or a mirror polished with human skin to make it an effective scrying-glass. Even in the practice of casting sortes, the best results are gained by using human bone. Karswell is far from the first to realise that the divining power is strongest and lasts best if it feeds off human life rather than human death. His great achievement, arrived at through much experimentation, was to keep the strain on the subject's body to a tolerable level."

Subject. I watched her face, marked as it was by years of pain, and the hand she unconsciously cradled. "But eventually the strain becomes intolerable," I said, more statement than question.

"Of course. Everything wears out."

"Are you—"

She didn't wait for me to finish that sentence; she barely let me begin it. "Karswell gave me the lesser burden. I am very well, thank you."

"Because you are his daughter?"

She gave a little exhalation, not quite a laugh. "Good God, no. Because Simon was stronger than I, and the experiment had more chance of success."

I took a deep breath. "Are you in contact with him at all?"

"Karswell? Why on earth would—" She broke off, eyes narrowing. "What have you in mind?"

"You and Simon have both said that you do not know how to end this. It seems to me that there is one man who might."

She shook her head. "He will not help you. He is vengeful to the last degree. No slight is so small that it can be overlooked. The least insult must be repaid a thousandfold. I expect he has been waiting for this moment for years. I imagine his dearest hope is that Simon or I will ask for his help, so that he can add insult to injury in refusing, or wreak greater vengeance in a pretence of help. Don't ask Simon to appeal to him, Mr. Caldwell. You must not ask him that."

"I won't," I assured her. "I would not ask it, and I am quite sure he would refuse."

"I think there is very little you could ask that Simon would not grant," Miss Kay said, a dispassionate statement. "Which is why you must not ask it of him. I want your word."

"You have it. I will say nothing of this to him."

She gave me a penetrating look. "And you must stay away from Karswell. He's dangerous."

"Of course," I said. "I quite understand."

It was easy enough to track Mr. Karswell down. I had made it my business to befriend the Remnant's more talkative members from the beginning—one should always have the information-gatherers on one's side—and Mrs. Phan proved able to tell me a certain amount of his career. He had moved to Oxford some two decades ago, and found some parasitic position on the great oak of the University there, from which he had been evicted on the publication of a *History of Witchcraft* in 1889.

"Disgraceful," Mrs. Phan said. "I do not know *what* he thought he was doing."

She was a lady of Indochinese birth, short of stature and of patience. As the only woman on the club committee, as well as the only individual of colour, she was on occasion treated dismissively by new members, although not twice.

"He published this as a general work?" I asked. "For public consumption?"

"As a scholarly work. It was most foolish."

"Why would he do that?"

"Fame I expect," Mrs. Phan said dismissively. "A person of great self-regard, Mr. Karswell. Verry great." She rolled her Rs beautifully in the French manner. "He wished to achieve an academic position with it, and failed. It was poorly written. *And* it contained a great deal of information that he should not have shared. We were obliged to…remove copies from circulation." She ducked her head in a little gesture of mournful respect that I doubted she would have shown to men who had been similarly removed from circulation. "It was not a good book, not at all. But I do not like to destroy a book."

"Naturally you do not," I agreed. "And Mr. Karswell?"

She gave her characteristic little hiss, blowing air through her nostrils. It had just a slight quality of dragon to it. "What do you want with him, Mr. Caldwell?"

"A word. Advice. His help."

"He is not a helpful man. He looks for offence, and takes it. And he does not like your friends." She frowned. "Now, why are you asking me for information, instead of them?"

"Because you are the best-informed woman in London, of course. Can you assist me in finding out what I need?"

It was not easy to leave Simon. Once the affliction took hold, it worsened quickly. At first only the most powerful cries of the dead had damaged his skin, and thus he had been able to conceal his pain from me. As it progressed, the cries left more and deeper wounds; now, even the slow, steady background scribble was beginning to leave white grazes behind. Soon those would slice into his skin, I knew. Blood would bubble up. He would tear apart.

I cannot write of my feelings on this. I knew, had always known, that his life was full of danger. I had faced death with him frequently enough; I had more than once braced myself to lose him. But I had expected it to be *suddenly*, in the report of a gun or the flash of claws. Not like this. Not this slow, terrible, inexorable worsening.

Miss Kay confined him to bed, to keep his skin still, and filled the room with wards and talismans to fend off any roaming spirits. It would not work for long. "They come to him," she muttered to me. "They need to speak."

Simon did not speak. He loathed physical weakness in himself, and his body's slow betrayal was an intolerable thing, bringing shame as well as pain. Or so I inferred, at least, because naturally he did not choose to discuss it.

"I will be away for a little while," I told him. "Something I have to do."

He didn't ask what. I think he was probably relieved not to have me there, may have thought I was being tactful. Left to himself, he would have died alone, crawling into a hole like a wounded animal, rather than be seen in his weakness by any man, and particularly me.

But it was not left to him.

I did not telegraph. No need to let Karswell prepare. I took a train from Paddington to Swindon, and from there a closed carriage brought me to Lufford Abbey. The pale Cotswold stone of the ancient building glowed in the afternoon sunlight, but though the ancient building was pleasing to the eye, it grated on the nerves. The air had a rustling dryness around it, like the touch of ancient skin.

I rang the doorbell. A maid answered eventually. I handed her my card and was left waiting on the doorstep for some ten minutes, staring at the heavy oak door, until at last it opened once more.

"You can come in. Sir," the maid added, reluctantly.

I was escorted to a drawing-room, furnished with pieces of great age—heavy wooden chests and settles—and a single comfortable modern armchair, in which a stout, elderly man sat, waiting. He did not stand.

"Mr. Robert Caldwell." he said. A calm, entirely ordinary voice. This was the man who had mutilated Simon.

"Mr. Karswell. Thank you for seeing me."

"I could hardly resist." He wore a very slight smile, suggesting intense if suppressed satisfaction. "I am of course familiar with your worthless and contemptible scribbling."

That set the tone for the conversation. I sat, without invitation. "I'm pleased to hear it."

"Sensationalist yellowback rubbish." Karswell dwelled lovingly on the words. "I suppose Feximal is content to have his character exposed by your nonsense, if it brings profit. The man was ever vulgar."

"He's dying," I said. "You've killed him."

The smile on Karswell's lips broadened. "Ah." A hiss of satisfaction. "The runes are wearing through at last? I had wondered. I must say, I thought it might have been sooner. But now it has begun, I expect the decline will be swift."

"It is. He is, I can assure you, suffering as much as you could wish."

"No," said Mr. Karswell. "No, I doubt that very much."

I made myself swallow, because my throat was cramping. "He has suffered from what you did to him for twenty years now. Have you not had your vengeance already?"

"He and my daughter revolted against me. Destroyed my experiment. Years of work taken from me by their disobedience. My success snatched from my grasp."

"And you couldn't start again and replicate it on other subjects. Why was that?"

He shot me a look of extraordinary malevolence. "I turned my attention to other studies."

I let that go. "Mr. Karswell, let me be frank. I need your assistance."

The smile of satisfaction on his face broadened unspeakably. He sat back, lacing his hands in front of his straining waistcoat. "I thought you might be here to beg."

"You put the runes on Simon. You have knowledge shared by no man alive. You must know of something, some way, to stop it."

He simply smiled. Waited.

"Whatever your price," I said. "Name it. I will pay, whatever it may be. I don't ask you to remove the runes. Just to stop the damage they are doing. It must be possible. Please."

He blinked once, slowly. "Did he send you to grovel on his behalf?"

I shook my head. "He doesn't know I'm here. He would be furious if he knew."

"And why, then, are you here, Mr. Whatever-your name-is? Why do you care?"

"Because he is my friend, and I love him dearly. I cannot let this happen, no matter how angry he will be."

"A friend who disregards his expressed wishes," Karswell mused. "Not much of a friend, it seems to me."

"His only friend. I am all he has, and I must fight for him, because no other man will. You say *not much of a friend*. Perhaps I am not. He will never forgive me if he knows I have come here; he would rather die than owe his life to you." I was sitting forward in my chair, speaking urgently; now I threw myself back. "Perhaps you are right. Perhaps it is my duty as his friend to respect his wishes. I should go."

Karswell held up a hand. "You are too hasty, sir. You have travelled some distance to see me; you must have considered this."

"Considered, yes," I said bitterly. "But I did not realise. You condemn my scribblings, sir, but you contaminated Simon with your own. You came close to destroying him as a youth; now you have achieved it as a man. Your acts disgust me almost as much as your cruelty. I find I do not wish to owe you anything, not on my behalf and still less on Simon's. You shall not contaminate the last days of our friendship, and I withdraw my request to you." I stood, jerkily. "He accepts his fate with courage and fortitude. I can do no less. Good day. I shall show myself out."

He let me get to the door before he said, softly, "What if I could find a way?"

I stopped, didn't turn. My stance presented a picture of irresolution, hand hesitant on the doorknob, head bowed. I have no doubt my face would have betrayed my true feelings.

He will never do a kindness, Mrs. Phan had told me. *But if you can make him believe he is doing a cruelty...*

"I cannot remove the runes from his skin," Karswell said. "I cannot silence the voices. But... Have you ever seen a tree struck by lightning?"

"Of course."

"Have you seen a church steeple struck?"

"If you have a point, kindly make it."

"The church steeple has a lightning conductor." There was a purr in his voice. "The power of the skies runs through that, alongside it, and dissipates itself in the earth. Without it, every steeple in the land would be a blasted ruin."

I turned. "You are suggesting that Simon needs...a lightning conductor?"

"You may put it so." He was smiling still, a glint of malice behind the round spectacle lenses. "But there are conditions. The conductor will have to be a living being. One who will take upon himself all the pain of it. Every lightning strike will go through him instead of through Feximal."

"With...the same effects?"

"I have no idea," said Mr. Karswell, with satisfaction. "One would have to wait and find out."

"This being," I said. "Who...?"

He shook his head, very slowly. "Ah, yes, Mr. Caldwell. Who will pay the piper? It shall be my faithless daughter, or it shall be you."

My heartbeat seemed uncommonly loud, thumping in my ears, pulsing against my collar. "Miss Kay or I."

"If Feximal wishes to live, he will see the price of it, paid by those closest to him, every day." He hissed the last words, transported by malicious pleasure. "He will know that he owes his life to me, and that your suffering pays it. Unless, of course, you are not a good enough friend to take that burden on."

I should like to write that I answered at once, that I seized the opportunity to help my lover, that my only hesitation was a dramatic device to conceal my urgency from this terrible man. It would not be true. I had seen the pain on Simon's face. I knew his strength. I knew I did not possess anything like his fortitude. I have never borne pain with grace.

And this was cruelty indeed. To put Simon under such an unwanted obligation, when his desire was always to protect me… He would be angry, I had no doubt of that. Brutally angry, savagely resentful. It would change everything between us, if he even permitted it.

And I did not want to let a malevolent occultist work on me as he had Simon and Miss Kay. Christ knew what he intended to do, but the light in his eyes suggested it would be bad.

He'd do it though. I had reason to know that. Simon and Miss Kay, still little more than children, had appealed to the great occult investigator Hesselius for help when they had thrown Karswell out. A pity they had not done so before. Hesselius put Karswell under interdict, Mrs. Phan had told me, binding the man not to continue his physical experiments on living subjects. I should have to bring my case to the Remnant's committee for permission, assure them that I had no greater desire than to let this lunatic do his will. And Karswell would once more have the opportunity to work on human flesh. He would not turn that down.

He would not, and I could not. But I felt my gorge rise at the thought, and the bile was sour in my mouth as I said, "I will do it."

"You will not," Simon said. "You will *not*. Christ above, Robert, what the devil were you thinking! How *dare* you do such a damned stupid thing! I should rather cut my own throat than give you over to that maniac—"

"You're going to die!" I shouted over his tirade. "Do you not understand that? You're going to die, and you want me to *watch*?"

"You think I want to live at this price?" he roared.

He looked drained. Eyes sunken, face pale; bandages visible round his exposed skin and bulking his form under his dressing gown. He shouted at me from a sitting position because it hurt him too much to stand.

"I should damned well hope so!" I shouted back. "I should hope you want to live, and to bring peace to lost souls and an end to other people's troubles, and to be with me, Simon. Do you *want* to leave me alone?"

"That is the most contemptible blackmail I have ever heard."

He had a point, at that. Under other circumstances I would have embarrassed myself. "What do you expect of me?" I asked, at a more moderate volume. "Do you think I can see you afflicted like this when I can help you—?"

"*You* cannot help me," Simon snapped. "Karswell can, or claims it. I do not want his help."

"Nor do I, and if we had any other choice I should not have gone to him. But we have no choice and I have a solution. I can *help*, Simon. Why can't you accept that?"

"It's not… I don't…" Simon was struggling. He never did find this sort of conversation easy. "For God's sake, Robert. How can you imagine I would let Karswell get his hooks into you?"

"How can you imagine I would let you die?"

"I am grateful for the time we have had—"

"Well, I'm not," I said. "Answer me this, Simon Feximal. You have told me this will kill you. We can all see that. Do you acknowledge you need help? Even if you don't want it, even if you will not take it, can you not admit that you are in need of it?"

"I grant this is hardly a comfortable position," he growled.

"Answer the question!"

He stared at me, brows furrowing. "If you must have the words, yes. I need help. I won't take Karswell's."

I ignored the second of those remarks. "You need help. You admit it. Do you remember a promise you made me, Simon? Near on four years ago, when I came to you in my own time of need, but I did not want your aid?"

Silence. Silence that stretched an uncomfortably long time, until, very softly, he said, "God damn you."

"'Accept my help now, and I swear to you, when the day comes that I need help, I shall ask for yours and accept it.' That's what you said in this very house. Don't dare give me 'but', blast your eyes. I had your promise."

"I did not mean *this*," he forced out through his teeth.

"I don't care what you meant. You will, you *must* accept my help, or go to your grave having broken an oath to me."

He shut his eyes. I honestly think he would have been tempted to strike me, if he had had his strength. Simon has never liked to be constrained.

"I made you that promise as a courtesy," he said finally. "There was no reason for you to refuse my help except foolish pride. The circumstances now are different."

"Entirely different. Then, we barely knew each other. If I had gone, you would not have been bereaved. You didn't love me then."

"I don't like you now," he rasped. His voice was thick with pain, fury, humiliation and a terrible weakness. I was hurting him because I was too selfish to mourn him.

"There is no way through this, but for one of us to give in," I said, into the ragged, raw-edged silence. "If I give in, you suffer, and die. If you give in, I suffer—"

"And live to regret it," he interrupted. "Have you any idea what Karswell may do to you?"

"Not really. And I am well aware you cannot bear the idea of my pain. But do not insult me by imagining that I can bear yours." I propped myself against the mantel, suddenly exhausted. "Simple as this, Simon: we began our association when you gave me that promise. Will you end by breaking it?"

He exhaled, long and hard, clenching a fist. "Damn you, Robert. God damn you. I shall not forgive this."

"Then I shall summon Karswell," I said, and left him.

Karswell's return to Fetter Lane was hedged about with caution. Miss Kay, whose disapproval of my proceedings was second only to Simon's, insisted on being present. The look she gave her estranged sire when they met would have made a better man go to his knees with shame. Karswell returned it with an expression of scorn.

The procedure was to involve a cartouche, a small piece of metal, which was to be embedded in the back of my hand. Karswell created the thing from what he called a blood alloy: Simon's blood, and mine, mixed with certain curious metals. It looked like a plain dull grey metal lozenge, fringed by spikes that gave it a resemblance to a clawed millipede.

"Mr. Caldwell is to be the lightning conductor," Karswell explained. "Under normal circumstances, the power will run through him harmlessly. *Almost* harmlessly. I dare say it may be a little uncomfortable. Of course, you will have to stay close. A hundred feet, perhaps. And when the contact is strong, physical touch will be needed, flesh to flesh." He hissed those words at Simon. "Mr. Caldwell will bear your pain while you watch, like a coward—"

"And will do it willingly," Theodosia Kay interrupted, voice cool. "Get on with it."

Mrs. Phan and Dr. Silence attended the procedure. That had been a condition of Karswell's permission to do the work, to ensure that he played no malicious tricks, and I was glad of it. The more people present, the less possible it was for me to change my mind. Dr. Silence's quiet authority and Mrs. Phan's open disdain also seemed to lessen Karswell somewhat. He made one attempt to speak to Simon, a few words of a taunt, but Mrs. Phan said, simply, "No," and the occultist snapped his mouth shut once more.

Simon was so weak by then, bandaged, bloodstained, white faced. We crowded into the bedroom where he lay: Miss Kay staring intently into her nails, Mrs. Phan and Dr. Silence flanking the bedstead. I sat in a chair by the bed, a wooden-framed one with arms, and my wrists tied down to them. Karswell had insisted on that. He had another chair, and a table, with the cartouche and the instruments he needed. Bowls. A scalpel. Needles.

I cannot write of the procedure. I thought I could, I have tried, half a dozen times, and the floor is littered with crumpled sheets as a result. The fact is

What he did

The process

I can tell you it hurt. I can tell you I screamed, that I bit my lip till the blood ran, and Miss Kay fetched a leather strap on which I could bite down, that it hurt in my flesh and bones and soul as the terrible metal fangs pierced my hand and I felt its probe reach down into my nerves, into my very essence. I can tell you that Simon's face was as unbearable as the pain, and that he leaned over and reached for my other hand, angry and so very weak as he was, and held it through the procedure, and that his grip felt like my only connection to sanity.

Let me be clinical. Julian Karswell embedded a small metal cartouche in the back of my left hand. That was all.

It was not all. I felt its malignity. I felt it put roots through my hand, a connection made to the world beneath the world. Worse, I knew, with sickly knowledge, that the connection would never be unmade: I had come to the attention of the great forces now. Before I had been touched by powers, now I was tainted, marked forever, and as I held Simon's hand I felt the presence of the dead whisper across my own skin.

But I held his hand, and I lived through those long hours, and so did he.

I do not wish to write more of this.

Karswell was not permitted to stay in the house, of course. He returned the next day. I sat in the drawing-room, curled over my left hand, which throbbed in a way that felt infected, though I had no doubt the infection was purely spiritual. Miss Kay stood by me. Simon still lay in bed. I had not asked after him. He had not wished to see me.

"That seems to have taken," Karswell said, examining my hand. His thumb dug cruelly into the swollen flesh, and I bit back a cry. "I hope you are pleased with your work, Mr. Caldwell. I wonder if Feximal will be happy when he knows, every day, that you endure what he was not able to bear."

"Ah, my father," Miss Kay said. "What a mighty revenge you have wrought. All you have achieved is to let Simon know how dearly he is loved. You underestimate Mr. Caldwell's courage and devotion as much as you overestimate your own cunning, and for the same reason: your entirely misplaced pride. You are a worm, and you will leave my house or I shall throw you out." She gave him the coldest smile I have ever seen. "I don't need Simon to do that for me now."

"*My* house," Karswell said, and she struck him. She hit with her left hand, those dark, deep nails out, and Karswell recoiled, clutching his face with a cry as she took another stride forward to stand over him.

He straightened, taking his hand from his face. The long scratches on his cheek welled with blood. There was rage and fear in his expression, nothing but contempt in hers, and I saw the moment that something broke in him as he met her eyes.

"Get out," Miss Kay told her father again, pointing with a black-nailed finger, and he shrank from her as he left.

Five days later, we tested the connection.

Simon had not spoken to me in the interim. He had recouped his strength, lying in bed, and I had slept fitfully in the other room, curled around my hand, wondering what I had done. A couple of times I got up in the nights and went to sit in the corridor, by his door, so I could hear him breathe.

The cuts had healed. There were no new ones. The cartouche worked. If he never spoke to me again, it would be worth it. I sat alone on the floor of a draughty corridor and told myself that it had been worth it.

Simon stood now, scowling, stripped to the waist. The runes moved as they always had on his skin. His chest and arms were still bandaged, and the visible skin was lined with scratches and cuts, little and big, some stitched, some healing. The colour was back in his face, gaunt though he looked. Everything else was falling apart, but my Simon lived.

"Well," I said. "Let us try it."

Simon nodded. He tipped his head back, face tightening, murmuring something in jagged syllables, a calling. I felt a faint tremor of movement through the air, in a way I had not before, even as the writing on his skin leapt to frantic life. He inhaled sharply, and I reached out and grasped his hand with my own.

That was…a shock. There was a second's stillness, then the power surged through me, bitter-cold, ice along my blood. The cartouche burned with cold on the back of my hand, and I could not help a gasp.

"Robert?"

"It's all right," I managed. It was not all right; it hurt. That nauseating sensation of an alien presence in one's flesh that one can get from a splinter, but worse. Quite considerably worse.

Bearable, though. Bad, but bearable, and the scrawling on Simon's skin left him undamaged. "By God," I said. "It works."

"Apparently."

"Well, get a mirror."

"I beg your pardon?"

"The spirit. We might as well look at it, since we're doing this."

Simon gave me a look compounded of half a dozen forms of annoyance. "For God's sake, you—we are both barely convalescent. Later."

He tried to pull his hand away. I took tighter hold of it. The cold gnawed through the cartouche, sickeningly invasive.

"What's done is done, Simon. And I know you are displeased with me, and God knows I understand why. But may I remind you that we will need to be within a hundred feet of one another for the rest of our lives if this is to be to any purpose. If you intend to keep sulking, that is going to be uncomfortable."

"I am not sulking!" Simon shouted, making the walls ring. "I am *angry*."

"Sulking."

"Oh, for—" He turned abruptly, his back to me, pulling his hand away, and I could not hold back a grunt of relief as the contact broke and the cold drained from my bones.

"That. You see?" His voice was muffled. "My God, Robert, I have been tainted all my life by what Karswell did. I had wished you to stay clean."

My heart plunged at those brutal words. It took me a moment to form a response. "You…you see me as contaminated, now? Am I less to you because I chose this?"

"No!" He spun round, with a spectacular scowl on his face. "*I* am the less for allowing this to happen to you."

"You did not *allow* me. I do not require your permission to act, and I wish to God you would stop—"

"Treating you like a child," he interrupted. "So you keep saying. Damn it, can you not understand—?"

"I understand perfectly," I interrupted in return. "It is a misery to see me in danger. You would take on any suffering to spare me pain. You would rather risk your own death than mine."

"Of course I would. A thousandfold. You *know* that. Why in Christ's name could you not accept it?"

I sighed. "Because, you overbearing ogre, I feel the same way."

We stood in silence for a moment, and then Simon's shoulders dropped from their tense position. He walked over, put his hands on my shoulders, very carefully, then ran a finger up my neck. "Does it…does it hurt when I touch you?"

"Of course not."

"You don't feel anything? Any pain?"

"No, not at all," I said, and then the import of his words dawned upon me. "Oh my God."

"That has only just occurred to you?" he enquired sarcastically. "That every physical contact between us might have been tainted by the other world?"

It had not occurred to me at all. Between my terror of what might happen to Simon and of what might happen to me, I had not even thought about other matters. My legs felt weak under me at the thought of what might have been. Christ, if Karswell had known about our relationship, if he had known how much he could have taken from us—

I would have sought a chair, but Simon's powerful arms closed round me, with unusual care.

"You will never, ever be so damned rash again," he growled into my hair. "You will never do such a stupid thing or put yourself in such a man's hands. *Never.*"

"I will do precisely as I see fit at all times," I mumbled into his chest. "Don't let go of me."

"I am never letting you out of my sight again. Imbecile."

"Well, you can't," I pointed out. "A hundred feet, he said."

"Closer than that." Simon tugged at my hair, pulling my head back, and stared down into my eyes. "My God, Robert. You irresponsible, reckless fool. I am *furious* with you." His mouth came down on mine with passionate hunger, lips colliding hard with mine, and I gave myself over to his kiss with overwhelming relief.

I did not expect our new circumstances would be easy. I did not expect thanks for my sacrifice. (Indeed, I never got them. My ever-graceless Simon.) But I knew in that moment, as he kissed me with such angry, loving care, that I was forgiven for my presumption in saving his life, and that was all I needed.

I was never to meet Mr. Karswell again, thank God. The conclusion of his tale can be found in a somewhat dramatic account by Professor Montague Rhodes James, published under the title "Casting the Runes". Professor James's publishers are clearly as shamelessly sensational as my own. I like to think that Mr. Karswell would have been irritated by that.

You will see, if you care to look it up, that his end was every bit as bad as he deserved.

Turn of the Century

I will not pretend that things were unchanged, afterwards. Simon treated me like the most precious porcelain for months, to my increasing fury, until I was compelled to provoke him out of his fit of chivalry (by underhand means which I shall not detail here; suffice to say that a little jealousy spiced things up nicely). Even once he was forced to accept that I would not permit his consideration, he worried.

In fairness, our relationship was taking a toll on me. Simon, at thirty-eight but free of the constant draining effects of the runes, was as healthy as a horse. His grey hair merely made him look distinguished; his muscular form was powerful as ever. By contrast, I had the disfiguring scar below my eye, and the thrice-damned cartouche in my hand.

It was not painful, in general; Mr. Karswell's professional pride equalled his malice. But I felt just a little bit drained, all the time I was with Simon, and when he leant on me, when the spirits spoke on his skin and I served as the lightning conductor for their force…well, suffice to say that my hair started to lose its colour at the beginning of the year, and was as grey as Simon's by December.

"Between this and the scar," I said irritably, gazing into the mirror, "it is a damned good thing I am with you, for I feel sure no other fellow would be interested."

"Lucky for them." Simon took me round the waist and pressed a kiss against my neck. "I should not permit it."

"I could dye it," I mused.

"Don't be absurd." He moved away to peruse the letter in his hand.

"It is hardly absurd. I am just turned thirty-one and look like an old man already. Can you tell me you don't mind? No, of course you don't mind; you would not notice if I shaved my head and painted it blue. Shall I do that, Simon? Paint my head blue?"

"Whatever you like, yes."

I shot him a glare, wasted because he was entirely engrossed in the paper he held, and turned back to contemplation of my features. I had yet to shave, and my beard was, regrettably, as grey as my hair. I was considering whether a moustache would make me look more authoritative or simply older when Simon handed me the letter.

"See what you make of this."

I scanned the sheet. Cheap paper, and cheap ink too: the nib had spluttered at several points. An uneducated hand. And a most peculiar plea.

"The man who runs the coconut shy on Rochester pier believes the fortune-teller is possessed by Satan. Why do you give me this spiteful nonsense? Throw it away."

"So I thought, but look at his accusations. When you discount the evident malice, what does he say?"

I read over the screed again. There was a great deal of malice to discount. The fortune-teller was, we were informed, an "unnatural thing", so sworn to the Devil's party that he could not set foot over the threshold of a church, and far too accurate (aided by Satan, of course). This, I had to admit, was unusual.

We had spite come to us constantly. Accusations based on race or religion (that Jews did this, Catholics that, and lascars the other) were frequent. Some letters gave the impression that their authors were unbalanced, or the worse for drink, or both; a few were pure hatred. Our morning's post often left me feeling really quite jaundiced about my fellow man.

Of course our profession made it a little harder to tell what was a valid complaint and what spite or fantasy. We once ignored a series of letters complaining that the neighbouring house was full of snakes, only to learn that the writer was telling the literal truth. But in general, the malicious communications were of the same repellent type.

To accuse a fortune-teller, that most meretricious and deceptive of creatures, of excessive truth-telling…that was different enough to catch the eye.

"Why not give it to Miss Kay?" I suggested. "She is the expert on divination."

Simon offered me a rueful smile. "Too late. She gave it to me."

That meant she had decided it was our task to assess the fortune-teller, to warn off a false claimant or bring a real one to her attention. Or, of course, to deal with whatever might arise should this be a case of demonic possession after all. I gave a resigned sigh and returned my attention to the question of a moustache.

We arrived in Rochester on the afternoon of the thirty-first of December 1899.

It was a strange time. The Queen who had given her name to our era was very old now, and change was in the air. Extraordinary inventions—motorcars, electrical devices, telephones—were discussed as though they might become everyday things. Women were agitating for new rights. The *fin de siècle* mood had been as popular as decadence always is, but a new century was dawning, with all the promise that any birth brings, and as we stood on Rochester Pier with the wind whipping cold air from the sea across our faces, it seemed to smell of the future, of life, of hope.

Rochester was in celebratory mood. It is not a large town—though it is of course a city, for it boasts an ancient cathedral, as well as a castle. These great buildings are incongruous in what is otherwise a little enclosed place, the market area set within medieval walls, the town itself huddled behind fortifications from the Napoleonic wars. Its location at the mouth of the Thames estuary leading to the sea had made it vulnerable to invaders, from the ancient Danes to the recent French, but its docks and shipyard were thriving, and its narrow ancient streets were bright with celebration. There were coloured lanterns, and fireworks, bonfires and stalls. It was as bitterly cold as one might expect of a waterside town in the depths of winter, and the darkness was closing in, but that did not stem the holiday spirit of the revellers.

This felt, in truth, more like an excursion than work. I bought a bag of roasted chestnuts which we cracked and ate as we walked along the pier, a working space turned to pleasure on this momentous date. We passed puppeteers and jugglers and dancing dogs, stalls selling spun sugar and a great carousel with painted horses that gleamed with red and gold.

"There's the coconut shy," I said reluctantly. "I suppose we should see our informant."

He was one Ephraim Jenkins, an oily sort of fellow who cracked his knuckles continually and was very willing to repeat his claims.

"Something wrong with that Seer, as he calls himself," he told us, in conspiratorial tones. "Don't look right, don't sound right. Against nature, that's what I say. One of those Oscar Wilde sorts, *if* you ask me."

"I did not," Simon said. "And if you have brought me here for gossip and spite—"

"No, no, no, sir, not at all," Jenkins put in hastily. "I was just saying—"

"*Just say* something to the point," I suggested. It was tempting to let him annoy Simon to the point of retribution, but I preferred to have done with this and go home. "You claim this Seer is too accurate."

"That's right. Knows stuff he shouldn't know. *Couldn't.* Says things, too, the nasty little spying, peeping—"

"What sort of things?" Simon interrupted.

Jenkins declined to be drawn to specifics on this, but his veiled allusions and offended mutters suggested that the Seer had made observations about his personal life which were both accurate and unwelcome.

"Anyone can find out gossip," I said. "What was this about the church?"

"Ah, sir, that's the proof, and I saw it with my own eyes. Christmas Day, service at Rochester Cathedral. All the folks going in. There he is in his heathen robes, part of the crowd...." A dramatic pause then Jenkins intoned, "He couldn't pass the threshold."

"Meaning what?" Simon demanded. "Passed out, fell to the floor, burst into flames, turned and left? What?"

"Cried out like he'd been bit by a snake, turned and ran," Jenkins replied, somewhat sulkily.

"For which there could be a dozen causes," Simon said. "You are obviously malicious and of remarkably little use. I recommend you apply yourself to your own business and not your neighbours'. Good day."

"Have I mentioned that I am very fond of you?" I enquired, as we turned away from the coconut shy.

"Why? Look, I think that's it."

The tent Simon indicated was a small, rather shabby affair in threadbare purple velvet, with a bored barefoot urchin minding the entrance. A faded board announced its occupant to be *The Seer of All Secrets*, and as we watched, a lady emerged from it in a state of extreme high dudgeon.

"Bloody cheek!" she announced, face reddened with rage, rouge and gin—"lady" was perhaps a generous description. "Not worth a farthing! The *nerve* of it. And I'll tell you what's more—"

The urchin handed her some coins, with the weary air of one used to giving refunds. The lady inspected them, sniffed, tossed a few more imprecations into the tent-flap, and stormed off.

It was doubtless a waste of time but we might as well be sure, having come here. We made our way to the tent flap, where the barefoot boy barred our entry, announcing, "One at a time, please, gents, and it's thruppence," in shrill tones.

I glanced at Simon. "Shall I?"

"By all means."

I dropped a coin into the grubby, outstretched hand. The guardian child leaned slightly to the side, thus indicating that the gateway was open, and I ducked through the velvet flap and into the musty tent.

The space was small, and low, reeking of cheap incense. A table at its centre, covered with a gaudy cloth, held a crystal ball with a crack running through it, as though it had been dropped. Before it was a rickety stool, which I took. Behind the table sat a person.

It was impossible, from the shadowed, smooth features, the robes, and the pleasant alto voice, to tell whether the Seer of Secrets was male or female, or both, or other. As we were to learn, neither "he" nor "she" is quite appropriate for that remarkable person; I prefer to do violence to grammar rather than insult to nature, and use a singular "they".

They looked at us, with very old eyes in a very young face, and spoke in a fluting voice that I can only describe as *mystical*. "I am the Seer of Secrets. What is your name?"

"Robert."

"Robert. Give me your hands." They extended their own hands over the table to me.

If this Seer were a fraud, as the threadbare trappings and affected tones suggested, that would be made instantly clear by their reaction, or lack of it, to the cartouche. I put out my hands.

The Seer took hold of them for a fraction of a second, snatched their own hands back as if burned, recoiled from me with a cry of fear and fell off the chair.

"Good God," I said, peering down at the confusion of cheap satin and thrashing legs. "Are you all right?"

"What the bloody fucking hell was that?" demanded the Seer, in tones that held a lot more East End than previously. "I mean—" That was back to the fluting voice, then they evidently decided the situation was beyond rescue. "Bugger."

I reached out my right hand to help them up. They waved it away, scrambling to their feet, looking at me with wary eyes.

"I shan't hurt you. Sit down." I extended my hands again. "What did you see? Don't bother with the voice."

They gave my hand a prod with the tip of a finger, not touching the cartouche. "Cor blimey, mate. Who did this to you?"

"Nobody you need worry about."

"Well, you say that. Lor' love a duck, what *is* this? It goes…" They stopped. They looked up and out, at the tent flap. Then they said, "Whyn't you ask him to come in?"

"Him?"

"Him this goes to. The connected one."

"Simon!" I called. He stepped through the flap a moment later. "Simon, this is the Seer of Secrets."

"Jo," the Seer offered, slightly shamefaced. "Just Jo."

Simon held out his hand. Jo narrowed their eyes, which were of a warm golden-brown shade. They held out their own slim fingers in a decidedly cautious fashion, touched them to Simon's and snatched them away with a wince.

"Well, now. So you're Robert, and *you're* Simon, and there's ghosts all round you both. I don't need to be much of a fortune-teller for this one, do I? Hello there, Mr. Simon Feximal, what brings you here, like I don't know."

"What do you think brings us here?" I asked.

Jo put their elbows on the table with a thump. "I've been getting it right again," they said, sounding very young and very hopeless. "I ought to make it up like everyone else, but I can't help it. I mean, I try, really I do. If I look into the crystal and talk about sweethearts and riches, everyone's happy. But…" Voice down to a whisper. "It's not true. It's not what I see."

Simon placed his hand on the table. "Show me what you see. Something that you could not know from Robert's writing," he added. We had had my books quoted back at me more than once.

"One of your ghosts?"

"If you will."

Jo touched Simon's hand. Their eyelids drooped. "Plenty here, ain't there? Eels, smells, rats…glass eyes? Dead man's fingers. *Drowned* fingers. Silver. And a noise, thump thump thump, it's a horse, a black horse—the *horse*!" They shrieked the last words. "Oh my God!"

"Well, that seems conclusive," Simon remarked.

Jo had gone pale. "That was—did he really— Oh, God, oh God, no."

"Don't waste your sympathy," I said. "He deserved his end."

Jo shook their head dumbly. There was a stir behind us and the urchin crept by, to Jo's side, eyes wide with alarmed defiance.

"'S all right, Sam." Jo put an arm around the child's shoulders. "'S fine."

"You advertise yourself as a fortune-teller," Simon said. "Do you see the future?"

Jo grimaced. "People say *see* like you're watching the play but that's not how it is. I have pictures, images, feelings, you know?"

"I know," I said.

"Yeah." Jo frowned at me. "You do, don't you? *You* see things. And you're not…" The child Sam poked the Seer in the arm with a grubby warning finger.

"Not what?" I asked.

"Listen." Simon spoke over my words. "We were called here by one of your neighbours who objects to your use of your talents, and is right to do so. You are dabbling in darkness. You are reaching out to dangerous forces without protecting yourself or considering the risk to those around you. Have you *any idea* what you might have summoned? What you might have let through?"

Jo shrank back. Sam grabbed their arm, glaring at Simon.

"No, I don't," Jo said, in a thread of a voice. "I got no idea. I didn't ask to be like this, I never wanted it, I can't help it. I touch your skin and I *see*. I don't want to but I can't stop and I don't know why and— Am I evil?" That was blurted out in a sudden desperate rush.

"I beg your pardon?"

"Evil." Jo hunched their shoulders. "Everyone says so. Devil's get, devil's work, they all think—"

"*I* don't," Sam announced shrilly.

"All except Sam." Jo gave the urchin an attempt at a smile. "I don't *feel* evil, and I don't mean to be it, but, Mr. Feximal, if this ain't the Devil's work, what *is* it?"

"Of course you're not evil," Simon said testily. "Or perhaps you are, I have no idea. But if you are, it's not because you have visions."

Jo did not look comforted by that. I stepped in. "What Mr. Feximal means is that evil lies in actions. It is something you do, not something you are. *I* am certainly not an evildoer, if that was your question. Or very rarely, at least. Will you tell us about the cathedral?"

Jo flinched. "You heard about that."

"Neighbours are the same everywhere. What happened?"

"I tried to go to church," they whispered. "Christmas Day service in the cathedral. I like carols. And…and when I passed the threshold… Oh God." They had both hands to their mouth in remembered horror. "There was blood all over the door."

"You had a vision?"

"Blood. And pain, and screaming and…and… You ever seen those old pictures, the really old ones, of devils and demons at work on sinners? All knives and tortures?" Jo swallowed convulsively. "It was like that. That's what I saw. I tried to visit a church on Christmas Day, and I saw hell waiting for me."

There was silence for a moment. Sam clutched Jo's arm in mute comfort, staring at us as though we owed them a solution. I will admit, I had no idea what to say. I had seen a great deal too much to offer blithe reassurance.

Simon, who has never offered blithe reassurance in his life, was frowning. "Had you been to the cathedral before?"

"No."

"Have you been inside other churches? Other places of worship or sanctified ground?"

"Yes."

"Without such visions?"

"Yes," Jo repeated.

"Well then." Simon stood. "Let us go and see what is different about this one."

"*Do* you think it is the cathedral, rather than—?" I jerked my head back at Jo, who followed us as we strode through the dark streets. They were huddled in a thin coat, those absurd robes flapping around their heels. Fortunately, it was dark enough that they did not attract as much attention as they otherwise might have. Sam scurried to keep up.

Simon shrugged. "I have met many men and women on a straight course to perdition, and none of them had the slightest difficulty walking on consecrated ground."

That seemed reasonable; looking back at Jo's thin, frightened face, I could only hope it was right.

Rochester Cathedral is a magnificent thing, a huge grey ancient Gothic edifice. It loomed against the sky in a suitably ominous fashion. Simon stalked up to the doorway and crossed the threshold without hesitation.

"Well, come on."

Jo stared at the open doorway, with its faint glow from the interior. "What…what if I can't? What if I can't go in and I see it again and I *know*?"

"What if you never find out?" I asked. "Do you prefer to live the rest of your life in fear of damnation?"

"Better than knowing, ain't it?"

"I shouldn't think so at all."

Jo considered that. I gave them a reassuring pat on the shoulder. "You really ought to let Mr. Feximal deal with this. Don't keep him waiting."

Jo nodded, took one deep breath and turned to the doorway. It was, I think, one of the more courageous acts I have seen in my life. They took four steps, crossed the threshold and stopped dead.

"Well?" Simon asked. "Jo?"

"Nothing." Jo turned, an incredulous smile dawning. "*Nothing*."

Sam gave a shrill whoop and hurled himself at Jo, who caught him and swung him round. I may have been smiling myself, somewhat. "Well, that is pleasing. So what *did* happen, Simon?"

Simon was standing astride the threshold, shifting his weight from foot to foot. "I cannot tell. At what point did you have this vision, Jo? On the threshold itself?"

"I'm not sure." Jo released Sam. "It was crowded, lots of people. I was about there." They indicated a spot a few feet from the door.

"No you wasn't," Sam said. "You was right here." He hopped over and planted his filthy bare feet squarely by the door. "Right here, 'cos some swell shoved you and you banged into the door, remember?"

"No…"

"Well, you had your funny turn then," Sam pointed out. "But *I* saw it."

"You saw Jo touch the door?" Simon repeated. "Let us—"

"Excuse me. May I help you?"

The speaker was an elderly man in the black gown of a verger. He was giving our odd little group a highly doubtful look. I suppose that was not unfair.

"The door," Simon said. "What is its history?"

"Well, it is a very ancient—"

"The bloody tale," I suggested, having an inkling where Simon was headed. "The terrible thing of which you prefer not to speak."

"I prefer not to speak of— That is, we do not encourage such wild fantasy," the verger said, somewhat ruffled. "It is a sensational myth, nothing more."

"Go on," Simon and I said together.

The verger glanced between us, mostly at Simon, and gave up. "I suppose you know that doors such as these were often covered in oxhide. There is a folktale—nothing more, I am positive—that during the old times, one Danish invader was captured by the locals in the act of pillaging the holy sanctuary, and subjected to a most disgusting punishment."

"Flayed," Jo whispered. They swayed slightly; Sam took their weight, as if by habit. "They flayed him alive and nailed his skin to the door. Didn't they? It wasn't hell I saw, it wasn't devils. It was *people*."

"It frequently is, in my experience," I said. "Simon, what are you doing?"

"Looking for the remnants of skin." Simon was peering closely at the door. "I think, here—"

"Oh, for heaven's sake. It's cold, let us go." I herded our little party down the stairs, away from the horrified verger. "There, Jo, are you reassured?"

Jo nodded. "I suppose. Yeah. Feel a bit stupid, to be honest."

"Not stupid: ill informed," Simon said. "You have remarkable powers of divination but you must have knowledge if you are not to endanger yourself and others. You cannot go on as you are."

Jo turned their face away as we walked through the cathedral grounds. "Yeah. I know that. But there's just me and Sam, and we got to eat somehow. What else can I do?"

Simon looked at the pair, at their worn clothes and patches, and perhaps he thought then of two other children who had huddled together with nobody to turn to. He glanced at me. I nodded.

"Come to London," he said. "You need a mentor, and my colleague is perhaps one of the best diviners alive. She may be able to teach you. She will certainly find someone who can."

Jo stopped, under the glow of a gas-lamp. "You mean it?"

"I will take you to her. She will know what to do for the best."

The look on Jo's face: hope warring with uncertainty. "I hear you, Mr. Feximal, but, no offence, there's lots of people want what I can do. And I got Sam to think about, I got to be careful. So let's have your hand."

Simon nodded approval and put his hand out once more.

"And you," Jo told me. "Right hand."

"Why?" I asked, offering it.

"Because you're connected." Fingertips brushed the back of my hand, very lightly, then settled more firmly. "Oh. *Oh.*"

I glanced at Simon, whose expression was intent, and it occurred to me too late to wonder what this strange youth might see between us.

"I see… I see the stories, and the telling of them. Darkness…no, shadow." Jo's voice was vague, abstracted, as though their mind was elsewhere. "Living in the shadows, when the shadows cast the light." Their eyelids flickered oddly. "Light in shadow, silent words, but they'll come. And the light comes after. Light on the blue. There *will* be light…but it's a way off yet. And there's a long night coming first."

We stood in silence a moment longer, before the Seer removed their hands and gave us a rueful half smile. "And what that meant, you tell me. But I reckon I can trust you gentlemen. So I'll go talk to your colleague—" Sam tugged at their sleeve. "With Sam here, 'cause we go together, and we'll see what happens. How about that?"

"Good," Simon said. "I cannot promise what my colleague will say but I can promise you that we will not simply take away your livelihood. You will have a new start, whatever it may be."

"A new start for a new century," I added. "And may it be a brighter, better place than the old."

"Yeah," Jo said slowly. "Here's hoping."

They did not sound quite convinced.

We left the Seer and the urchin in Rochester, with an appointment to come to Fetter Lane in the New Year and a little assistance to cover the cost of the train ticket. Our own train back to London seemed to dawdle endlessly; the streets were crowded with revellers when we returned to the metropolis; and it was close on midnight when at last we lay together in bed.

"Will they come, do you think?" I had been unsure whether we ought to bring the pair with us, just in case.

"Undoubtedly," Simon said. "Jo's situation is not a pleasant one. It is an uncomfortable thing to have connections to the world beneath the world, and far more so without support or knowledge. He—she?— will need a mentor."

"Would Miss Kay do that?"

"For gifts like those?" Simon snorted. "She will mentor, cherish, and fight to the death to prevent someone like Karswell getting hold of that youth."

She doubtless would. And it seemed probable that Jo needed a protector. Our inflexible, rulebound world was not kind to those who stepped away from man or woman's allocated position.

"What do you think he—she—damn it, I shall say *they*—meant about the light?"

Simon shrugged, and pulled me to his broad chest. "I don't know. If I have learned anything from Theodosia, it is not to live by premonitions. They are too often treacherous. In any case..." He pressed his lips to my forehead. "I need no vague assurances of the future. I am very well here and now." He trailed the kiss down to my earlobe. "Did you say you were going to dye your hair blue?"

"Something of the sort."

He exhaled with puzzled amusement. "I suppose it is a new fashion? Well, if you must."

"You would not object?"

"If it strikes you as a good idea. Blue or brown or grey, it is all the same to me, so long as you are content."

I rolled over and up so that I straddled his chest, watching his face as the runes flowed under my thighs. "I am content. Extremely. How could I not be? The only way I could be more content is if you, Mr. Feximal, would bestir yourself and see in the new century with me."

Simon clasped my hips with his warm, strong hands, so firm, with such unconscious ownership that I shivered in his grasp. "I dare say I might do you service. Will you do me one in return?"

"With the greatest pleasure."

"Don't dye your hair blue. I like it grey. I like the contrast."

"With what?"

"It gives you gravity, when you are all levity."

I contemplated him narrowly. "I could swear that is a joke."

"Not an original one, I fear." He looked pleased with himself, nonetheless.

"Still." I bent to kiss him. "And we had better get on if we are to match your strokes to those of the clock."

That we did. Simon's arm round my neck, cradling me, I embracing him; the both of us gasping our pleasure. We clasped each other, close as any pair could be, with soft cries and half-formed words and whispers, rocking together. "This is how to see in the century," Simon murmured in my ear. "This is how to spend one."

And as we made love, there was a roar from outside, the sound sweeping along the crowded streets like rolling thunder, and the church bells began to chime all over London.

We brought Jo to live in Fetter Lane—it is a large house and Miss Kay did not wish to lose such a treasure—along with the ubiquitous Sam, who assisted Cornelia with the housework while acquiring an education. Jo was a delightful and lionhearted young person, and their gifts rapidly became indispensable to our work. Sam was an ordinary, bumptious, rumbustious scapegrace, ever tumbling into scrapes, cheeking Simon and Miss Kay without the slightest fear. (This did them both a great deal of good, in my opinion.) Between the two youngsters, the cold house came alive in a way that I had not imagined possible.

I have written a great deal of our early years; I find I have nothing to add on our later ones. Our working life remained dramatic and dangerous, but Simon and I had reached an equilibrium, a mutual understanding matched with steady, loving contentment. We were scarred, and grey, and we had been through much, but we had been through it side by side and were happy to be so.

I should conclude my story here, with the bells of the new century, and the bright dawn of a hopeful, peaceful future. That is part of the joy of crafting a tale: one may end on the perfect moment and leave it shining in the reader's memory as the final word.

If I stopped our story here, all would be well forever.

I cannot.

The End

I began this account of my and Simon's secret life in September 1914, with the world falling into chaos around us. Matters have not improved since. As I write, Russia is in upheaval; the Kaiser's forces are on the attack. America has joined the fray. God knows when this will end, or how.

Simon and I are soldiers now, of a kind, though we are both well over recruitment age—Simon will be fifty-six in a few weeks, if we live to see it; his hair honestly greyed by now, his powerful shoulders beginning to stoop a little. Needless to say, we did not volunteer. I am, I hope, a patriot, but I see no love of England in this harvest of her youth. It is a blood sacrifice, no less, and the young men who bravely shoulder guns for England, or indeed Germany, are as much victims as though they were bound to a stone altar in a stinking cellar, with General Haig holding the silver knife.

You will be asking yourself why Simon and I fight this war, then, and I can only answer: Because we were compelled to. The Great Powers on both sides are attempting to leverage influences they ought not touch, of which the summoning at Mons in 1914 was merely the beginning, and every occultist in Europe has been exhorted or extorted to join in raising forces from the world beyond. We were not excused. Representatives of Whitehall came to Simon with requests that turned to orders; Simon refused with increasing ill grace; Sir Ranjit Singh himself visited Fetter Lane to change his mind, and failed.

"You no longer have the luxury of independence, Mr. Feximal," he warned Simon. "Your country requires your service. Germany has more active occultists in Wittenberg alone than we do in London. There is a war to fight and you are needed."

"I do not go to war with men," Simon growled. "Germany is not my enemy."

"She is now," Sir Ranjit said. "And I suggest you reconsider while the choice remains your own."

Simon declined, with finality. Two days later a Whitehall junior came to see us. This time we were informed that the Fat Man had kept records, to which Sir Ranjit had access. The official brought written testimony: from a hotel where we had allowed affection to outstrip discretion; from clubs I have not attended in twenty years; worst of all, a letter that I had written to Simon some ten years back. (I asked him, afterwards, why he had kept words of love and desire that could damn us both when any sensible man would have burned the blasted thing. He replied, "It was the thing you wrote for me.") He had kept the letter, and someone had stolen it from our home, and now it was waved in our faces with a threat of prosecution for sodomy and the attendant humiliation, shame and gaol.

Simon may be in his fifties but his right arm would still do credit to a man half his age. It did no good, except to relieve his feelings, but at least the Whitehall man went away with a badly broken nose to go with our bitter, reluctant capitulation.

We had packed Jo off in good time. The thought of our brave, fragile Seer used as a crystal ball by some oafish general was unbearable, and Miss Kay removed them before the outbreak of war which, needless to say, Jo had seen coming. Sir Ranjit informed us that it was a treasonous act to deny Britain the use of such powers. Perhaps it was; if so, I cannot regret that I am a traitor.

Sam is serving on the same battle cruiser as Gene Robey. I do not wish to think of that.

So here we are, Simon and I, fighting the hidden war, in which occultists on both sides compete to raise forces against one another, as if there were not enough madness loose in the world. Simon has refused to take an active part in this evil, no matter what the threat, so instead we are stretcher-bearers, conscientious objectors on the front lines of invisible battles, fighting the symptoms because we will not be the cause. We struck down the ghouls of no-man's land that infested the trenches of Normandy last year. We walk the trenches, among the rats and barbed wire and through the mud, with shells booming around us. The ghosts scream day and night. Simon's skin is unspeakable; my left hand unusable with the constant, throbbing cold pain. I cannot go more than twenty yards from him now for fear of breaking the cartouche's connection. I do not want to.

I have seen many dreadful things in my life, but this war is as close to hell as I have ever been. And I think, on the whole, this is the end.

We will do our duty until this insane conflict ends, or until it ends us. Either way, we shall not return to England. I dream of warmth, blue skies and peace, lapping seas, and a lonely cottage a very long way from other people. Somewhere unravaged by war, if such a place still exists in Europe. Somewhere Whitehall will not find us, and the voices of the dead will drop to a whisper, and two ageing gentlemen may share a house in peace, without prying eyes and the threat of shame in a country that makes a fetish of death and a crime of love.

So, then. I shall send my dog-eared bundle of manuscript to my solicitor to be passed to you, and return to my war beneath the war, and when it is over, my name and Simon's will be listed as either deceased or missing in action, and you will not hear from me again. You may publish this account at such time as the law permits, or destroy it, or do anything in between. It hardly matters now.

But I had to tell the story, Henry. I had to let someone know who I was: not merely Simon's assistant, his chronicler, his poor scribbling friend, but the great love of a great life. That I may have lived in his shadow, but I was always by his side. That I was as needful to him as air.

Simon kissed me this evening, a snatched kiss in a canvas tent, and said, quite calmly, "I love you."

"Do you know," I told him, "it has been twenty-three years and you have never said that before?"

"Have I not?" he asked, slightly surprised. "But you knew."

"Of course I knew. I have always known."

"Well, then," he said, with mild exasperation, and put his arm round my shoulders.

If Fate grants us another twenty-three years, preferably in comfortable retirement, that would be very welcome. But if it ends tonight, as long as we go together, I shall feel entirely satisfied with my lot.

Either way, dear Henry, it has been a pleasure working with you, except for your relentless pedantry on the matter of the Oxford comma.

Yours ever,
Robert Caldwell
Passchendaele
October 1917

A note from the Editor

Simon Feximal and Robert Caldwell were listed as missing in action on the rolls of honour at the end of the Great War. No bodies were found, but then, so many men ended in unmarked graves or shell holes, finding burial only in the mud, or the bellies of scavenging things.

As a matter of record, in the year 1921 Miss Theodosia Kay realised her considerable assets, made over half of her fortune and the Fetter Lane property to the individual known as Jo, and took a steamer to Naples. There she disappeared, quietly and permanently. It is possible that she came to an unfortunate end in that teeming city of thieves, an ageing woman travelling alone as she was. It is equally possible that she chose a solitary retirement on the Italian coast and felt no need to maintain ties with England.

And, I have sometimes thought, or dreamed, it is possible that Miss Kay vanished with a purpose, and a destination. Some little Mediterranean cottage, perhaps, far from the world's notice. A place where a bright-eyed gentleman and his older companion might live in ghostless quiet, and spend their days together watching the sunlight on the sea.

Henry Scott
Editor

Acknowledgements

This book exists in large part because I wrote a story, *Remnant*, with Jordan L. Hawk, to whom I owe huge thanks. In this story, set just after "The Writing on the Wall", Simon and Robert meet Jordan's series characters Whyborne and Griffin (to mutual dismay), and Robert provokes Simon out of his fit of chivalry by underhand means. *Remnant* is available free from Smashwords.

The *Secret Casebook* was written in a spirit of loving homage to the Victorian occult tradition and the pulp fiction it produced. All the following can be found free on Project Gutenberg.

Mr. Karswell, shamelessly appropriated into my service in "The Writing on the Wall", is the villain in "Casting the Runes" by M.R. James, which you should read right now. Thomas Carnacki and the Saaamaaa Ritual are the creations of William Hope Hodgson in *Carnacki the Ghost-Finder*, which is a lot more fun than Robert would have you believe. Dr. John Silence appears in the short stories of Algernon Blackwood. The sinister Dr. Nikola features in three novels by Guy Boothby. The Diogenes Club and the Fat Man who belongs to it are the creations of Sir Arthur Conan Doyle.

Some of the stories in this collection are inspired by British folklore.

The legend of Peter des Roches and King Arthur ("Butterflies") is a very old one. Peter was real, and his tomb can be seen in Winchester Cathedral. My thanks to Gill Vickery for bringing this to my attention as a delightful children's story, and my apologies for ruining it.

The story of Vortigern's palace ("Remember, Remember") is part of the ancient Welsh Merlin cycle. Many bridges and palaces across Europe are supposedly mortared with blood.

Dando and his dogs ("Devils on Horseback") can still be heard in the skies around St Germans in Cornwall. It's probably wild geese.

The Rat Queen ("An Eye for an Eye") is a unique London tosher's tale, as recounted by the Victorian tosher Jerry Sweetly on his deathbed. He really did have a daughter and a granddaughter with differently coloured eyes. I have adapted the tale to my purposes; the original appears in *The Lore of the Land: a Guide to England's Legends*, by Jennifer Westwood and Jacqueline Simpson, which is a marvellous resource for anyone interested in English folklore.

Several Kent and Essex churches are said to have had their doors covered with the flayed skin of Danish invaders instead of the usual cowhide ("Turn of the Century"). Samuel Pepys records this legend from his visit to Rochester Cathedral in 1661.

The story continues in the new standalone series Green Men...

England, 1923. The Great War is over, the Twenties are roaring in, the Bright Young Things hold ever more extravagant parties. It seems as though the world has changed for good. But some far older forces are still at work, and some wars never end.

The occult battles fought in the War Beneath the War have torn the veil protecting our world from what lies outside. With most of the country's arcanists dead, and the Government unwilling to face the truth of the damage done, a small group pledged to an ancient duty must protect England from supernatural threat.

Set in the world of KJ Charles' award-winning *Secret Casebook of Simon Feximal*, the Green Men series covers a motley crew of occult experts, jobbing ghost-hunters, and walking military experiments as they fight supernatural and human threats, save the land, and fall in love.

Spectred Isle
Green Men book 1

Archaeologist Saul Lazenby has been all but unemployable since his disgrace during the War. Now he scrapes a living working for a rich eccentric who believes in magic. Saul knows it's a lot of nonsense...except that he begins to find himself in increasingly strange and frightening situations. And at every turn he runs into the sardonic, mysterious Randolph Glyde.

Randolph is the last of an ancient line of arcanists, commanding deep secrets and extraordinary powers as he struggles to fulfil his family duties in a war-torn world. He knows there's something odd going on with the haunted-looking man who keeps turning up in all the wrong places. The only question for Randolph is whether Saul is victim or villain.

Saul hasn't trusted anyone in a long time. But as the supernatural threat grows, along with the desire between them, he'll need to believe in evasive, enraging, devastatingly attractive Randolph. Because he may be the only man who can save Saul's life—or his soul.

Books by KJ Charles

A Charm of Magpies series
The Magpie Lord
A Case of Possession
Flight of Magpies
Jackdaw
A Queer Trade
Rag and Bone

Society of Gentlemen series
The Ruin of Gabriel Ashleigh
A Fashionable Indulgence
A Seditious Affair
A Gentleman's Position

Sins of the Cities series
An Unseen Attraction
An Unnatural Vice
An Unsuitable Heir

Standalone books
Think of England
The Secret Casebook of Simon Feximal
Wanted, a Gentleman

Green Men
Spectred Isle
Last Couple in Hell
Damned Young Things

9 781999 784607